MAN ON!

'No,' Grenet told Greg in his soft, southern French accent, 'leave my football clothes on. I like to wear them, even now.'

Like Greg, Grenet had not changed out of his kit since practice and he filled it with an agile-looking, masculinely lithe body. His dark-skinned, classically Gallic features had a lustful, almost absent expression and his closely shaved hair and goatee gave his good looks a tough-guy edge. Greg thrilled at the sight of this handsome man and to gain release from the sense of pent-up sexual pressure inside him he began stroking himself, enjoying the feel of his cock beneath the silken material of his own training shorts.

MAN ON!

Turner Kane

This book is a work of fiction.
In real life, make sure you practise safe sex.

First published in 2000 by
Idol
Thames Wharf Studios
Rainville Road
London W6 9HA

Copyright © Turner Kane 2000

The right of Turner Kane to be identified as the Author of
this Work has been asserted by him in accordance with the Copyright,
Designs and Patents Act 1988.

www.idol-books.co.uk

Typeset by SetSystems Ltd, Saffron Walden, Essex
Printed and bound by Mackays of Chatham plc, Chatham, Kent

ISBN 0 352 33730 3

One

The crowd cheered as Greg Williams, Middleton United's star centre-forward, swerved past another defender and strode closer to the goal. If he could just manoeuvre around Brian Dalton, the only player left in a position to challenge, he'd be up for a shot. But Dalton was too close, heading towards him quickly with a look of determination on his face. Greg glanced across the pitch to see one of his team-mates in an open space. Thinking fast, he flicked over a perfectly aimed pass just before Dalton collided into him, taking him down. The roar of the crowd signalled that Middleton had scored, all thanks to a shot Greg had set up. He felt ecstatic but also in agony. Something in his leg had obviously twisted.

'Sorry mate. Eh, are you all right?' Dalton asked as he removed the weight of his six-foot-four, lithely muscular frame from Greg's body.

'No – I'm going to need some help.'

Dalton waved a warning to the side of the pitch. 'Least you got the pass in. It was a good shot.' He bent over to offer a handshake in apology. Greg couldn't help but let his eyes pan up those dark-skinned, hairy legs to the crotch of Dalton's shorts. The shiny white material, slightly mudstained at the side, bulged quite beautifully, hinting at a rather thick cock hiding inside.

'No hard feelings, then?' Dalton asked.

Almost, Greg thought. But not the kind you mean. He smiled, then winced as another shock of pain shot through him.

'What's all this, then? Let's have a look at what's wrong.'

Dean Macdonald, the physio, had arrived. Dean was a short but broad-shouldered man who was obviously as friendly to the gym as any of the players on the field. He had a thick-jawed handsome face below a mass of tousled dark hair that Greg always enjoyed seeing close up.

'It's my leg. All along here.' Greg pointed along his left thigh.

Dean blew on his hands and rubbed them together. 'You'll have to excuse my cold fingers.' He beamed a white smile as he began to massage the tightened muscles. His touch was gentle but firm and Greg all but forgot the pain, enjoying instead the sight of a gorgeous man's hands pulling at the flesh of his upper leg. He wanted the man to go higher and higher to where the fine blond hairs got thicker and darker, would have loved to see those cold fingers slip up his shorts and begin to wander around. Greg felt a tightening of the material at his crotch: suddenly there was significantly less room for manoeuvre. He desperately began to think of something, anything else to take his mind off the two beautiful men at either side of him. A football pitch, surrounded by two teams and thousands of fans, was hardly the place to be discovered with an erection. But fortunately enough, Dean managed to find the root of his problems.

'Ow. Ow! That's it. That really hurts.'

Dean stopped fondling. 'Well nothing's broken.'

'That's a relief.'

'You've just pulled a muscle.' Dean looked directly into Greg's eyes, his smile at its most attractive, then added, 'You lucky thing!'

He patted Greg on the knee, and asked if he wanted a stretcher or whether he could manage to walk.

'I think I'll be okay,' Greg said. 'If you give me a hand.'

Dean leaned across, wrapping a strong arm around the footballer who made a similar motion, putting his own arm around the back of Dean's neck. Though he flinched occasionally, and slightly, as they slowly vacated the pitch, Greg's thoughts were more occupied by the comfortable warmth of the body next to him, the meaty shoulder he could feel through the sweatshirt, the devastatingly gorgeous face barely inches from his own. Greg was becoming more and more eager for the showers. He was sorry to be taken from the game but rather glad to be going to the locker-room before the rest of the team. He needed to be naked. And alone.

As he neared the tunnel leading to the dressing-rooms, the crowd cheered once more. Greg waved his free hand in acknowledgement of their appreciation. Both he and the audience knew that his injury wasn't too serious and that it would be a wait only until next Saturday for him to be on the pitch again.

Inside the locker-rooms, Dean helped Greg to a bench. 'How's it feel sitting down?' he asked.

'Not too bad.' A lot of the pain had subsided already. 'But I don't think I'll be ready to go back out by the end of the match.'

'You're right there,' Dean laughed. 'What you need is rest.'

The room was empty apart from the two of them. The journalists and other players would not be arriving until the game had finished which, allowing for injury time, wouldn't be for at least thirty minutes. Greg took in a deep breath through his nose. He loved the smell of the changing-rooms, the warm musk of the hundreds of men who had changed there making it seem as if the very tiles on the wall were impregnated with testosterone.

'Tired, eh? Here, let me help you off with those.' Dean squatted down. 'Don't want to risk any more strain.'

He smiled that smile again, then began tugging at the laces on Greg's boots. He took a moment to scratch at a dried mud spot. His movements were as careful as when he was massaging and Greg began to wonder if Dean shared the same love of sports kit he did. Dean waggled the boot's tongue a little, then eased the shoe off, resting Greg's foot on his thigh.

'I've been running around quite a lot.' Greg could feel the wetness between his toes as the air reached them. 'I hope it doesn't smell too bad.'

Dean sniffed around the thick white sock for a while, taking obvious pleasure in the sour stench before announcing: 'Gorgeous!'

He pulled gently at the sock, peeling it off seemingly as slowly as he could. Greg was rather unsure of the situation. He had never been entirely certain of Dean's feelings towards him. He had thought several times before that there had been looks and, as there had been on the pitch, comments to suggest Dean might be interested in him more than on a simply professional level, but he had never acted on his suspicions. The signs now appeared once more to have an aura of come-on about them, but Greg didn't want to make a move in case Dean was merely being helpful.

Dean had now taken off the second boot. He ran a finger up Greg's instep making the entire leg jump in reflex action. He eased both hands into the top of the sock and dragged it towards himself, then took the entire foot in his hands. It felt distinctly wonderful to Greg to have the moistness of his sweat rubbing on to another man's skin.

'And now, we'd better get these off.'

Dean reached for Greg's shorts but Greg took hold of his hand as it clutched at the hem. Even if Dean was hitting on him, now was neither the time nor the place to take him up on it.

'I think I can take it from here,' he said.

Dean looked rebuffed (Greg wondered whether it was a look of disappointment) and stood up.

'Just kidding around, Greggy.' He play-punched Greg, not too hard, on the shoulder. 'You get a shower and I'll be back at the end of the match to bandage that leg up, all right? I'd best get back out there. They'll be wondering what I'm up to.'

Dean left rather quickly. Next time perhaps, mate, Greg

thought, marvelling at his self-control. His heart was pounding and he found that his hands were shaking with excitement. He took off his shirt and stood up. His stiff cock sprang out of his shorts as he pulled them down and he tugged at the end a couple of times, enjoying the feeling but still slightly nervous that someone might catch him at it. He decided it would be best to hit the showers. At least whatever he got up to in there would be hidden from immediate view.

Greg entered the tiled corridor at the back of the locker-room. A series of sprays were mounted on the wall at both sides. Greg turned the tap for the water and the place began to steam up immediately. He found the showers maddeningly erotic, being a place where he was so often surrounded by the beautiful naked bodies of his team-mates. Frequently when masturbating he had centred his fantasies on the behaviour after the match, imagining that the celebratory hugs, the commiseratory pats on the buttocks, the kidding and remarks about each other's dicks would turn more overtly sexual and that he and the rest of the lads would end up in one huge horny orgy underneath the jets of water. He turned his mind to such matters as he squirted out a palmful of shower gel and began to soap up.

Greg's body was lissom and well exercised. He was blond and light skinned, and though his tight pectorals were free from hair he had a decent, dark growth around his cock and balls. He looked down at his throbbing penis, a good seven and a half inches long, and a foreskin that had crept back over a deep pink oval of glans. It had a slight shine of pre-come. Greg fingered a drop that hadn't been washed away, gently brushed it over and around the head and then underneath, rubbing back and forth at the spot where all his pleasure seemed to be concentrated. He let out a slight 'oh' of pleasure, then closed his eyes, feeling the heat of the shower pound upon him. He gripped fully the hard muscle that extended out of his body, squeezed slowly up so the foreskin rubbed over the end, then pulled back, all the while thinking just how good it would be to have someone else to do it for him, to have Dean's fine hands back to touch him all over again. Gradually, Greg increased the rhythm of the back and forth action, sometimes focusing on the last inch of himself, other times moving along the entire length so his little finger ended up buried in his pubes. With his free hand he began to feel the rest of his body. His nipples were erect now: he circled one with a finger then gasped a little as he pinched it. He moved down, enjoying the masculine feel of the ridges in his stomach muscle and the line of hair that led downward from his belly button. He scratched at a hard, thick thigh, then gently pulled at it with the entire width of his palm, imagining it was one of Dean's rough but tender touches. He cupped his hairy balls and massaged a while, panting faster as the sensations in his penis got stronger and stronger. In his mind he saw Dean, naked and behind him. Greg moved his hand over his bottom and directed his middle finger between the split of his cheeks to his anus. He began to tease the hole, and was ready for the thrill of insertion when a deep voice spoke and he stopped, surprised.

'You enjoying yourself?'

Greg spun around, taking his hand from his backside, but not releasing the grasp on his penis. It was Dalton, the guy who had tackled him earlier. Dalton was naked, and had his shower gel in his hand, apparently ready to get clean. Greg began to panic that he had let time slip away unawares, that it was the end of the match and that the other players would be arriving like Dalton had. Getting caught masturbating in the showers was bad enough but he would never live it down if he was found in this state by the rest of his team.

'Er – I wasn't expecting anybody back yet,' Greg said slightly timidly. He let go of his cock, which sprang up and bounced a couple of times. Dalton grinned at it.

'Obviously not. Don't worry though. There'll not be anybody else here for a good twenty minutes or so. I'm only in because I got sent off. The ref didn't like that tackle I did on you. Or the one I did on Jackson afterwards.'

Dalton was known as one of football's hard cases, always in trouble for being too aggressive on the pitch. At his height he was an intimidating figure, but he was also one that Greg had always found electrifyingly manly. They had showered together before, the last time their two teams had clashed, and Greg remembered just how irresistible-looking Dalton's body was: the tight pecs; deltoids that veed impressively; biceps like tennis balls. And that knob! Not so long, but thick, really thick like nothing Greg had ever encountered before. And was it his imagination or had it twitched a couple of times since Dalton had made his entrance?

'It's not going down, is it, mate?' Dalton nodded at Greg's still-rigid member. 'Only one thing for it. You'll have to finish off.'

Greg looked surprised, but Dalton just laughed.

'Don't mind me. I know how it is after a game. I'm always fucking horny as well. Must be all the exercise. Go on, get some soap on it before the rest of them arrive. You never know, I might join you in a bit.'

Greg began fondling himself again, although in a some-what reticent manner. Was he misreading this situation as well? Could it really be that Brian Dalton, the notorious tough guy of the footballing world, wanted to see him wank off? Once more, as he had been with Dean earlier, Greg was half scared of making a wrong move, in case Dalton's actions were purely amiable laddisms that if taken the wrong way could end up in some troublesome repercussions. But he was also excited in the extreme to be playing with himself in the presence of such a hunk of masculinity. He chanced a look over and to his amazement found Dalton was living up to his promise: he too had started to masturbate, tugging at the wrist-thick monster that was already almost at full stiffness.

'What are you staring at, golden boy? Never seen anybody else do it before?'

Dalton seemed almost angry and Greg wondered whether he was heading for a beating. But he just couldn't take his eyes off that gorgeous prick.

'No, it's just that . . . Well, it's so big!'

Dalton smiled, and moved a little closer. 'Yours isn't so small. Here, let's have a better look at it, just to compare.'

Both men took their hands away from their crotches, their penises bobbing gently as they did so. Dalton moved so that his erection ran parallel to Greg's own, almost touching it, the large bulbous head merely centimetres away from Greg's black mass of pubic hairs.

'See,' Dalton pointed out. 'You've got a bit more length. And I've got the width. But they're both pretty decently sized.'

Greg couldn't help but throb a little as he looked down at the big blue vein that snaked along Dalton's piece, right from the circumcised tip to the hefty, round, hairless balls that just begged to be mouthed.

'I've got an idea,' Dalton said slyly. 'I know something that will bring us both off quickly.'

Greg was pleading inside for what he hoped was about to happen. Surely now there was no danger of a problematic outcome.

'What's that then?' he questioned, mock innocently.

Dalton took hold of Greg's right wrist and made Greg grab his erection. Then he took hold of Greg's own dick and squeezed it playfully.

'This,' he said smiling. 'This should make us come in no time.'

Greg could hardly believe it. First Dean, and now Dalton. It must have been his lucky day! But as he began sliding his fingers up and down the hot, wet skin, Dalton doing the same to him, he accepted what was happening soon enough. The sheer joy of being in the slowly moving masculine grasp was too great for him to do otherwise. He began alternating his view between the sight of what was going on down below and the strong, slightly stubbled jawline and piercingly blue eyes of Dalton's almost unbearably handsome face. What made the situation all the more erotic was that Dalton kept reciprocating the gaze, looking back right at Greg, sometimes giving a cheeky grin, always panting a little, sometimes letting out a happy 'oh yeah' as they wanked. Greg wondered what it would be like to kiss Dalton, and taking a chance that now almost nothing was out of the question, arched his head forward a little. To his relief, Dalton responded, pushing his hard lips against Greg's own, then probing a tongue in his mouth. Greg moaned as the unshaven skin rasped against his face and he felt himself being dragged into a full-body embrace. It was so good to be in those arms, to feel those taut muscles pressing against his own, to have a steely cock warm against his belly. Greg stroked Dalton's broad back and shoulders, fingertips slipping over the shower drops to the roundness of his buttocks.

Eventually Dalton pulled away. 'The lengths you have to go to to get a snog out of a bloke these days!' he joked.

Greg laughed, fully at ease. They hugged again and returned to their mouth play. After a couple of minutes Greg began to move downward, first brushing his lips against Dalton's thick neck, then gently biting at his chest and at the tattoo on it. He stopped briefly to tongue a nipple, making Dalton quickly take in a breath, before he slowly licked along Dalton's ripple of abs. Greg found himself on his knees, with Dalton's manhood leaking streaks of shiny pre-come merely centimetres from his mouth. Looking upward once more at Dalton's begging gaze, he darted out his tongue to take a taste. The salty sensation brought a wave of pleasure over him. He moved a hand to tease his own slippery end as he manoeuvred over the beautiful pink orb, up and down the shaft, underneath the crease of the head before finally taking it all in right to the back of his throat. It was no mean feat: Greg's jaw began to ache instantly from stretching to accommodate the size. But the hot length felt so good in his mouth he simply didn't want to stop.

Dalton was groaning now, loud deep moans that echoed around the showers. It sounded as if he was almost ready to orgasm. Greg felt that way too, although his enjoyment was so great that he would have preferred to go on all night were it possible.

'Please, Greg,' Dalton interrupted. 'I'm nearly there. But I don't want to, not yet.'

Greg stopped sucking, but kept a good hold of the cock in front of him.

'I want to fuck you, mate. I want to shoot while I'm up your arse.'

Although he was slightly worried whether he could manage something of such a width, Greg nodded. He wanted it inside him, no matter how much it hurt.

Greg lay down on his back, placing his hands on the back of his thighs at the knees so that his eager butt-crack was exposed to the world.

'Just what I wanted to see,' said Dalton. 'That's a gorgeous hole, mate.'

Dalton put his head between Greg's legs and rested his nose at the base of Greg's balls so that his mouth was directly between Greg's buttocks. Greg felt so turned on at the heat of Dalton's breath panting out on to his anus. He shut his eyes in ecstasy as Dalton's tongue began its warm wet washes, easing its way around and around and then inward. He gasped as he was opened up even more, aided by an accompanying thick finger, and then, on relaxing, he simply lost himself in the incredible feeling. Soon three fingers were inside and Greg was unable to prevent the deeply pleasured noises he emitted with each thrust.

'I'm ready,' he said, at last. 'Please, Brian. Put it in.'

Dalton disappeared for about half a minute, rolling a condom over himself as he knelt back down. He swung Greg's legs over his shoulders then pushed forward gradually. Greg had never felt anything like it before, never been stretched to that extent by anyone and it felt like nothing on earth. He grabbed at Dalton's broad back as the tool slid in and out. He pulled Dalton's face closer so they could kiss once more. He grabbed his own sticky prick and began to jerk it off, his knuckles running against Dalton's hard belly. The bucking got faster and faster; the two men's grunts began to synchronise as their movements increased in intensity. Greg's balls bounced with every penetration; Dalton was now pulling out completely before ramming back inward, all the time growling 'Yes! Yes! Yes!' Greg felt the dick inside him tense and then explode as Dalton convulsed in his arms. And then he too reached his peak, yanking himself dry, the come splashing upward all over Dalton's well-defined chest and then dripping down onto his own.

Spent, Dalton remained inside Greg for a while. They kissed as if to punctuate the act, then laughed at each other and the happiness of their afterglow.

'I suppose we'd better get a proper shower now,' Dalton said, before delivering a final kiss, then pulling out.

Greg heard the locker-room door bang open, then the noise of cheering crowds that told him that the game was over.

'And not a moment too soon!' He winked, knowing that now they could both shower in safety.

A couple of hours later Greg was in his car, driving along at a comfortable pace. He had been given time to rest his leg and so had decided to spend part of it with a visit to his mother. And despite a little twinge of pain where he'd been tackled, he felt pretty relaxed already. The afterglow the afternoon's sex session had given him still warmed through his body and he had that special feeling of being mellow and happy, of being thoroughly relieved.

He had not been driving ten minutes when his mobile phone beeped, breaking his calmness. He pressed the hands-free button and began to speak.

'Hello. It's Greg.'

'Hi, Greg. It's me, Steve.'

It was Steve Glenn, Middleton United's manager.

'Oh, hi Steve. What can I do you for?'

'I'm sorry I didn't manage to catch you after the match, but publicity was calling. I've got something I wanted to have a word with you about.'

'Really?' It sounded ominous.

'Yeah, it's that business we were talking about. Well, I've just been on the phone to Weston City and they want to have a word with you. They're interested in the transfer. Very interested. I think you could have a contract with them by the end of the week.'

'What? That soon? What about United?'

'Don't worry about us, son. We wouldn't want to hold you back. And let's face it, you're too good now for a team like us.'

'Well, I don't know what to say. It's such a surprise.' Greg was pleased and rather taken aback with the suddenness of it all.

'How about thanks.'

'Thanks Steve. And I really mean that.'

After making their goodbyes, Greg let out an enthusiastic cheer. It was fantastic news. He was moving up to the top of the league, at last fulfilling his dreams of a lifetime by becoming a key player in a world-class football team. He could barely believe his luck. First, the surprise and fun of the time he spent with Dalton and now this. He pressed his foot down on the accelerator and the car speeded up. He was eager to get home, to be somewhere he could share his good mood generated by the day, surely one of the greatest of his life.

Greg's mother lived in a terraced house in one of the older and less well-off districts of Middleton. He had often suggested she move out to one of the safer, newly built areas a bit further out of town. After all, he was more than capable of helping her out with the rent and she really didn't need to be living somewhere so spacious now that he had moved out. But she insisted. It was the house she had moved into when she had first left her parents and there she was staying.

As he drove up the narrow street, his expensive car a somewhat incongruous status symbol in the area, Greg had to admit that his mother had a point. Despite the fact that he had not lived around there for a good few years, the place still felt like his true home. He had many good memories centred around that part of Middleton, and felt his life would be missing something if he had no reasons to go there again.

Greg parked the car outside his mother's house and got out. He had a weird but pleasant feeling every time he knocked on the door of the house where he used to live, one of extreme familiarity with the place and yet knowing all the while just how distanced he was from it. His mother answered quickly.

'Oh Gregory!' she said as if surprised. 'Come in love. Oh you! Come here!'

She pulled Greg into a hug, smacking loud kisses on to his cheek. It was only a few weeks since Greg had seen her last, but however short the gap between his visits he always got the same warm welcome.

'I've got your tea in the oven, love. It won't be long till it's ready now. Do you want a cuppa?'

'Yeah. That'd do nicely.' Greg closed the front door behind him, wiped his feet on the mat before he was ordered to do so then followed his mother into the kitchen.

Greg's mother was in her early sixties. Her hair was almost

fully grey now and her glasses were worn permanently and no longer just for reading. She wore a blue sweatshirt and jeans: comfortable-but-not-past-it-wear as she liked to call it. She had already flicked the kettle switch as Greg entered the room.

'So how's my darling?' She smiled at him with a true mother's love. She had given birth to Greg in her forties: he was her only child and as such held a very special place in her heart.

'Fine,' he said, then realised his underestimation. 'Great, actually. In fact I've got some news. I got the transfer.'

'Oh that's wonderful, love. I'm so pleased for you.'

'It'll mean a lot more money coming in.'

'Don't you get enough already?' Greg's mother always appeared surprised by how much her son earned. No one in her family had made such a success of themselves, she reminded him regularly, never mind at so young an age.

'A lot more money to spend on necessities,' Greg hinted.

'Now don't start,' Greg's mother warned sternly as she took cups and tea-bags from the cupboard. 'I'm happy enough where I am.'

'OK, OK.' Greg laughed, thinking that perhaps he would broach the subject of her moving later. 'I'll not break the atmosphere of good news.'

'Does it mean you're going to be famous? I mean not just in Middleton?'

'Potentially. I might even have my face on a collectible sticker soon.'

Water was poured, milk and sugar added.

'And what does Eddie have to say about it?'

Eddie was Greg's boyfriend. Although Greg's mother appeared to like Eddie well enough, she often implied that he was not destined to be the real one for her son.

'I've not told him yet. There's plenty of time for that. I'll let him know when I get back.'

Greg's mother had never had any problem with her son's sexuality. She was a sensitive woman, one that really knew people, and she had recognised early on that Greg was never going to be your average man. But she had accepted it without trouble, realising that his coming out was less like losing a son, more like gaining a homosexual, and she was far too independent to let other people's opinions worry her at all. And when Greg's father had shown that he was never going to be able to come to terms with it, he was thrown out, with Greg's mother never looking back for an instant.

'Matty rang earlier. He must be psychic. He always knows when you're coming back.'

'Oh really?' Matt was Greg's oldest and best friend, a person that Greg felt he unfortunately never got to see enough of any more, now that he had other commitments in the way.

'Yes. It seems you're not the only one with big news.'

Greg sipped at his tea. 'What do you mean?'

'Oh, I'd better let him tell you.'

Greg realised he wasn't going to get anything else out of the woman, who had begun busying herself with plates and knives at the kitchen table.

'I'll give him a call after we've eaten.'

'It's ready now.' Greg's mother opened the oven and a stomach-rumbling waft of steak and kidney pie filled the room.

'Lovely, Lila.' In an affectation that Greg felt was generated by their closeness Greg had called his mother by her first name since he was a teenager. 'Home cooking,' he continued, as he seated himself in front of his plate. 'Nothing can beat it.' But his thoughts flicked back to the salty taste of Brian Dalton's hard cock, and in his mind he amended what he had said out loud. There was almost nothing that could beat his mother's food. And what did, he had experienced in the showers that very afternoon.

Two

The Black Bull was never a busy pub, even on weekends. That night Greg found it, as he always did, populated by a mere handful of locals. Apart from the odd redecoration the place had barely changed since his parents first began taking him there for Sunday lunch as a child. Then, as now, it was the same old faces: couples out for a drink after work; a group of ageing lads meeting up to reminisce; a gaggle of young girls getting drunk too quickly and laughing about their boyfriends. Maybe the lack of change was the reason why Greg never got any hassle about him being a famous face of the local team on his return visits. People either knew him from the past, or simply recognised him and nodded a hello, but no one approached him to cause trouble, or ask for an autograph. Unsurprisingly, he liked the pub. It was an easy place to come back to, a good one for him to take one of his few but well-earned breaks.

At the bar, Greg ordered a pint. The barman, who had been manager of the place for the past twenty years or so, exchanged a friendly greeting and a joke about Greg's limp before handing him the lager. Feeling at home, and pleasantly relaxed, Greg was now in a very good mood to meet Matt, who he found alone in an alcove by the jukebox.

'Matt?' he asked, in an attempt to get the man to look up from the rim of his glass. Matt did so and grinned briefly before laughing 'C'mere' and pulling Greg into a tight hug. Matt was a truly huge man, his size and the muscles on his body coming as a result of his regular physical work as a labourer. Although their relationship had always strictly been on the level of friends, Greg recognised the fact that the man was the type he always fell for: rough and ready, with puppy-dog eyes to die for. It felt good to be in those strong arms of his friend, to have his fingers clutching at that strong builder's back. Unfortunately the clinch didn't last particularly long.

'How's your leg, anyway? I forgot to ask you on the phone.'

The two men sat down, facing each other.

'Oh, it'll heal fast enough. Nothing serious.'

'I saw what happened.' Matt went to all of Middleton's matches. At least the ones that Greg played in. 'And the tackle after it that got Dalton finally sent off. He's a real fucker that one.'

And don't I know it, thought Greg.

'Nice goal though. We wouldn't have won it if you hadn't set that one up.'

'Well, I try, you know.' Greg took a sip of his drink. He could tell Matt was avoiding talking about what he really wanted to, but didn't really know how to bring up the subject without awkwardness. Instead, he decided to reveal his own news.

'I ought to give it my best, anyway, these being my last few games for United.'

'You what?' Matt asked, confused.

'I'm getting a transfer. To Weston City. By next month, I'll be playing at the top!'

'Blimey! You never said anything! Congratulations! And cheers!'

Matt raised his pint and the two clinked glasses. To an outsider, the mood would have seemed happy enough, but Greg was concerned. Having known Matt for a number of years, he could easily sense the signals that indicated something was wrong. Now his worry was confirmed by the way Matt's grin faded quickly, how the man returned to staring at his drink.

'Matt, Mum said you had something to tell me. Something you told her the other day.'

Matt sighed. He was avoiding eye contact. 'Yeah, I have. It's a good thing really.' At last he raised his gaze to look at his friend. 'I'm getting married.'

'What?' Greg began to laugh. 'I would have thought it was something a lot more terminal the way you were carrying on.'

Matt grinned, a little.

'Anyway, nice one mate. It looks like I'm not the only one who needs to celebrate.'

'I don't know. It's just that – It was Sarah that asked me. I barely remember agreeing. One minute everything's the same as always, the next she's picking a ring out for me to buy her, she's choosing a dress, a suit for me, where it's all going to happen –'

'Is it all going too fast?' Greg thought he had discovered the problem. 'You and Sarah have been going out for a long time now, you know.'

'I know that. But we're still so young. There's still so much I want to do. So much I want to explore.'

'Sarah always was pretty pushy. Especially when she got an idea in her head.'

'Yeah, but she's going to end up pushing me away if she's not careful.'

'Have you spoken to her about it?'

'She's not one for listening too much either, when she wants something.'

There was a slight pause, which gave Matt time to return his look to the top of his glass. Greg extended an arm to squeeze at his friend's chunky shoulder and Matt's eyes met his own once more.

'Don't worry,' Greg said. 'We'll sort something out I'm sure. Have you set a date?'

'It's in a couple of months.'

'That soon? Well, you're bound to get nervous. They say everyone has doubts.'

Matt shook his head. 'I'm having doubts about everything.'

'What do you mean?' Greg asked.

Matt took in a deep breath, as if what he was about to say was truly difficult for him.

'I'm not even sure I – What I mean to say is – I don't know if I really like –' Matt's eyes were everywhere except at Greg, and he was blushing as he finished his sentence with the word 'Sarah'.

Greg was taken aback, but also more than suspicious that there was something else that Matt had not revealed.

'That's a big doubt,' he said. He was worried and, not knowing exactly the words to say right then, decided to buy some time to think about it. 'And don't think I'm avoiding the issue but I think we'll need another drink to discuss it further. Same again?'

Matt nodded. If Greg had turned around as he headed off, he would have realised immediately what was wrong with Matt. Matt's stare was frozen, fixated at the level of Greg's muscled backside, watching the thighs tight in blue denim, splitting into a manly stance as they reached the bar, the look revealing without question what was really going to hold him back from his impending marriage.

Later that night, the men were still talking. Last orders had gone, they had finished their final pint and now they were walking up the hill to their respective places of rest. Matt had not yet revealed the full truth but had spent the evening alluding to it. He still appeared down. Greg was doing all he could to cheer him but by the time they reached Matt's parents' house he had far from succeeded.

'Do you want to come in for a bit?' Matt asked. He still lived with his Mum and Dad, as he did not yet make enough money on the building site to truly have a go at living on his own. 'I've not stopped making a classic cuppa.'

'Yeah, that'd be nice.' Despite all their talking, Greg knew that Matt's problems were not all sorted out. He had an idea what was at the root of them but had said nothing, instead deciding to wait for Matt to get to that point on his own.

The house was terraced, like Greg's mother's. It was small but Greg remembered it as having a happy, family atmosphere that meant it seemed more cosy than poky.

'We'll have to be quiet,' Matt whispered as he dead-locked the door. 'Mum and Dad are in bed. Go through into the kitchen and I'll put the kettle on.'

Greg obeyed. He knew the procedure from the many other times over the years he had been round there for an after-night-out drink. He sat down at the old table and prepared to listen some more.

Matt leaned against the breakfast board, and folded his arms across his chest so that his thick, hairy forearms bulged out like legs of ham.

'You know,' he began, 'there's something about this marriage business that I've been holding back on.'

The kettle began to hiss as it heated itself up.

'I guessed as much. But if you don't want to tell me that's fine.'

'No, it's – Before, when I said I didn't know if I like Sarah, that was a lie. I do like her, I really do. Just perhaps not enough, that's all. And there's something else, someone else that's in the way of me and her that I really have to do something about before anything goes any further.'

'Who is it, Matt?' Greg was hoping that now everything would come out into the open. 'Come on, you can tell me.'

Matt moved across the room, and placing one hand on the table bent over so that his face gazed directly into Greg's.

'It's you, Greg. It's my feelings for you that are giving me doubts.' Matt pushed forward and the two men's mouths met, gently at first, just brushing at each other's warmth and the slight wetness of saliva on their lips, and then their tongues touched, slowly rasping over each other. Greg wanted more, but before thirty seconds had passed Matt had pulled away.

'I'm sorry –' he began as he stood up once more, then turned around.

'Don't be. It's just a surprise, that's all. I had no idea you felt like this until tonight.' Until the kiss, Greg had no idea how he felt either. The act had brought up to the surface so many feelings that had been bubbling away inside him. He realised how much of a disappointment it had actually been when Matt announced his engagement, how it would hurt to finally lose this big, rough bloke to marriage. Greg was glad Matt had done what he had; there was a new development to their relationship and it felt so right, so good. He stood, then wrapped his arms around Matt's huge body and breathed into his ear.

'It's a surprise all right, Matty.' Greg put his palms upon the hard blocks that made up Matt's chest and began to tickle the nipples. 'But it's a good one. Oh yeah, it's a really good one.'

Greg licked the edge of Matt's ear, then moved down to bite the lobe. He felt Matt's body wriggle slightly and his bubbled buttocks press backward against his own hardening crotch. He began to explore the crevasses of the ear with kisses and strokes, first at the top, then from side to side and downward, until he reached the opening. As he carefully wiggled his tongue inside, Matt panted hornily. Greg felt Matt reach to take his hands in his own and move them downward, over the bulge of stomach muscles, then he held them at the pack of denim between his legs. Greg kissed at Matt's neck, at the bristly hairs at the edge of his jawline as he grabbed at the rigid rod beneath the unyielding material. Touching a guy's cock in that way was always good, not really knowing how big it was, what it was going to look like, just trying to guess by fondling it. From what he could make out, even under the constriction of his clothing, Matt was quite a well-endowed man, a wielder of a good three-and-a-half-inch (in circumference) man-thing that pressed a good way down his thigh. Greg kept squeezing the end of it, feeling it throb heartily as he ran his fingers back upward to the balls. He dragged a fingernail down the teeth of the fly, then with both hands tugged at the contrasting softness of what apparently was an oversized pair of nuts. He couldn't wait to see what Matt would look like unhampered by clothing. Matt turned around and smiled.

'This time,' he began, his crotch pleasingly standing to attention, 'it'll be better. I'm not so nervous now.'

He kissed Greg again, but not so warily as before. This time mouths locked hard, tongues firmly implanted and writhed, and hands grabbed at young, hard bodies. Eventually Greg pulled away and started to drag Matt's T-shirt out of the waist of his jeans. Matt raised his arms to reveal a perfectly developed body, with thick patches of hair at the pits. Greg pulled at Matt's belt buckle, undid it and slid the leather out through the straps. Although he could barely wait to see Matt's piece out in the open, he also wanted to take his time. The anticipation was just so delicious it wasn't to be wasted. He eased open the top button, slowly zipped down the fly, then pulled the jeans over Matt's huge thighs to knee level. He knelt so that his face was level with Matt's white Y-fronts, which were as heavily and tightly packed as a grocery bag containing an entire week's shopping. Suddenly, he remembered where he was.

'What about your parents?' he asked, worried about interruptions.

Matt shook his head. 'Don't worry. As long as we don't get too noisy they won't come down. Me and Sarah used to do it downstairs all the time. Besides, it's always better if you're scared of getting caught.'

The mention of Matt's girlfriend made blood surge to Greg's cock. It turned him on to think that his friend had known only women before, that the penis in front of him had only been inside vaginas and women's mouths, had been only straight and now was eager for its first man. For a moment Greg lost sight that Matt was his friend and saw only that he was taking a man's gay virginity. It was something he had done before, but only once and as such represented an area of forbidden and rare pleasure that was of extreme excitement for him.

He placed his fingers in the elastic of Matt's pants, pulled down slightly to expose a line of curly hair then moved his face on to Matt's still-covered genitals. He loved to have a man so close, to have the hardness of an erection, the softness of huge balls pliant against his cheeks and lips, his closed eyelids. He shoved his chin right underneath Matt's packet, rubbing his nose and forehead against the warm white material, positioning the clothed cock so it stroked across his face as he moved upward. Matt was moaning more regularly now; Greg glanced up and saw his friend had got that sexy, open-mouthed begging look that he had seen so many times on other guys, but had never expected to see on Matt.

'Please.' Matt was desperate and Greg knew what was wanted. He too found it hard to hold back any longer and so eased down the Y-fronts. At last Matt's monster cock bounced free. As Greg had thought, it was a good nine-incher, really meaty with a bit of a curve to one side. It was a slightly darker colour than the rest of Matt's body. The foreskin came right to the end to create a pocket of wrinkles, which by that time was holding a decent backlog of shiny pre-come.

'Looks like you're quite excited,' Greg said as he tasted his friend's fluids. Matt groaned as Greg took the head of the cock into his mouth, enjoying the sensation of the stiff, greasy muscle, feeling his jaw muscles extend even wider so that he could take in more of it. He closed his eyes as the tip of his nose headed towards Matt's dark bush, grabbed his own crotch at the joy of having another man fill his throat so well. All the while sucking, he pulled back to give himself the opportunity to speak.

'Fuck me. Fuck my mouth, Matt.'

Matt shuddered with enthusiasm, then began to do as he was asked. It was as if he was scared at first, not thrusting too hard or too fast, so Greg took hold of his beefy arse-cheeks and pulled the man towards himself to demonstrate just what he was capable of taking. Matt began bucking faster and deeper, letting out a small 'oh' every time he was in as far as he could go. Greg was horny as anything now, listening to the clicks and smacks of his sucking as the dick jammed again and again into the back of his throat. He returned to playing with himself, not caring that it was still in his jeans, his other hand tickling and fondling Matt's hairy plums. It wasn't long before Greg could sense the tensing of Matt's body and he knew what was going to happen. With a final deep bang forward, the cock in Greg's mouth began to shoot, jerking wildly and repeatedly as the streams of hot, salty load burst down his gullet. He swallowed again and again; the orgasm seemed to go on forever but he loved having the pulsating wet member in his mouth so much that it could have done for all he cared. But all too soon, the throbs lessened in frequency and intensity and Greg felt the softening dick pull out.

He looked up and smiled. Matt seemed flushed and relieved, and yet also appeared a little bit sheepish.

'That was the first time I've come in the presence of another man,' he confessed, breathless.

'And how did you like it?' Greg stood up once more.

'It was better than I could ever have imagined.'

Greg laughed. 'Well, there's plenty more where that came from. C'mere.'

They kissed again. Greg knew he would still taste of come, and it turned him on to know that he was giving Matt his first sample of man-juice. He felt so hot now he knew he would have to do something about it or he would have a messy pair of trousers to deal with.

'Ever touched a guy down there before?' he asked.

Matt shook his head.

'Are you ready to?'

Matt nodded.

'Then take it out, Matt. I want to feel your hands around me.'

Matt fiddled with Greg's belt and, obviously enthusiastic to see his friend's manhood in all its glory, quickly pulled Greg's pants and jeans down over the erect member. Greg watched as Matt's face fell open in awe. Greg wasn't as big as his friend but he knew Matt just wanted some dick at last and the harder and readier it was the better.

'Is that what you wanted?' asked Greg.

Matt licked his lips in anticipation. His own cock was rising again. 'It's beautiful.'

'Touch it,' said Greg. 'Go on. Please. Touch me.'

Not taking his eyes off the trembling shaft, Matt reached out for his first real feel of another male's privates. The fingers were cautious, as if frightened the thing would blow off in his hand if he were too eager.

'Go on,' encouraged Greg. 'Grab hold of it. Grip it like you would your own.'

Matt did as he was told and Greg winced with mounting tension.

'Now wank it. Back and forth, that's it. And feel my balls.'

Both men were highly excited now: Matt obviously extremely thrilled at his initial foray into gay love, Greg enjoying directing a homo virgin around his sexual parts. But great as the experience was, Greg wanted more.

'Turn around, Matt. I want to feel me inside you.'

Matt looked surprised, and as if he was about to refuse. Then his face melted as if he realised that that was what he wanted too. He turned around, leaned over the kitchen table, then spread his sturdy glutes open with both hands.

'Is this how you do it?' he asked.

'Oh yeah.' Greg smiled at Matt's naivety. 'That just looks wonderful.'

And it did. A gorgeous pink moon of masculinity with its split guiding Greg's gaze to its star of a pucker. Matt's hungry hole winked in expectation. Greg greased up his middle finger with spit. He tickled the anus, circling round and around before cautiously inserting, initially only to the first joint, then past the knuckle and finally shoving it all the way in. Matt was giving out a low-level groan constantly now.

'Are you okay?' Greg asked just to make sure. He was answered only with a 'mmm'.

With this encouragement Greg tried a second finger, relishing the sight as it too disappeared up the chute. He began to hand-fuck Matt, sliding back and forth until the muscles slackened so he could slip in a third digit.

'Are you ready for more?' Greg asked. He himself was more than ready.

Matt nodded. Greg removed his hand and, manoeuvring his quivering manhood into place, let it rest a moment up Matt's crack.

'Please,' Matt begged. 'Do it to me now. I want it inside me.'

Greg quickly took a johnny from the back pocket of his jeans and put it on. Finding the right place once more, he pushed forward a little, savouring every moment of the tight hole easing over his cock-end. He took it slowly, knowing every movement ahead was a step closer to the deflowering of the man in front of him. And with every push, Matt let out a little grunt, his rectum giving just that little bit more until Greg was swallowed up entirely by the virgin arse. For Greg, the view was fantastic: Matt's wide triangle of a muscle-bound back leading right down to those huge hard cheeks in which he had buried his own cock.

'Are you ready to get fucked now?' asked Greg. 'Do you want to know what it's like to be screwed by another man?'

'Yes,' Matt said with a pant. 'Oh yes.' Greg began his thrusts, slowly at first, because Matt's fuckhole was still so tight, then quicker and quicker as Matt relaxed. Greg leaned over so that his body covered Matt from behind. Neither man had ever thought they would be this physically close together and it felt fantastic to be breaking those boundaries. Greg placed his hands around Matt's own. Soon enough they were moved down to grasp Matt's re-hardened dick.

'So you like it up you then?' Greg gasped as he pumped, and began once more to fondle Matt's piece.

'Oh yeah, Greg. I love being fucked.'

With those words, and realising he had well and truly introduced his friend to his side of the tracks, Greg became horny to the point of not being able to hold it in any longer. He felt his cock get really hard. Every sensation in his body centred on the head banging away at his friend's arse.

'I'm ready, Matt,' he warned. 'I'm going to shoot.'

'Me too,' Matt said. 'Make me come too, please.'

Greg was now drawing all the way out and shoving right the way in with each fuck, just as Dalton had done to him earlier in the day. He felt his balls tighten and he started to come off. It was an orgasm that started in his toes, then rushed all over him and into his crotch. He shoved his dick up as far as it would go as it frantically spurted, each burst more pleasurable than the last, the hot come coating him inside the prophylactic that gripped him. Matt stood up slightly as he too began to shoot, each jerk shuddering throughout his body, his arse rhythmically clamping around Greg's cock even more, his come dribbling over Greg's fingers on to the tablecloth over which they leaned. At last and with a sigh, the judders of joy stopped for the both of them. Greg withdrew, and the two men kissed.

They paused and left their embrace to clean up the worst of the mess with the tablecloth.

'I'll have to get this in the wash before Mum sees it.' Matt began gathering up the table covering, apparently somewhat distracted.

'You're right there.' Greg put himself back into his pants and jeans. 'That'd give the game away in no time, wouldn't it?'

He sat down, feeling drained, but relieved. And then, still joking, said, 'To tell you the truth I'm a little bit disappointed.'

Matt turned his attention from the buttons of the washing machine and looked confused.

'After all, it was a cup of tea you invited me in for, wasn't it!'

The men laughed, and Matt switched on the kettle once more.

A couple of hours later, after much, much talking, Greg finally began to make a move. He had not wanted to go at all. The change in his and Matt's relationship was a good one and it had brought with it warm, comfortable emotions that he enjoyed greatly. Being tucked under Matt's hefty but gentle arm as they chatted about the past and future, about big topics and small ones, felt wonderful. It seemed to Greg as if his life had been a journey down a long, long road and then bang, almost without knowing it, he had arrived home. Greg understood what the blossoming, quivering motions at the pit of his stomach meant. It was the beginning of love, and he began desperately attempting to read Matt's actions and words for signs that his friend felt the same. Certainly the cosy situation made it seem like Matt was in the same boat. But Greg couldn't be sure without asking outright and, not wanting to unsteady the pleasant but fragile new area their friendship had entered, he didn't pursue the idea too far.

Despite having been given the time off to rest, Greg had got a lot of things to sort out as a result of the impending transfer. Eventually the big day he had ahead of him could be avoided no longer, and he left for his mother's home to prepare himself with sleep.

In the morning, he found his mother had risen even earlier than he had, and was preparing an unwanted but inevitable fried breakfast in the kitchen.

'Morning, Lila,' he said, kissing the woman on the cheek, feeling a spit of hot fat spark against the back of his hand as he got too close.

There followed a brief but significant pause. 'You were out late last night, weren't you?'

'Er, yes.' Greg knew instantly what his mother was getting at. 'You know Matt and me. We always have a lot of catching up to do. Did I wake you up when I got in?'

'No, no. Not really.' Lila shuffled the sausages in the pan nonchalantly. 'He's all right then, is he?'

'Yeah, he's fine.' Greg sat down at the table, picked up a piece of toast from the rack and began buttering.

'No troubles with that girl of his?'

'No. Didn't mention anything.' Greg could tell his mother suspected something but he wasn't about to reveal any of what had happened between him and his friend, and instead he turned his attentions to the morning paper.

There followed an uneasy breakfast. Fortunately, knowing his mother's inquisitive mind well, Greg was able to weave around her veiled insinuations as if they were defenders on the pitch and, as he kissed her farewell on the doorstep, he left her none the wiser for her prying.

The next couple of days were busy ones for Greg. He had several meetings with his personal adviser about the impending transfer and by Friday morning, Greg found himself on his way to Weston for his introduction to the club along with the signing of his new contract.

The drive took a couple of hours and the journey was all

motorway until Greg hit the city itself, where a confusing maze of roads led him out the other side to his intended destination: the huge imposing building that was Weston's stadium, Helmsfield Park. As he drove around it he couldn't help but be awed by the ground's size and architecture: the combination of concrete, metal and design had retained its impressiveness over the several decades it had been in existence. His heart jumped a beat as the club's name and insignia in large relief on one of the side walls came into view. He was about to become a vital part of the Weston legend and he was proud to think that soon he would be wearing that very badge on his chest.

Attempting to contain both his excitement and his nervousness, but still wanting to succumb to the rollercoaster ride of it all, he pulled into the car park of the building's offices. As he got out, he heard a woman's voice calling his name.

'Mr Williams! Greg! Over here!' A blonde, bubbly-haired woman approached with an outstretched hand. 'Hello there, Mr Williams. I just popped out to see if you'd arrived. I'm glad you made it.'

Greg accepted the handshake. 'I'm sorry I'm late. I got slightly lost.'

'It's the one-way system. I know, it's a nightmare. Never mind, you're here now. Trevor's just taking a few calls at the moment so if you'd like to follow me, I'll take this opportunity to show you around.'

The woman set off towards the glass entrance doors in the side of the building.

'My name's Suzie, by the way. I'm Trevor's assistant, so any immediate enquiries you can just ask me.'

Suzie led Greg into the building.

'Here's reception. That's Celia behind the desk, and Sean who actually ought to be working.'

The reception area was well spaced and welcoming, with a seating area near the door. Suzie made her way to the lift and, pressing the button, began glaring through her large round glasses at the young, dark security guard who was leaning over the desk, casually chatting. Greg waved a hello at Celia, then quickly glanced over the guard's uniform, a beige shirt tucked into brown trousers that fitted snugly over an obviously well-worked-out body. Sean seemed to reciprocate the interest, his friendly gaze penetrating Greg's own for just long enough. Unfortunately, there was apparently little time for proper introductions.

'Come on, Mr Williams.' The lift doors slid open and Suzie entered. 'All the way to the top.'

'See you around.' Greg shrugged at the lost opportunity as the doors closed, and he made a mental note to acquaint himself better with the staff as soon as he got the chance.

Greg stood looking out of the huge glass windows of the VIP lounge. He felt surrounded by luxury. The design of the large room was sleek and modern, decorated in pale coordinating shades based on Weston's club colours. An unmanned bar ran the length of one wall: the clusters of chairs and tables suggested that this was as much a space for socialising as watching the game. Greg had no doubt that the lounge provided an appropriate space for those who could afford to be there. And the view was truly magnificent, a perfectly advantaged perspective over the pitch. Greg marvelled at the giant stadium of a capacity far greater than the one at Middleton. He felt a shiver of anticipation and trepidation that one day soon the crowds that filled those seats would be watching him, cheering him on and hoping he'd pull through for them.

'I bet you can't wait to get down there, can you?' Suzie had moved to join Greg at the window. 'Well, it won't be too long now. You've got your first game with us at the end of next week.' She pushed her glasses back up the bridge of her nose and turned around.

'Right, through that door,' Suzie said, and pointed like an air stewardess at an open door on the far left, 'is the press conference room. There is a direct route from here to the dressing-rooms, but it's long and winding down the back stairs, and I've just been paged by Trevor to say he's ready now. So if you'd like to continue following me –'

'Ever been a museum guide?' Greg joked as he entered the corridor.

'Do you think I qualify?' Suzie laughed. Greg had decided he liked the woman. She made him feel relaxed and at ease even though the events of the day were somewhat intimidating.

'It's not long now,' Suzie explained. 'He didn't want his office too far away from the bar. No, I'm just kidding. Trevor's a lovely man. I'm sure you'll get on like a house on fire.'

Suzie led him to a door that bore the legend TREVOR BROWN: WESTON CITY FOOTBALL CLUB MANAGER.

'Here we are then. Do you think you'll remember your way around?'

'Yeah, no problem.'

'Well, if you do have any trouble you know where to come. Right, I'll leave you to it. See you, Mr Williams.'

Suzie disappeared quickly, her high heels clicking as she left. Greg faced the door. With his guide now gone, his anxiousness returned. Even though the deal was clinched and all that was needed was his signature on the contract, there were things that worried him. Could he really cut it at such a high level, with all the publicity and pressure it would bring? But there was only one way he would find out, he decided, and that was to go ahead and try. He knocked on the door. Hearing a loud 'Come in!' he entered to find his new manager rising from behind a large wooden desk. Though the two men had met only briefly during transfer talks, Trevor's face was very familiar from the countless television and newspaper appearances he had made. An ex-player himself, Trevor had a build that was impressive: he was slightly bulkier than the average footballer as a result of his age but he managed to fill his suit more than appealingly. Now he was in his forties, a sprinkling of grey hairs had begun to appear just above his sideburns. But though the lines on his face were deeper than when he was known as one of the main heart-throbs on the pitch, he still retained his notorious pin-up looks. As the two men shook hands, Greg couldn't help but momentarily forget his concerns and simply enjoy the thrill of looking at those beautiful eyes and that famous dimpled chin.

'So, the big day is here at last.' Trevor's smile was welcoming and his cockney barrow-boy accent charmingly manly. 'I hope you're as excited by it as I am.'

'Definitely.' Greg sat down.

'Itching to get started, are you?'

On more things than you think, Greg thought as he replied effusively in the affirmative. He felt aroused and flirtatious but there were other, more pressing matters at hand than his sexual desires.

Trevor picked up some papers from his desk and handed them over. 'This is the contract. Just a formality, really. All the ins and outs as we discussed them, but now they're in print. So if you'd just like to check through and sign where it says.'

Greg began skim-reading the contract. He knew what it said, having seen a draft already and having gone over the points very carefully with his adviser. As he read, his stomach twisted with the returned tensions, although this time, with the facts in front of him, they were undercut with a definite tingle of elation. This was the moment he had been dreaming of for almost his entire life. From the five-a-side games he had played in the street as a child, through the way he had proved himself as a contender in school teams to his apprenticeship that led to his inclusion in Middleton's first team. The drive and determination, the commitment he had always shown and the sacrifices he had made had all been to reach this point: to be able to play at the top. Greg couldn't believe that the time had arrived at last, when the simple act of writing his name on a piece of paper would bring the fame and fortune and the opportunity to achieve what he had always wanted. He leaned forward to rest on the desk, placed the nib of his pen in just the right position above the dotted line.

'What are you waiting for, son?' Trevor asked after a few moments had passed. 'Something wrong with a sub-clause?'

'No.' Greg shook his head, and let the ink finally run out over the page. 'I was just savouring the moment.'

Trevor laughed, stood up once more and stuck out his hand.

'Welcome to the team, Greg! You'll be the making of us. There'll be no stopping us with your legs on board.'

'Thanks. I'm glad to be here.' Greg's head felt light with exhilaration.

'Now that's done, how's about some lunch? I got Suzie to organise us a table at Androtti's. We can't hang around too long, though. There's a press conference scheduled for two thirty.'

'Things move fast around here, don't they?' Greg opened the door and the two men left the office.

'Your feet won't touch the ground, mate. Believe me, I've been there and done it. But don't worry.' Trevor put his thick arm around Greg's shoulder. 'I'm sure you'll love every minute of it.'

Greg immediately felt better with such an attractive man next to him. 'No doubts about that, boss man,' he revealed. 'Suddenly, I've got no doubts at all!'

*

Back in the car park the two men found a surprise that put a halt to Brown's plans for the afternoon. Greg's car had been clamped.

'You're fucking joking me!' The famous, grumpy, controlling side of Brown, the part of him that made him such a feared as well as respected manager, seemed to be making an appearance. 'It must be because you haven't got a pass for the car park. This is all I need. We're late already and I've arranged to meet Howe and Baker there. Damn it!'

'It's no problem, Trev. It's not like they've scratched the paintwork or anything.' Greg squatted at the locked-up wheel and checked the framework around it in an attempt to reassure his new boss that things were OK.

'We'll have to take my car into town. We can sort this out later. Sorry, Greg. Not much of a welcome to Weston, is it?' Brown ran his hand over his hair in frustration. 'Those bloody security guards! I warned them you were coming!'

Security guards? That sexy uniformed guy who had been standing in the reception earlier on? Suddenly the clamp seemed even less of a problem to Greg.

'Listen, boss. Don't worry about it. You go for lunch. I'll stay here and sort this out and we can meet up later for the press conference. I'm not that hungry anyway.'

'But I wanted to introduce you and Baker. He's a good bloke to know in this line of business.'

'There's plenty of time. It's only my first day here, after all.' Greg put on his best, chilled-out grin.

Brown looked as if he was thinking hard. 'Are you sure?' he asked, obviously eager to get away.

'Yeah, I can handle it. And when I think about it I'd rather get this out of the way. I don't like the thought of my baby caged up like that.'

'Cheers, Greg.' Brown headed off to his own car. 'I could do with a few more easy-going players like you on the team. It'd make my life one hell of a lot easier.'

He got in and drove away and Greg waved him off.

Greg made his way back to the reception area. Celia, the receptionist, was most deferential and apologetic, but he attempted to allay her worries with amiable smiles and a relaxed manner. He really wasn't upset by the incident, he told her, he just wanted to know what he had to do to solve the problem. Celia directed him to the security guard's office down a hallway on the right. Greg went to it, hoping that Sean was still on duty.

He found the office easily and knocked on the door. Receiving no answer after a second attempt, he turned the handle. Inside, he found a small office, one wall of which had a number of television screens mounted on it that showed different areas of the stadium. They were meant to provide an overview of the building inside and out so that any incidents or troubles could be kept under control, but at that particular moment Greg found them redundant. They were unmanned, the person obviously supposed to be keeping an eye on them asleep at their side, his feet up on the desk. Greg was amused at the sight of the security guard, his snores rumbling away and his head lolled back in complete release. Sean was a truly gorgeous man. Greg guessed he was in his late twenties and over six foot tall. He had a very handsome face with dark hair and skin that gave his looks a Spanish air, and his massive frame was exercised and well shaped. His uniform emphasised his masculinity and he looked smart and sexy dressed in it. His short-sleeved shirt had epaulettes, and pockets at the front; his tie was tight and he had a dark, peaked cap that he had taken off and laid on the desk. Greg wondered how much the smile Sean had given him earlier on that morning had meant and, wanting to glean some more background information, he forced out a loud, hearty cough.

Sean sat up with a start. Greg tutted, mock-dismissively. 'If Trevor Brown had found you like that you'd be for it.'

'Er – sorry.' Sean rubbed his eyes and blinked a few times.

'I was just on my break.' Sean had a deep-throated voice and a rolling Yorkshire accent that sounded very, very appealing.

Greg laughed at the man's excuses. 'I believe you!' he said sarcastically. 'I bet you've not missed anything, anyway. Not many people around here when there's not a match on.'

'That's right.' Suddenly Sean looked worried. 'You're not going to tell anybody, are you?' he asked, somewhat concerned.

'No, mate. Don't worry about it. You're in too much trouble already.'

Sean looked confused, and Greg quickly explained what had happened. Sean began apologising profusely for his mistake.

'Sorry, Mr Williams. I'd forgotten all about you. It's just that some people use the car park illegally when there's overspill from the local shopping centre and I thought you were one of them. I'll get it sorted out immediately. I hope it hasn't caused you too much bother.'

Sean stood up and reached for a cabinet above the monitors. Greg noted how pinchable his pert buttocks looked as he stretched upward.

'The release key is in here,' he explained. 'It'll not take long to free your motor.'

As he opened the door to the cupboard, a magazine that had been placed inside fell out and on to the desk. It was creased and well thumbed, and from the image of a lingerie-clad woman on the front cover Greg could immediately tell what it was.

'Oops,' Sean said deferentially. 'It's not my day for impressing the new man at work, is it.'

Greg moved closer to the security guard. He picked up the porn mag, feeling disappointed. 'So this is what you get up to on your breaks as well?' he joked.

Sean looked chagrined. 'Well, you know . . .' He shrugged. 'But not with that, though. It must be one of the other fellas'.

Left it in the key cupboard for a joke or for later when it's his shift. That sort of stuff. It's not really my style.'

Greg felt encouraged once more. 'Oh.' He put the magazine down. 'It's not my style either.'

Sean stopped fiddling around with the rows of keys and looked directly at Greg as if he was trying to work the footballer out. Greg turned around to sit on the edge of the desk.

'So what do you look at when you want to, you know, pass the time?' he asked, hoping for an appropriate response.

'I don't know.' Sean appeared to be a little embarrassed and as if he was under duress. He finally found the key he was looking for and twiddled it on his finger. 'Er, whatever is around.' He shrugged.

'Oh, come on.' Greg pushed further, knowing he was on to a good tip. 'Big guy like you must have your preferences. What pushes your buttons when you're not whiling away the hours sleeping?'

Greg licked his upper lip slowly, all the while looking directly into the security guard's eyes. Again Sean looked as if he was trying to understand where Greg was coming from, and then, as if he had come either to a decision or a realisation, he delved under the desk and pulled out another magazine from a bag hidden there. He threw it on to the table as if he was challenging Greg to look at it.

'This is the sort of thing that butters my muffins, mate,' he said defiantly. 'How about you?'

Greg picked up the skin rag and began flicking through. To his delight, he found it contained a series of photos not of naked women but of men. It was quite a hardcore publication and its pictures depicted actual sexual acts between the good-looking body-builders on its pages. Looking at it, especially in the presence of another man who was every bit as attractive as the guys in the magazine, began to turn Greg on and he felt his prick prime with rushing blood.

'Oh, right,' he said as if surprised. 'You end up in here on your own having a quick one over this?'

Sean nodded. 'From time to time. You know, when I get bored.' He seemed a little more self-assured now and his cockiness was very appealing.

'Wouldn't it be better if you had someone in here with you?' Greg asked.

'You haven't seen the other security guards.' Sean shook his head. 'Not my type at all. So I can't answer your question because, truth is, I've never tried it.'

'Really?' Greg placed the open magazine on the desk. 'Well, I guess it's about time that you gave it a go. Come on.'

He flicked through the pages until he found a picture that he particularly liked. It was a close-up of a pretty, blond man. His mouth was opened wide and he had two large penises placed upon his outstretched tongue. 'How's about that one, then?'

Sean nodded in approval, smiling.

'All right. Let's get down to business.' Greg was very horny now and his penis was fully erect as he opened his fly and eased it and his balls out of his trousers.

'Now you,' he encouraged. Sean did as he was told, his huge hands tugging at his zip and then delving inside. He pulled out his piece. It was hard, about seven inches long and had an oval, pink head with a deep slit at the tip where its opening was. His big balls dangled beneath and patches of dark pubic hair stuck out at the side of them. The genitals looked great poking out the front of the brown nylon security guard trousers. Sean ran his fingers over the end of his cock, then gave it a couple of tugs.

'That's a nice one you've got there,' Greg said nodding at it. 'Mind if I have a go?' He reached over.

'Be my guest,' Sean beamed.

The thing was hot to Greg's touch and it jumped into his

grasp with a vehement throb. He began to pull at it, wanking slowly, Sean's breathing becoming heavier as he did so.

'Go on. Me as well.' Greg shifted his hips around so that his prick moved closer to Sean's trembling fingers. The security guard took hold of the filled meat and gave it a good squeeze. Greg gasped at the touch and at the sight of Sean's hefty hand that clasped his body.

'See,' Greg murmured. 'I told you it would be better if you had someone here with you.'

The two men began jerking more enthusiastically, Greg sometimes looking at the filthy picture in front of them, sometimes at the hand upon him but mostly at his new friend's solid member as he felt along it. He found the guard became sticky quite quickly, a white bubbly mess collecting on the bell end and on his fingers. His taste buds activated, his desires became such that wanking alone just wasn't enough.

'Oh, fuck the porn, mate.' He grabbed Sean by his meaty shoulders and turned him around. 'We've got it right here.'

Greg planted his lips full on the handsome man's mouth. The kiss was energetic. He accepted the entirety of Sean's tongue into him almost immediately. They pressed their bodies together and Greg enjoyed the rubbing of the uniform against his engorged penis, the unyielding muscles of Sean's body as they chomped away at each other. He nibbled at Sean's neck with his teeth, then began working his way downward, pecking and licking over the chunky pectorals and feeling with his tongue for the point of Sean's nipples. He yanked off Sean's tie then began unbuttoning the man's shirt with enthusiastic fingers. Exposed, Sean's body was stunning. He had a brawny, developed torso covered in fine dark hairs. It looked great framed by his workman's shirt and Greg left it on him as he smooched further and further down, over the man's belly until he had reached his shiny belt buckle and the guard's prick beat away at his neck. Greg was now squatting and he looked up at Sean's desirous, almost distant expression as he rubbed his cheek against the man's dick. He stuck out his tongue, and steadying the thing with his fingers, licked over the dripping end. Sean throbbed away from him and then beat down again. Greg pressed harder, taking a full lick, swallowing the first taste of the man's heated, potent juices and then opened his jaw wide to accept him. Sean moaned as Greg pushed downward, immediately taking the length fully inside him. Greg gulped and writhed around with his head, and the sounds the guard made signalled that what he was doing was received gratefully. He sucked back and forth a couple of times, really dampening the shaft with his saliva and then stood up once more in the hope that he would get some similar action in return.

'Fucking hell!' Sean puffed, obviously excited. 'You've done that before, haven't you?'

'A few times,' Greg chuckled. 'Now why don't I see how experienced you are?'

'Wait on a minute. I've got an idea.'

Sean got down on the floor, his dong wobbling around as he moved to lay on his back. 'How's about a bit of sixty-nining? That way there's no waiting around for your turn.'

'Clever boy,' Greg said, getting into position. He slipped his trousers and underwear over his shoes and then knelt with his knees at either side of Sean's head. He eased himself downward and felt a long wet lick run up his left thigh, rasp up the side of his balls then continue up his erection, right from base to tip. It felt like pure magic and to show his appreciation he bent over and stuck his face in Sean's crotch once more. He began sucking hard and fast and his munching felt all the better as it was happening to him at the same time. He looked down between his legs to see the handsome face dragging up and down his length, sucking at his balls and biting at his thighs. He could feel fingers up the crack of his bum, playing around, trying to find his entrance. His anus was tickled as he gobbled away, then prodded and then finally penetrated fully by a digit. He felt his dick twang out of Sean's mouth then the licks get further and further back until there was hot breath warming his split cheeks.

'You've got a fucking fantastic arse, mate,' Greg heard from behind him. 'Will you . . .?' Sean paused as if afraid to ask his question, and then blurted it out, agitated and embarrassed. 'Will you sit on my face? Please?'

Greg moved to sit on his haunches so that his backside was cleaved fully just above Sean's lusty face. 'It'll be my pleasure,' he said lowering himself. He felt a long, slow lap drag along his chasm and he quivered at the moist, tender touch. Like the fingers before it, the tongue quickly found his hole and he sensed its probing deeper and deeper inside him. He began bouncing up and down slightly, screwing himself with the extended mouth muscle. Sean was wanking now, and Greg found the man's other hand creeping along his thigh until it found his thickened cock. It was a wonderful mix of sights and sensations and soon Greg was horny enough to shoot.

'I'm near,' he said, taking hold of Sean's mighty wrist to suspend his jerking. 'How about you?'

'Just one more thing, mate,' Sean huffed. 'Wipe your arse all over me. That'll bring me off. Wipe yourself all over my face.'

Hearing such a filthy request from such a hot stud brought Greg almost to the brink but focusing hard he pushed downward once more and began shuffling around. He could feel the security guard's forehead, his nose and tongue prodding against the inside of his split bottom. He became more and more wet with saliva as he squirmed this way and that, the stubbled cheeks and chin of Sean scraping against his arsehole and at the base of his balls. He loved to look down at the huge man, face obscured by a backside, his neck protruding out of the base of his squat. Quickly the pounding grasp upon Greg's dick became too much and he began to ejaculate. He watched as the spray of jism gushed out of his beating horn, pumping long stripes over the security guard's chest, one globule hitting the man's belly button directly and filling it with a milky pool. He felt his arsehole contorting repeatedly as the eating at his entrance continued and his orgasm seemed to reach higher peaks of bliss. And then he was joined in his pleasures. Sean's prick began to gush, his load flung in all directions by the jerking fist around it. It jumped again and again, the cream flying over Sean's clothing, drips highlighting his dark trousers and making a mess of his torso. Unable to let so much spunk go to waste, Greg bent over and took a good lick of Sean's belly as his climax faded. Whether he tasted his lover's or his own wad he didn't know or care: the succulent flavour had the same stimulating effect whoever had made it.

Emptied, Greg sat up once more. His legs felt very trembly after his orgasm but he remained in his position for a few seconds longer. He gave Sean's face one long, last, squashing rub, clenching his cheeks so that he grabbed the man within them before he finally stood up and began redressing.

'How was that for a break, then?' he asked, zipping up his fly.

Sean's face was red with pleasure. He took a handkerchief from his pocket and began drying himself, paying particular attention to the blobs on his legs.

'Better than a trip to the cafeteria any day,' he laughed.

Greg bent over to kiss the man. He could taste and smell himself on Sean's lips and face and the contact felt all the sexier because of it. He pulled away and, looking at his watch, remembered that there were things to be done before Trevor Brown arrived back from his lunch.

'Now about this clamp,' he began, picking up the release key from where it had been dropped on the floor. 'I hope I'm not going to get one every time it's your shift.'

'Nah,' Sean's sultry looks broke into a grin as he got to his feet.

'That's a shame,' Greg joked, giving the guard's buttocks a playful slap. 'Because I certainly enjoyed paying the fine!'

Three

Hours later Greg was on the road back to Middleton, somewhat relieved to have finally escaped being the centre of
attention. The entire afternoon had seemingly focused on
him. There had been what felt like hundreds of people he
had been introduced to, and then at the press conference a
good stint of interviews to build him into a new star. It was a
fantastic, thrilling ride to have so many hopes pinned on him,
and so many people suddenly interested in who he was and
what he had to say. It had taken a lot of concentration to
come out with the right comments and make himself look
worth the attention and now he was tired and ready to rest.
As he drove, he wondered whether he was heading to the
right place to relax. Not only was his flat in chaos, being half
packed up for the move to his new place in Weston, but
there had been such a change in his relationship with his live-
in boyfriend, Eddie, recently that he no longer felt truly
comfortable being there. Of course, he could pinpoint the
exact cause of the shift in his feelings. It was what had
happened between him and Matt earlier on in the week. The
sex and new-found intimacy had brought up strong emotions,
much stronger than anything that had existed between him
and Eddie. Greg knew that as a couple the two of them just
weren't going to make it. More than that, it was unfair to
Eddie to pretend otherwise any longer. He knew what he had
to do, and despite his weariness, he knew he was going to do
it that night. He was going to tell Eddie outright that their
relationship was through.

Greg threw his large, heavy sports bag on to the sofa with a
soft thud.

'Eddie?' he shouted. 'Are you in?' He had thought he had heard noises as he had arrived in the flat and assumed his boyfriend was already home. He wanted to get what he had to say out in the open as quickly as possible and though not angry with his lover was impatient for him to appear from whatever nook he was hiding in.

'Coming!' a muffled voice said from the bedroom. Turning quickly, Greg accidentally stubbed his foot on one of the large boxes occupying the lounge floor. He swore agitatedly. Though his flat was a sizeable one, it still couldn't cope with the mess caused by its contents being packaged up and left in such disarray.

'Hello, love.' Eddie emerged as Greg was taking off his shoe to rub his painful toes. He bent over to kiss Greg on the cheek, then moved to stand in the centre of the room with an apprehensive look on his face. Eddie was a slim, toned man whose face, like that of a singer in a pop band, was definitely more pretty than handsome. He wore a white dressing-gown at the opening of which a hairless chest peeped through and above that the perfect, pale skin of his elegant slender neck.

'I was just about to take a shower when I heard your key in the door.' He cringed, then ran his hand through his dark, fashionably messy hair. 'Oh, sorry Greg, that's bullshit. What I mean to say is that I've got something important to tell you.'

Eddie appeared frustrated and obviously worked up. Greg wondered if now was the time to drop his bombshell, but deep down knew that he couldn't avoid it.

'Me too,' he offered, by way of warning.

'Me first.' Eddie seemed unmoved by the interjection, and began pacing what space was left of the room. Greg had encountered this side of the man before, the side that put what he had to do and say above everything else. The offspring of a rich family and rather spoiled by them while growing up, Eddie continued to act accustomed to getting his own way easily as he progressed into his twenties. Greg knew the two of them were total opposites in that respect. Greg's social background had meant he had worked hard for everything he had got in his life. But it was the differences between himself and Eddie that he found undeniably attractive. Eddie's once-weekly coiffured hair, the rounded vowels and public-school sense of manners, even the controlling, superior way Eddie was acting at that moment just sent a thrill directly to Greg's privates. That he, a real working-class lad had made it with someone so far over the class divide was so erotic that he didn't mind, and secretly enjoyed Eddie's selfishness in taking the driver's seat now.

'I really don't know where to begin. There's no easy way to put it for you.' Eddie stopped pacing and looked directly at Greg. 'I suppose we both know that things between us have cooled off lately. And the thing is, for me – Well, it doesn't seem like such a bad turn of events. Which is not to say, of course, there are any bad feelings creeping in. It's just that I think that sometimes relationships come to a natural end. And ours has done exactly that.'

'So you won't be making the move with me to Weston?' Greg asked, rather relieved that his intention to end the relationship had been pre-empted.

'I'm afraid not. I've made other plans. It seems so under-hand now.'

'Don't worry about it,' Greg reassured, secretly glad that Eddie was unwittingly making his life a lot easier. 'To tell the truth, I've been having feelings along the same lines.'

'Still friends, then?'

'Yeah, of course. No problems there.'

'How about a hug, then?' Eddie opened his arms, and Greg stood up and sank into them. 'Oh, baby, we had some good times, didn't we?'

'We certainly did.' Greg remembered the occasions when he'd been in Eddie's clinch and he'd been more than just a friend, when the odour of the fashionable aftershave Eddie always wore and that he could smell right then had intermingled with the smell of their sweat and lovemaking. Greg felt warm, and happy, and slightly aroused.

'You'll keep in touch, now that you're a big star?'

'Sure.'

'Good. I'm glad about that.' Eddie arched his neck around and whispered directly into Greg's ear. 'There's something else I have to tell you.'

Greg enjoyed the sensation of warm breath on his neck, the easy quality of being comfortable next to a familiar body.

'There's been someone else. For a while now.'

Startled, Greg pulled away. 'What?' he questioned, surprised.

'I'm sorry. It was nothing to do with you. Or us. It just happened.'

Greg, in shock, scrambled for answers. 'Well, who is it?'

'Someone from work. No one you know.'

Greg turned away, feeling rejected.

'Listen, like I said, it was nothing to do with you.' Eddie took hold of Greg's shoulders and began to massage them affectionately. 'I don't think either of us thought we would be together for the rest of our lives, did we? And when things developed between Alan and me well, it felt right in a way that our relationship didn't. I hope you won't begrudge me that. And besides, I bet I wasn't the only one who was unfaithful during our relationship.'

Greg couldn't help but acknowledge Eddie's arguments. They were ringing true, echoing as an almost exact copy of the experiences he had been through the past few days. He too had found something in someone else that had not existed between him and Eddie, and that had been the reason he had wanted to move on. And when he thought of the time in the showers with Brian Dalton, with Sean that afternoon and even more of the fantastic sex he had had with Matt, he knew that to be hurt was also to be hypocritical.

'You're right. I've no reason to be mad at you.'

Eddie raised his hand and began to caress his ex-boy-friend's face.

'Hold your horses, Greggy-boy. I'm sorry but there's one more thing I've yet to reveal.'

Eddie seemed slightly playful. Greg was suspicious but in a better and more relaxed mood. 'What now?'

'Remember what you just said: "I've no reason to be mad at you".' Eddie clambered over several boxes as he moved away from Greg.

'Where are you going?' Greg laughed nervously. 'Come on, what is it?'

Eddie stopped, making himself a barrier between Greg and the bedroom door.

'Well, the thing is, I just wasn't expecting you back so early.'

Greg realised what was implicit in the statement: Eddie's new love was still in the flat!

'You're joking!' He was more surprised at Eddie's audacity than shocked at the betrayal.

'No.' Eddie giggled, obviously having realised the situation was okay. 'I'm sorry. This is all rather ridiculous.'

'There's only one thing for it.' Greg, feigning angry determination, started towards the door. 'Me and him, settling this right now, man to man.'

'No, don't go in there!' Eddie grabbed Greg's body and the two play-wrestled briefly. 'He's asleep!'

'Oh I see,' teased Greg. 'Asleep in my bed. And I should let him stay there? Not likely!' He managed to get a hand on the door handle. 'I won't wake him, honestly,' he pleaded. 'Just let me through. I only want to see what my rival looks like.'

'Are you sure?' Eddie relinquished his hold.

'Yeah, trust me.' Greg placed a peck on Eddie's cheek, slowly turned the door handle and edged into the room.

The bedroom was as messy as the lounge, with its furniture and other contents being boxed up and placed haphazardly all around. The bed remained in the centre of the room. Its cream-coloured duvet was rumpled and lay at the side of the man Greg presumed to be Alan. The man's trousers and boxer briefs were pulled down to his ankles and though his shirt and tie were loosened he still wore his navy, expensive-looking suit jacket. Experiencing the phenomenon that occurs to all sleeping men, his exposed cock was erect and pointing straight upward. Eager to get a better look, Greg tiptoed further inside. The prick angled enticingly away from two large, spread-eagled thighs, and closer up Greg could see it much better. Above two hefty bollocks, out of a ring of dark pubic hair it stood unrestrained. Brown in colour, it was mapped in thin veins that wound up to an almost perfectly spherical head. Looking upward, Greg saw it belonged to a well-built man with tanned skin. The man's face was handsome, topped with chocolate-brown hair and, defying Greg's expectations, looked older than he had imagined. The man's oblivious state combined with his exposed manhood felt unbelievably sexy to Greg. He had just turned back to Eddie to indicate that Alan was truly a worthy adversary when he tripped over a box he had not been at all aware of and fell to the ground with an almighty thud. Greg swore in embarrassment as Alan sat up with a start. On seeing the unfamiliar man scrambling around on the floor, Alan got up and began struggling with his pants and trousers, his big hard prick bobbing around at fly level as he tried to put himself away.

'Sorry, I didn't mean to wake you.' Greg got to his knees, relishing being so close to the aroused crotch. 'I was just enjoying the view.'

'You must be Greg.' Alan finally zipped up, causing a sizeable mound to poke forward from his groin. 'Listen, I'm sorry we're meeting like this.'

'I'm not,' Greg interrupted, smiling. Like Eddie, Alan

spoke with the clipped upper-class sounds that turned Greg on so much. That the voice came in such a broad-shouldered, good-looking parcel meant Greg was in full-on flirt mode.

'Don't worry,' Eddie entered the room and sat on the bed. 'I've told him all about it. Everything's fine.'

'Are you sure?' Alan's manner was that of someone who was used to a position of authority and he commanded the room with confidence. 'Listen, both of you, I've just woken up. I suppose it's all a little much, first thing.'

'It looks like some of you was fully awake before we arrived,' said Greg, who had begun to feel very, very horny. He had never had an experience with an older man before. 'Now I see we have two choices here. Either the situation takes an awkward turn or it goes down a path that is much more fun. What do you two think?'

After a pause, Alan nodded at Eddie.

'Go on then,' Eddie directed. 'Get over there. I want to see you do to him what you used to do to me.'

Greg crawled on all fours until his head was inches away from Alan's bulge. He looked up directly into Alan's eyes and face, saw that his skin was no longer as taut as, and creased differently from, a young man's at the collar of the crisp white shirt. He thought of Trevor Brown that afternoon and how the difference in their ages had been so arousing to him and knew that the imminent proceedings were going to be lots of fun.

'Take it out, man,' Alan demanded sternly. 'I can see how much you want it.'

'Oh yes, sir!' Greg was half-humorous in his acquiescence but he was also very titillated at being bossed around. 'I really want it!'

He began caressing the mound in front of him, enjoying the feel of the solid man-flesh within the Bond Street materials. He gave the cock a good hard squeeze, making Alan gasp with pleasure, before fiddling at the shiny gold buckle of the leather belt. Loosening enough slack, he bit down hard on the belt and pulled back, savouring the rich smell of the Italian leather as the belt's arm popped out of its hole. Taking Alan's waist in both hands, he tugged at the fly button with his lips, savouring the smooth feel of the shirt and trousers against his face. He paused momentarily with his face pressed against Alan's crotch, feeling the clothed tumescence throb at his cheek, then drew the zip downward with his teeth. The trousers fell to reveal Alan's well-shaped legs once more. His white boxer briefs were tight around his thick thighs and the Y at the front was extended and mis-shapen from what was happening inside. Greg looked upward once more, knowing how good half-naked men could look. The one in front of him was no exception, standing there in his shirt-tails and gazing down with the hungry look horny men get. Not wanting to make the man wait any longer, Greg slowly eased the briefs downward and Alan's prick sprang outward, bouncing and pulsating into freedom.

Greg heard movement behind him and he looked to find Eddie moving across the bed.

'Carry on. I'm just getting into a better position,' he said, lying a mere couple of feet away and placing a hand within his dressing-gown at the same time. Knowing he was being watched so closely turned Greg on and he too began fiddling at himself.

'Don't do that,' Alan said dismissively. 'I want all your attention on me.'

Frustrated, but also inflamed at the restriction, Greg returned to the job at hand. Close up, Alan's knob looked even better than it had earlier on. Greg brushed his face against the length, feeling the heat slap against one cheek, then the other. With finger and thumb around the base, he licked directly at the end of the prick, first at the clear bubble of pre-come that had collected in the urethral opening, then at the first inch or so beneath the head. He began moving up and down it, wanking the man off with his curled wet tongue.

'Oh that's good, man,' Alan panted in appreciation. 'That's really, really good.'

Greg looked over at Eddie who was now completely naked and was rubbing his erection slowly. Staring directly into Eddie's eyes, he pulled at Alan's cock with his fingers, dragging its loose skin and head into his open mouth. Being watched by one man while having his mouth used by another made him feel so hot and once more he slid a hand up his own thigh to where his hard tool struggled against his jeans.

'I said no!' Alan sounded stern now and, showing he meant business, he yanked Greg's head back by the hair.

'Sorry!' The jerk pinched at Greg's scalp not badly, but just enough. He liked the idea that he was doing something wrong, and the slight pain added that extra, sexy notion of shame to the goings-on.

Alan began wiggling his broad hips around, teasing Greg's open mouth with his prick. The sensation was overwhelming: having such a beautiful and ready piece of flesh just out of his reach, sometimes brushing slightly against his lips and tongue, always pulling away if Greg managed to grab too much of it.

'You really want it, don't you?' Alan asked.

'Oh yes!' begged Greg. 'Please just let me suck you off.'

Greg grunted with joy as the thing was finally realigned with his mouth. Initially plugging him with only a couple of inches, it suddenly thrust forward. At first Greg thought he would gag, but his throat quickly accommodated and he was electrified at being so completely filled with hot man. He could hear Alan moaning as the man fucked back and forth, sometimes pushing all the way in so that Greg found his face pressed against that hairy, greying crotch. It felt fantastic to be used in such a way and Greg began to understand how

Eddie could fall for someone who knew how to screw so well. He felt so turned on now that his penis practically hurt, bound as it was by his clothing and remaining as yet untouched. He was about to sneak another attempt at touching himself when he felt something warm prodding around at the back of his neck. As Alan pulled out once more, Greg turned to find Eddie standing at his side.

'That looked so good I thought I'd get myself a piece of the action.'

Greg took in the full gorgeous sight of Eddie's long-limbed, smooth-skinned body and the thin but lengthy prick and was glad that he was going to get one more fuck out of the man before they truly split up.

Greg's two lovers moved to stand side by side. They contrasted beautifully: one older and experienced, semi-clothed, the other fresh, youthful and totally naked. Both, however, as Greg knew, had one important thing in common: the need to have a greedy mouth attacking their meat.

'What are you waiting for, man! Get to it!' Alan impatiently clipped the back of Greg's head with his open palm.

Again feeling sheepish and shamed, and definitely hornier for it, Greg did as he was told. At first he stretched his mouth so that he could fit the ends of both knobs in, wrapping his moistened tongue underneath them as they slipped and slid around. Both were dripping quite readily, and Greg shivered with pleasure every time he got a taste of that greasy juice. His cheeks filled every time the cocks crossed each other and pressed against the insides of his mouth. Sometimes one would escape the grip of his lips and slip out with a wet pop and he would have to chase it back into position with his fingers, the excess of saliva he was producing oozing down his chin. His own prick was aching like hell now. He would have given anything to feel himself up just a little bit but rather than risk another scolding he took his mind off his own pleasure by concentrating on that of his lovers. He began sucking them individually, taking one right to the back of his throat then the other, and building up a steady rhythm as he did so. He felt around to the crack of both men's arses with his index fingers, enjoying how Alan's bum was hairy while Eddie's was smooth, and searched for their individual puckers. Finding both almost simultaneously, he inserted his fingers and the room echoed with the moans of increased delight. He continued to alternate a little longer, until he felt Alan grab at his head and, realising the man was near to coming, he shoved his finger in as far as it would go.

'Oh yes, that's right, man. Finger-fuck me while I screw your face.'

Greg did as he was told, drawing and withdrawing his finger in regular movements as Alan did the same to his mouth. At the other side, Eddie was wanking furiously and was so close that the top of his fist bounced against Greg's face. Alan was grunting louder and louder and Greg could tell how close the man was to coming off by the rigidity of the length that was in his mouth. The thrusts became faster and faster and seemed to go further and further into Greg and then at the point where the pumping of his mouth was as furied as he could take, he heard Alan issue a final, breathless order.

'Touch – yourself. You can – touch yourself – now.'

More than ready to obey, Greg grabbed at his own engorged pecker. He felt shocked: surely it had never been so hard, so responsive before. The release of the frustration of being deprived for so long was devastating and, surprised, he began to shoot at the first touches of his firm end, thrilling as the orgasm possessed him, and enjoying the sensation of the hot sperm exploding out against his thigh and wetting his jeans. Almost at the same moment, Eddie let out an ecstatic yell and Greg felt the man's spunk fly over his cheeks and neck again and again until he was fully coated by the shower of love-milk. Now there was only one orgasm left and Greg was eager to drink it down. With wet sticky fingers he grabbed at Alan's arse and began kneading as he jerked his head back and forth. He could feel the cock in his mouth tremble a second before finally the hot viscous liquid gushed inside his cheeks and throat. He swallowed again and again, loving every salty gulp as Alan's body shook with joy until within himself the burning fires of lust became quenched by the satisfying waves of afterglow.

'Well, I'd not expected tonight to turn out so smoothly,' Eddie said as he wiped himself clean with his dressing gown, then began dabbing at Greg's neck and face.

'Ex-army, by any chance?' Greg turned to Alan who was pulling up his trousers again.

Alan looked bewildered. 'Sergeant major actually. How did you know?'

Greg rubbed his head where his hair had been yanked and thought back to all the ordering around he had just endured.

'I don't know. Lucky guess, I suppose,' he joked. There was a silent pause, then simultaneously the three men started laughing, the ice between them having been well and truly broken.

Four

'Yeah, over there, mate.' Greg directed the burly removal man to the far side of his new lounge. The man bent over to place a teeming orange crate on the floor, his peach-like arse, tight under dirty denims, rising in the air like a celestial body rises into the sky. Greg could watch rough, well-built men doing manual work for hours and not get bored. He loved to see a good set of muscles stretching and expanding beneath tired, sweat-stained clothing, or the outline of a man's packet jiggling at the front of old tracksuit bottoms. But despite the enjoyments on offer in his flat that day, and the fact that his direction was required to give some guidance amongst the disarray of the move, he just had to take a break for a while. There was something he had to do, something he had been trying to do for some time now and he just couldn't put it off any longer.

'Listen,' he began, becoming a little taken aback by the charms of the burly man's roguish face. 'I need to take fifteen minutes so you'll just have to carry on as you think best for a while. I don't want to be disturbed so only give me a shout if there's any disasters.'

'All right mate.' The man winked. 'Where will you be if we need you?'

Greg headed off down the hallway. 'Locked away in here,' he said as he shut the bathroom door behind him. He could hear thunderous laughter as he sat on the edge of the bath. Having attempted to get away several times that morning only to be distracted by a table being taken into the wrong room or the sound of crockery being broken, he had figured that escaping to the bathroom would give him a decent excuse not to be interrupted. And the phone call he wanted to make was an important one, one that needed peace, quiet and his full attention. He took his mobile out of his pocket and dialled. A deep voice answered with a hello.

'Hi Matt, it's me.' Despite the length of his and Matt's relationship, Greg was so nervous he could feel the pulse beat in his neck. 'I'm sorry I've not been in touch sooner, but I've been so busy with the transfer and the move that I've just not had time. And I wanted to have a chance to talk to you properly.'

'Oh, right. What about?'

Greg sensed coldness in Matt's voice.

'Can you speak now?' he asked, trying to understand Matt's abruptness. 'Are you at work?'

'No.' Matt obviously wasn't about to explain further.

'Well, I wanted to talk about us, about what happened the other night.'

'There is no "us" Greg, at least not in the way you mean. I'm still getting married. I still want you to be best man, but that's as far as it goes.'

There was a loud knocking on the bathroom door.

'What? You can't be serious. What about all the things we talked about? What about me?'

Matt began talking but the sound was all but drowned out by the loud voice of a removal man asking where he should put the stereo.

'Look, Matt, I'm sorry. Can you just hold on a second?'

Greg opened the door brusquely and found one of the older workmen behind it, a large speaker in his hand and a surprised look on his face. 'Ten minutes. Ten minutes is all I ask.' He slammed the door and, replacing his phone to his ear, heard only the buzz of a dialling tone.

'Fuck!' Greg was confused and angry. What had happened to change the situation back to the way it was when he and Matt were simply friends? Could Matt not see that he was making a big mistake? Not knowing what to do, but deciding that to call back immediately in such a frantic, excited state would probably only exacerbate matters he sat back down to think. Mere seconds later there was another knock at the door.

'Look, I'm sorry mate,' a voice shouted, 'but we're having some real problems out here.'

Greg postponed calming down and flung open the door once more. He found a very pleasing view. It was the man whose bum he had been watching earlier. He was obviously overheated from the work he had been doing as he was pulling off his T-shirt to reveal a torso of rippling muscles, lightly covered in dark hair and a shiny sheen of sweat. If only Matt could see that, Greg thought, there'd be no doubt in his mind about what he should do. The beginning of an idea popped into his head, but was interrupted before it could be developed further.

'Are you OK?' asked the half-naked man, apparently bemused by having been stared at for so long.

'Yeah,' Greg answered, rather dreamily. 'I was only thinking about something. Now what was it you wanted?'

'I just need a bit of help.'

Greg looked over the man's scampish, ruffled hair, his unshaven face and his fantastic, moistened body and smiled.

'I'll see what I can do,' he said, feeling much, much better already.

Five

'Come on, lads. We want it faster and harder than that.'

Greg was hot and sweaty. Taking the trainer's encouragement to heart, he passed the ball with a strong accurate shot. He couldn't tell whether it was his nervousness at joining a new team or whether that morning's training session, his first with Weston, was actually a lot harder than it had been with his old squad. Not that he minded the extra exertion: it just made everything seem like that much more of a challenge and he was more than ready to welcome one of those.

It had been a good morning, all in all. Despite his tensions about starting his new job, in reality everything had turned out well. The other players had been friendly enough, he had pleased himself with his abilities during ball practice and the team's coach, Scott Kenner, had a stern determination to push his men that Greg appreciated. In fact, though he did feel worn out by it all, he was also very excited. He knew that at last he had reached a milieu that would bring the best out of him and he was looking forward to the chance to show exactly what he could do.

'Willy! Over here!' Again Greg booted away the ball with a direct, hard kick. He found himself grimacing with pain as he brought his leg down. The pass had been a little too hard, overextending the thigh muscle that he had injured in the bad tackle with Brian Dalton. He started limping as electric jabs shot along him, but wanting to prove his stamina he continued to play.

It wasn't too long before Kenner noticed the problem and ordered Greg off the pitch.

Greg stumbled away from the other players, unable to hide the intensity of the twinges he was experiencing.

'Is it your thigh again?' Kenner asked, reaching down to place his hand just above Greg's knee. 'I saw the match where it happened. That Dalton is nothing but a bad 'un.'

'It's nothing,' Greg lied. 'I'll be all right in a bit.'

'Yeah, you will be all right. It's nothing serious. But a trip to the physio will make sure it's fully sorted before your first match.'

Greg was disappointed at knowing he would be missing the rest of the day's training but he trusted Kenner's opinion. The coach was in his late fifties, his trademark bald head betraying his age, and had spent most of his life in football. The kind of sporting experience he had wasn't to be ignored and not wanting to risk further injury Greg headed off to the changing rooms.

'Physio's like you,' Kenner shouted after him. 'A new fella. Knows his stuff though. And I think he'll be a familiar face to you as well.'

Not fully understanding what Kenner meant, Greg turned with a confused look on his face. Kenner didn't explain further and instead simply directed Greg away with a flick of his hand before returning his gaze to the practice match.

As soon as Greg pushed open the door to the changing-rooms, he heard voices. The sound was not of a relaxed conversation, but of a muffled, half-whispered dialogue that made Greg wonder just who had something to hide. Not wanting to make his presence known, but wanting to discover what was going on, he carefully took off his boots and crept along as surreptitiously as his thigh strain would allow.

Reaching the end of the room's nearest wall, he popped his head around the corner. Immediately he found what Kenner had meant by a 'familiar face'. It was Dean Macdonald, the physio from Middleton. Greg had never expected to see the man again and definitely not in the state he was in at that moment. Macdonald was half-naked, wearing only tracksuit bottoms and trainers, the bulge at his crotch revealing his inflamed condition. He wasn't alone, either. Leon Grenet, Weston's first-choice striker, who had left practice early because of a hamstring complaint, was sat on the bench in front of the physio, his thick thighs spread and his hands fumbling in between them. Greg's heart skipped a beat. The two men were about to have sex, apparently unaware that he was looking on. His cock thickened in his shorts as he took in more of the view. He was familiar with Dean's body, although he had only seen it clothed before. Dean was a broad man with a body like a rugby player. His arms and chest were large and defined and he had a thick rug of dark hair that covered his torso from neck to belly. His lower body looked just as enticing. The blue, shiny tracksuit bottoms he wore were loose fitting except at the front where his erect penis was making them bunch up into a pleasant-looking bump. Greg watched as Dean placed his thumbs in the waistband as if to pull them down, only to get stopped by Grenet, who obviously had different ideas.

'No,' Grenet said in his soft, southern French accent. 'Leave them on. I like the look of it in them.'

Grenet had not changed out of his kit since practice and he filled it with an agile-looking, masculinely lithe body. His dark-skinned, classically Gallic features had a lustful, almost absent expression and his closely shaved hair and goatee gave his good looks a tough-guy edge. Greg thrilled at the sight of the two men and to gain release from the sense of pent-up sexual pressure inside him he began stroking himself, enjoying the feel of his manhood beneath the silken material of his shorts.

'Come here.' Grenet placed his hands on Macdonald's hips and pulled the man closer. Greg could see Macdonald's lump quiver briefly before Grenet pushed his face against it. Both men let out an initial blissful sigh of relief at the contact, Macdonald's track-suit bottoms rustling gently as Grenet rubbed against them again and again. Greg's prick throbbed as Grenet placed one hand under the still-clothed crotch and lifted two large balls into view. The indentation the package made was magnificent, an irresistibly full combination of hard and soft flesh beneath that oh-so-touchable clothing. It looked so good it was almost a shame when Grenet eased the elasticated waistline down to thigh level, allowing the rampant manhood to leap out.

Dean's unit was like the rest of him, broad, squat and hairy. His penis was thick with a huge, round, suckable head and his bushy balls filled Grenet's palm with ease. Greg continued to watch as his team-mate brushed his lips against Macdonald's purple end, darted out a tongue to lick up the sides, then finally took it in his mouth, uttering a satisfied 'mmmm' as he did so. The sight was truly astounding: one of football's top players in the instantly recognisable blue-and-white kit going down on one handsome hunk of a man. Greg had never thought he would see something so erotically beautiful but there it was, right in front of him. He was so turned on by it all there was nothing he could do but try to join in.

Deciding his leg could be sorted out later, he walked round the end of the wall, coughing as he did so. Startled, Grenet and Macdonald both tried to hide their erections and pretend nothing was going on. Greg smiled, attempted to give off an air of amiability and the men relaxed with Dean starting up a conversation.

'Greg! I was wondering when I'd bump into you. I got a move here too.'

'I'd noticed.' Greg gave Dean a good, long, up-and-down look before continuing. 'But we can leave the catching up till later. What's more important to me now is how I can get in on this little party you've got going here.'

'*Je ne sais pas, mon ami*,' husked Grenet. 'Do you have an invitation?'

'An invitation?' Greg acted mock surprised, then pulled down his shorts to expose his stiff cock. 'Will this do?'

Grenet eyed the freed meat. 'Not bad. But I'll turn it over to the committee.' He turned to Dean. 'What do you think, yes or no?'

'He gets my vote.' Dean had begun feeling himself up enthusiastically. 'Come on, then, Greg. I've been waiting for a bit of you for a long time now.'

Greg took his shorts off and moved over to kiss Dean eagerly on the lips. He too had been waiting to have sex with Dean for a long time, ever since that day back in Middleton's locker room when the physio had made a pass at him. Now, having Dean so close, his tongue squirming over his own, felt so good it was like breathing air after a long dive underwater.

Greg felt Dean's big hand take a hefty pinch of his bum and pull him in closer. Greg shivered, wrapping his legs around one of Dean's tree-trunk thighs, savouring the feel of the smooth tracksuit material against his naked cock and balls. He ran a hand over Dean's chest, stopping to pinch at one of the hard thick nipples beneath the wiry but yielding hairs. He continued downward over Dean's belly easing a hand to where Dean's muscle pointed skyward, firm and proud. Greg enjoyed the heat produced from between the man's legs, the matt of hair on the balls that he fondled tenderly. He shimmied his hips back and forth to pleasure himself, the loose skin of his knob dragging up and over and then down again with every dry fuck. He could feel Dean's fingers prodding around the crack of his arse, then the warm delight of his sphincter relaxing as Dean tickled his hole. He arched his lower back, causing his buttocks to rise up and outward so that Dean could slide into his body. The mixture of pain and pleasure at the intrusion was exquisite and he closed his eyes to concentrate on nothing else but that joy for a second.

'Hot stuff,' interrupted Grenet, who had his own penis

poking out the leg of his shorts so he could play with it with the tips of his fingers. 'Now how about me?'

'Let me see what I can do.' Greg bent over in front of Dean, enjoying the exit motion of the inserted finger as he did so.

'Now,' he said positioning his face close to the seated Frenchman. 'What was it you had in mind?'

Grenet kissed him hard and eagerly. The thought of knowing two sexy men's mouths in such quick succession fired Greg immensely and he returned the kiss with full, reciprocated passion. At the same time he could feel Macdonald behind him wiggling around at his opened bum-cheeks. The sensation of the hard-on along with the silky texture of the material against his arse and haunches was fantastic and he began rubbing back in return. He broke from Grenet's lips a moment to take in the sight of his team-mate once more. He stroked a hand over the man's shaven head, relishing the rasp of stubble against his palm. He grabbed at Grenet's muscular shoulders, then ran his touch over the football shirt, paying particular attention to the armpits that were wet with fresh sweat.

'Ah, it's the kit you like, no?' Grenet had obviously realised what was making Greg so horny. 'OK, my friend. How about you start to like the contents of my shorts?'

With one hand Grenet guided Greg's head downward. To steady himself, Greg gripped Grenet's muscled thighs, getting his face as close as he could to the genitals in front of him without actually touching them. He breathed out hard over the exposed inch of Grenet's penis causing the man to utter a moan of approval then began tonguing the hard impression in the man's shorts. Grenet had exercised himself well before leaving the pitch. His shorts were still slightly damp with sweat and Greg took in hearty breaths of the rich aroma. There was no smell that Greg liked better than that of the fresh perspiration of another man's crotch. Knowing the musk would be at its strongest around the balls, he pulled Grenet's legs upward then started nosing around the moist expanse of material, pressing hard enough so that Grenet would enjoy the contact, while he could gain greatest access to the horny scent. He could feel Macdonald behind him with playful, wandering fingers pleasuring his anus, eventually sliding the entirety of one, two then three large digits inside him. The delightful pain of being stretched and frigged made Greg pant and groan. He began taking as much of Grenet's balls into his mouth as he could just to have the feeling of men filling him at both ends.

'How about you fuck him for real now?' Grenet asked.

Greg turned his head to watch as Macdonald responded by taking a condom out of his pocket. He pushed the waistband of his tracksuit to his ankles then began to put it on. Greg loved to see a man rolling a rubber on. It combined the gorgeous sight of some guy touching his own cock with the electrifying anticipation of what was about to happen next. He even liked the look of an erection in a johnny – the sleek and alien, forbidden yet desirable quality it gave a guy's manhood was fantastic – and Macdonald rampant and pre-pared behind him was no exception. But looking was still no comparison to feeling and, unable to wait any longer, he squeezed open his cheeks in readiness.

As ever the experience of being penetrated by an actual penis was even greater than that of being entered by fingers. Greg let out a slow breath as he felt his rectum expand to take in the full extent of Macdonald's tool. As the man reached right up to the hilt, he contracted his arse muscles as tight as he could to give the signal that he was ready for action. Gradually, Macdonald started bucking his hips, Greg pushing back in reciprocation so that their flesh met together with brisk slaps.

Having sorted out the activities at one end, Greg began seeing what he could do about the other. At first he simply kissed Grenet, enjoying getting screwed by one man while being at the face of another. Then, desperate to be truly packed with male muscle he tugged Grenet's shorts down. He left them at knee level, knowing how good men in sports gear looked but allowing Grenet's genitals to be fully exposed.

'I want it in my mouth, Leon,' he said, breathless. 'I want to have meat at both ends.'

Grenet stood, waggling his thin, reedy dick with one hand and with a relieved moan of acceptance Greg received the bulbous end into his mouth, wanking himself furiously as it immediately sped further inward. The experience of two cocks at once like that made Greg horny like never before. It was as if there was a giant length running right through him from one end to the other and as the two men reached a rhythm, screwing in and out together in unison, he gave himself over completely to the sensation of monumental pumping, invading masculinity, and he slipped into another world of happy submission. He couldn't care less if anyone did walk in on them right then because the meeting of the male presence with his own in the way that he was experiencing at that moment was nothing less than sublime and his pleasure for a second was crystal perfection.

All three men were noisy by that point, their deep-throated utterances of rapture echoing around the tiled walls of the changing rooms as they reached their respective peaks. Dean was the first to make it, pulling out of Greg and yanking off his condom so he could shoot over Greg's back. Greg couldn't help feeling slightly disappointed at the absence of Macdonald from his body, but as the streams of hot man-juice pumped out across his skin his regret was replaced by the initial risings of his own orgasm. Knowing by the hardness of Grenet's cock and by the frequency and ferocity of his thrusts that his second love partner was ready, Greg let himself go in his hand, trembling as he felt the muscles all over his body tighten then relax again and again as the tool that he jerked at jolted uncontrollably. His own spunk flying up against his belly and dripping through the gaps in his fingers, he felt Grenet shudder against his tongue then detonate, letting free the hot tasty liquid into his throat with regular, almost mechanical judders. The heat and flavour of Grenet's jism were mind-blowing and Greg felt he could have drank on and on for days had not the inevitable calm arrived to the member in his mouth. Letting Grenet withdraw, Greg grabbed at him with a tight grip, squeezing out a last sticky drop onto his tongue, then licking his lips with a smile.

Satisfied, and more than grateful that he had arrived when he had done, Greg picked up his shorts from the floor and wiped himself off on them. None of the men spoke for a few moments: there was the atmosphere of relaxed, mutually acknowledged satisfaction between them that can be achieved after particularly successful sexual encounters.

It was Grenet who finally broke the silence. 'Well, that's my injury taken care of. How about you?' He patted Greg on his bare buttocks before pulling up his shorts.

Greg remembered why he had left practice. The pain in his thigh had gone, even the thought of it being removed by the steamy session that had just occurred.

'That's amazing. I thought I was in trouble earlier but, thanks to you two, I don't feel too bad at all. I guess that's what they must call sex therapy.'

The three men laughed. 'The power of the prick,' Dean added as he headed off to the door of the physio room. 'Well if either of you need any more doctoring you know where to find me.'

Greg and Grenet said goodbye then the both of them hit the showers.

They talked amiably as they washed themselves, having not had much chance for proper introductions since Greg's arrival at Weston. He found Grenet friendly with a laid-back charm that made Greg presume that he must be quite a hit with other men. He relaxed in the company, feeling at ease enough to reveal his concerns about playing for Weston. Grenet was more than reassuring, having made a similar, though geographically greater move two years previously. Greg discovered their experiences in football to be similar, both having become successes in the smaller sides of their home towns before being spotted for the big time. He took comfort in the fact that Grenet had initially had the same doubts he did and felt a lot less alone as a result. His new partner on the field appeared to already be someone he could turn to. The bond between them was important; as they would be playing so closely together the trust and support had to be strong and reliable. The success of their initial meeting made Greg more confident and he was sure that he and Grenet would be able to provide a striking force to contend with.

It was not until they heard the door of the changing-rooms bang open, signalling the arrival of the other players that Grenet's attitude and demeanour changed abruptly and he became secretive and extremely self-conscious.

'So what did you think of your initiation, *mon frère*?' he whispered to Greg as the other voices nearby became louder.

'Initiation?' Both Grenet's style of presentation and what he was actually saying bemused Greg.

'We've known about you for quite a while. I was chosen to try you out and I'm glad to tell you that you passed with flying colours.'

'Leon, what the hell are you on about?'

'Sh!' Grenet indicated that someone was nearby. 'No time to explain fully. You know the disused warehouse on the way to the ground?'

Greg nodded.

'Make it there after the match next Saturday. Whether we win or lose you'll be needed. Trust me, you won't regret it.'

'Regret what?' Phil Bowden, one of the centre-backs,

entered the vicinity, hit a shower button and began rubbing himself down.

'Nothing, my friend. Just introducing the new boy to the team.' Grenet winked at Greg who was intrigued but still none the wiser.

'You guys feeling better, then?' asked Bowden. 'We're hoping to go on and lift the trophy next week. We'll need you both fit for that.'

'Much, much better, *merci*.' Grenet smiled as he headed off towards a towel. 'No need to worry about us.'

'Yeah, Bowden, I feel the same.' Greg hoped that his voice had more conviction than he could feel inside him. His doubts were caused mainly by the odd way in which Grenet had behaved. The rendezvous had been arranged for after the important quarter-final cup game and Greg was sure that it wasn't just a coincidence (he was looking forward to the quarter-final and was thankful he wasn't cup-tied, as he had had a slight ankle injury when Middleton played in the cup). But as guarded as Grenet had become he was also sure that he wouldn't be finding out anything else, at least not until the following week.

Six

A few days later, Greg was relaxing in his new flat. He had more or less got all his things where he wanted and was at last beginning to appreciate the move he had made. The flat really was an impressive design, the wrought-iron girders from the original structuring contrasting with the exposed brick walls and the chunky floorboarding. Being on the seventh floor of the block meant that the large windows gave fantastic vistas over the city and Greg watched the sun get lower and lower in the sky as he lay on his large leather sofa. The place was really starting to feel like home to him and he was grateful for his new job for bringing about the money to afford such luxury. In fact, Greg could only think of one thing wrong with his abode as he settled down after another hard day's training. It was just too big to fill with only one person.

He knew exactly whose company he wanted there. The man who had brought such strong and fresh emotions into his life that significant night just a couple of weeks ago. He had enjoyed greatly the sex he had had with the other men since, the farewell threesome he had with Eddie, the sports kit fun that had gone on with Grenet and Macdonald but he recognised the activities were all simply pleasure-centred and what he had found back in Middleton was more, just so much more. Matt had been in the back of his mind since they had made love, dogging him like an opposing player he just couldn't dodge. He had been questioning over and over again what he should do next, but at that moment, the situation appeared nigh on impossible. He didn't know how, but he had caused a rift between them and the lines of communication had broken down. He had called, left many, many messages but it was to no avail. The object of his affections simply would not respond. It was a set of very frustrating circumstances made worse by the fact that Greg knew exactly what it meant. Not that Matt didn't reciprocate his feelings, far from it. For to undergo such an abrupt and violent about-face, he must have felt equally strongly about their relationship, if not more strongly. With a sensation of being lost and becoming somewhat down, Greg decided he needed to hear the sound of a friendly voice. He picked up his mobile from the side table and fiddled with a couple of the buttons.

The phone rang at the end of the line a good few times before a familiar female voice answered.

'Hello, Mum,' Greg said. 'It's me.'

'Oh hello, darling,' Greg's mother enthused. 'How's my little superstar?'

Greg laughed. No matter what happened his Mum still had two feet on the ground and he knew the ties between them would always keep him on an even keel.

'I'm fine. Just ringing to give you a progress report really.'

'Are they pushing you too hard? Things must have been a bit of a whirl for you lately.'

'You can say that again.' Greg proceeded to explain what he had been up to for the past few days, about the move, the subsequent shuffling around of his furniture and possessions and about his initial introduction into the world of top-division football. He had been exercising hard as he told his mother but he both liked the exertion and was becoming more and more convinced of his capabilities. He had been doing a lot of work with Leon Grenet to build up a pitch rapport between them and was pleased with the headway they had made. In fact, though he could feel the effect of the extra physical demands the past week or so had brought, in terms of football he felt mentally better than ever and his mother was delighted to hear it.

'That's my boy! I never doubted you for a second. They're

all cheering for you round here, you know. I've had so many people knocking on my door to say congratulations or to see where it was that you grew up. The local kids shout your name when they ride by on their bicycles and I always give them a wave.'

'Any reporters?' Greg was suddenly worried. His mother wasn't usually one for too much intrusion from outsiders.

'No, no, not yet anyway. And if there was do you think I wouldn't be able to handle them?'

Greg was certain his mother would be more than able to cope, but still would have preferred it if she lived somewhere that she didn't have to put up with such stuff.

'Well, if you ever want a return to peace and quiet . . .'

'I know who to ask.' Greg found his mother's determined independence admirable but slightly exasperating. Obviously sensing his disquiet, she changed the subject completely.

'Oh, while I remember, pet. Doreen popped round the other day with some of the wedding details.'

'Matt's mum?' Greg was surprised that Matt's family was getting in touch even though he was not.

'Yes. It's just a few things like an itinerary, the guest list for the stag night and so on.'

'Oh.' So Matt was avoiding him, but pretending there was nothing wrong? It all seemed cold and confusing.

'I'm sure it'll be lovely. They've picked a local church and I saw an outfit the other day that'd be just fine for the occasion.'

'Have you seen anything of Matt himself lately?' Greg interrupted, anxious for further details.

'No. Well, actually I did bump into him in town a couple of days ago. He was across the street though and I don't think he saw me.'

'It's just that I've not heard from him. For a good while now. And you know, well, you do understand how close we are . . .'

Greg knew that somehow his mother did understand exactly what his feelings were.

Lila sighed knowingly. 'Yes, my love. I'm sure Matt's just busy right now. Busy with everything. He's a man with a lot of choices to make and these things take a lot of effort. But don't you worry. He's got a good head on his shoulders. He'll sort things out in time and then he'll be in touch, pleased to see you as he always is.'

Greg let his mother's words sink in a while, knowing deep down she was right.

'Yeah. Thanks Mum.'

'Well, I'd best be off. I've got a washer full of clothes that won't get hung out by themselves.'

The two made their farewells and Greg returned his gaze back outside. The view was now a rosy sunset as if the world itself was trying to let him know that everything would turn out OK. Inside he knew that Matt was taking a wrong turn with the wedding and that it was up to Greg to make him realise it. He wished he could fit in a visit back to Middleton, but with his work schedule being what it was he just wasn't able to. He thought again of the idea he had had the other day while moving. It was risky and it could possibly mean a complete end to his and Matt's relationship but he knew it would take something so challenging to turn things the way he wanted them to go. Fortunately, there was plenty of time before the wedding to think everything over further. For now, he could relax a while and dream of fulfilling love in the glow of the evening sun.

Seven

The day of the quarter-final, Greg's first important game with Weston, arrived. They were playing Portham United, a solid team that threatened to give them a demanding match. Greg had been pretty nervous during the run-up to the game, his emotions swinging from elation to fear and self-doubt almost hourly. But luckily he remembered similar experiences from before his first professional fame. He had ridden a roller-coaster of intense feeling back when he was introduced to the public eye playing for Middleton but it had all disappeared, transforming into pure adrenaline as soon as he had got his feet on the ball. He was sure it would all be the same at Weston, the worries and insecurities turning to iron-willed determination at kick-off. All the same, he couldn't stop his hands from shaking and his body shivering a little as he and his team made their way out on to the pitch.

'You OK, my friend?' Grenet whispered in Greg's ear as they jogged out into the cheers of the crowd. He had obviously cottoned on to Greg's concerned face.

'I will be.' Greg knew deep down that he would be fine but at that moment, with the roar of the fans deafening on seeing the arrival of their heroes, he felt wobbly and very, very eager for the game to start.

Weston had won the toss and Grenet took the kick-off. Greg came into play almost immediately, comfortably manoeuvring around one of Portham's best midfielders and smoothly passing to a team-mate who had found a more advantageous space. Weston moved upfield. Grenet, leading ahead, became entangled by Portham's defence, dancing around the opposition's tackling attempts but unable to gain ground. Suddenly, Greg saw a chance. With Portham concentrating so much on Grenet they had left a space unprotected and he made for it, giving Grenet the 'back door' warning as he did so. The ball was passed his way. Greg sped to meet it, his heart thundering. He was in for a chance already, mere minutes into the game. The crowd blared out, wishing him on. And then his hopes were dashed. Due to clumsiness caused by his nerves one foot caught the ground too low and he tripped over on to the grass. He picked himself up straight away but by then it was too late and possession of the ball had switched. Greg couldn't believe it as he refocused on the game, with the ball steadily making progress away from him. He could sense his own fans' disappointment, and hear the mirth of the Portham supporters around him. Nearby, a couple of the opposition were smiling at him and Ian Charmers, one of Weston's own midfielders, was making a confused 'what-the-hell?' face at him. He felt let down by himself and embarrassed by his momentary lack of skill. His first few moments in a cup game for a big team and he had made a stupid, clumsy mistake an amateur would be ashamed of. Realising he couldn't let his negativity get the better of him, he decided there was only one thing he could do and that was to make up for his error quickly and with all the talents that he knew were within him.

Before long the ball was back in Weston's control and was returning into Portham's half. Newly determined, Greg strode out of the reach of a defender and receiving a pass from Charmers turned to find only one player between him and the goal. This time, he knew he could do it. Thinking fast, he arched the ball over the man in front of him, bombed towards it then bang, slammed it firmly into the back of the net. The crowd was ecstatic as Greg's team-mates sped towards him, leaping onto his shoulders so they could wrap their legs around his waist.

'That's one hell of a turnaround, Willy,' Charmers shouted, kissing Greg again and again. 'All is forgiven, mate.'

Greg could feel a restlessness in his shorts as the men clamoured to touch him. If this was his reward for scoring a goal, he thought, he couldn't wait until he had planted in a second.

The rest of the match was tightly fought and exciting. After the goal, Greg found himself settling in quickly. His uneasiness left him and he began to enjoy playing to the standard he knew he was capable of. The crowd became more and more worked up every time their new striker got a touch and by the time Greg, in the final ten minutes, scored a second goal, securing the game for his team, they were wild with delight at the discovery of this star and the future joys he would bring to Weston matches.

Needless to say, Greg rode on waves of elation as he left the pitch. His first big match for a new team and he had shown to himself and his team-mates that he had what it took to make it at the top. Most importantly he had shown it to his fans and the congratulatory chant they had made of his name after his second goal rang in his ears. That kind of appreciation was something he had waited his entire life for and his stomach burned with joy that it had arrived at last.

Back in the changing rooms, Trevor Brown was waiting for the team to arrive. He gave out a few back pats and words of encouragement to show his satisfaction as the players walked past him, specifically winking at Greg in a proud manner before starting a brief post-match speech.

'Well done to you all, lads. You deserved that win, there's no question about that. Some excellent playing out there today and it was great to see you working as a team. Keep it up and we'll walk the rest of the competition. Special mention to our new striker team.'

The players turned their heads towards Greg and Grenet. Greg felt embarrassed but honoured as Trevor continued.

'Notably the new kid on the block who despite some

obvious but understandable nerves, pulled through to do the business. Let's hear it for Willy. Well done, my son!'

An impromptu round of grateful applause went up, Greg fending off some amiable ribbing from his colleagues at the same time.

Before he left, Trevor spoke to Greg directly over the celebratory noise that had built up.

'The press will be after you, kidder. They'll be more interested in your fall than the goals you scored, but you're celebrity material now. Come and see me before you leave.'

As Brown's words sank in, Greg realising that his work that day was far from over, Grenet came over and gave him a hug. Both men were shirtless and Greg felt the tremors of arousal at the naked skin against his own. His nipples hardened as Grenet gave him a kiss on the cheek and he was turned on by the idea that what looked like mutual admiration and praise to the others in the team was secretly something much more to the two of them.

'And will you be coming to see me tonight?' Grenet whispered, grinning heartily.

Greg knew Grenet was referring to the mysterious invitation he had made not two weeks previously. He nodded and as he did so felt a sharp stinging pain in his left buttock.

'Are you two engaged now or can I have a turn?'

It was Charmers, grinning after having just flicked Greg's backside with a wet towel.

'Don't worry, my friend,' Grenet left Greg's embrace and returned to undressing fully. 'This one, he is anybody's.'

'Good,' Charmers was totally naked yet free from any self-consciousness. He too grabbed Greg into his arms. 'I like 'em easy. Nice one, new boy,' he enthused.

Greg was very horny now. Though he guessed Charmers' antics were simply playful laddishness, he couldn't help but enjoy them on a sexual level. The touching, the nudity, the football kit were all having their effects upon him and despite knowing that all he would receive by way of release in the meantime was a shower with several playful team-mates, he suspected that the evening's impending events would be providing him with something a lot more appeasing.

Greg spent a good hour with the press. Trevor was at his side at the conference and he had his adviser not too far away, so he felt supported rather than overwhelmed by the roomful of people focusing primarily on him. He felt he was developing a good rapport with the media, keeping answers to questions simple as he was grilled about the transfer, the game and his good looks. He appeared to be well liked. Although he could tell he was being groomed as football's new rising star, and though part of him would have preferred his job if it were football and football alone, he knew that promotion was all part of the modern game and he should start enjoying the attention. He knew the next day's papers would be full of stories about him. The turnaround of skills and confidence after his initial, anxious fall made for a good story and would all add to the creation of him as a character in the nation's consciousness.

It was past seven o'clock before Greg finally got to leave the ground. He was filled with trepidation as he drove away from the stadium able only to guess at what lay ahead of him. Fortunately, his destination was not too far away and before his dashboard gauge had clocked up two miles of the road that led to Weston city centre, he had reached the empty warehouse that Grenet had specified.

The building was an old clothing manufacturers that had gone bankrupt in the eighties. Many of its windows were smashed and a certain amount of graffiti decorated its dirty grey walls. As he pulled up he recognised Grenet's silver-grey convertible parked outside. It and the several other expensive cars that were around looked incongruous in the surroundings. It was obviously a location that was chosen only for secrecy and privacy and as Greg locked up, his mind raced over the possibilities that could be in store.

'Welcome, *mon ami*!' Greg jumped as Grenet called him. He had become somewhat agitated with both anticipation and the general alienness of the situation. Grenet started laughing.

'I'm sorry, I didn't mean to alarm you. I apologise for the way things must look. Like a gangster movie, no? Bang! Bang!'

Grenet made pistols out of his fingers and pretended to shoot.

'It's just that we like to keep things hidden. And well, who's going to suspect we'd be here?'

Greg looked around at the general grimness. 'No one, I guess,' he agreed.

'That's right. But don't worry. This isn't a place we use often.'

'Come on, Grenet,' Greg was getting impatient. 'You've been keeping me in suspense long enough now. Who is this "we"? What is this all about?'

Grenet let a benign look spread over his face. 'Come this way, my friend and all will be revealed.'

He led Greg through a side door into the building itself. The inside of the warehouse was large and empty. The evening light poured through the many window spaces in the walls and created patterns of shade and illumination that added to the atmosphere of mystery. Greg could see a number of figures standing around. All had faces he recognised. From the first glance, he counted at least four who were members of his own team. The rest were players from Portham United, the squad Weston had defeated that very afternoon. He noticed that the Portham men were still in their kit and he wondered why while appreciating the view.

'Glad you could make it.' On Greg's left, Charmers winked a greeting. 'Grenet says you passed with flying colours the other day. Seems you're as talented off the pitch as on it.'

Greg chuckled briefly, feeling bemused.

'Some explanations are needed, of course.' Grenet addressed the crowd with not a little authority. 'He's not just new to Weston, but he's also fresh to us.'

He put an arm around Greg's shoulder and began talking quietly to him. 'Welcome to our secret society. You may be confused, perhaps even a little fearful now but in an hour you'll be glad, *non*, ecstatic that you have been chosen to be a member.'

'Chosen? What do you mean?'

'Ah! We know things, important things about you and everyone who plays professional football. But don't worry. For you there is nothing sinister in store.'

'But Leon, you *are* worrying me. What the hell is all this about?

'It's a tradition that goes way, way back, before you or I ever dreamed of the soccer glories we know now. It goes back with cup games ever since they started, passed down from generation to generation in secrecy until we are given the honour to continue them.'

'But continue what?' Greg was still at a loss.

'It's a way of congratulating winners and commiserating with the losers. Basically, after every trophy match certain selected players of both teams meet up. The stage at which the game has been played determines what acts will be performed and whether you are a winner or loser determines what part you will play. It's not that complicated.'

'Are you serious?' Greg could barely believe what he had just heard. 'Can you really expect me to think that some of the most important players in the country end up having sex just because of a game? And that no one's ever discovered your secret society?'

Grenet shrugged. 'It wouldn't be a very good secret if they had. Like I say, it's just for fun. Many of the men involved aren't even gay, they're just carrying on the ritual. Relax. Just enjoy yourself. You've been a winner today.'

'Is he in?' Charmers had approached the two men.

'*Oui*,' Grenet nodded. 'Isn't that right, *mon ami*, you are with us?'

Greg looked across the room as he considered the question. He half-expected it was a set-up, some kind of joke because he was the new guy at Weston. But then he thought of the sex he had had with Grenet, the naked embrace and good-humoured pass Charmers had made in the changing-rooms after the match. Perhaps it hadn't been just manly teasing as he had thought. He took in the famous faces in front of him. Some were people he never even thought he would have the chance to play against, let alone have the possibility to experience sexually. All were handsome, cute or rough-looking, all were in their prime, and all were mouth-watering examples of masculinity. He paused his gaze on the youthful good looks of Portham's striker, Peter Hammick, a man with such boyish pin-up qualities he had his own best-selling calendar released the previous year. Greg felt giddy with desire at the idea of getting close, realising that even if he thought the whole thing was a lie he had to take the chance that it wasn't for the smallest possibility that he would get to fuck the man.

'Yes,' Greg affirmed his decision hoping that the rest of Weston were not about to pop out from some hiding place somewhere to ridicule his gullibility. 'I'm in.'

Grenet began manoeuvring Greg to a certain position in the room while the rest of the men formed a circle around him.

'Now as a new initiate, you have a certain job to perform. You get to start the ceremonies. And that means also that you have first choice. Choose only from the United side. We won today and it's important that our unity as victors is shared.'

Leaving Greg alone, Grenet walked to his place in the circle before prompting once more. 'Go on. Choose a player.'

It was the moment of truth. Greg knew exactly who he

would pick. All that remained was to discover what would happen next.

'Hammick,' he said, almost breathless. 'I want Peter Hammick.'

An understanding murmur rose from the men. 'You like the pretty ones, no?'

'I like 'em anyway they come.' Greg watched as Hammick stepped forward to approach him. 'But right now what I want is a bit of this.'

Hammick stood in front of him, his beautiful fresh visage mere inches from his own. Barely twenty, Hammick had skin that was blemish-free and taut. He had generous and friendly blue eyes framed by his short light-brown hair. Beneath his kit, Greg could tell there was a firm body and with a quick glance at the exposed skin between Hammick's shorts and socks he saw the striker's developed thigh muscles that betrayed his suspicions to be true. Hammick was really something. Greg felt on the edge of a precipice waiting to see how the man would react to having been selected.

'Here goes.' Hammick seemed a little nervous as he gently took hold of Greg by the back of the neck and planted a kiss firmly on his lips. The kiss was tentative at first, not full, and then gradually he felt Hammick loosen up and submit to his affections. Their tongues met and caressed. Again Greg sensed an initial wariness before Hammick once more relinquished his self-control and soon their mouths wrestled together, hungry for each other. Greg wrapped his arms around the man he had singled out and the move was reciprocated as they grabbed and felt at each other's hard flesh, Greg appreciating the touch of hard, young biceps and shoulders underneath the silky feel of a football shirt, the tight but yielding brawn of pert buttocks covered by used shorts. He couldn't believe his luck. All Grenet had said had been true.

Eventually Hammick pulled away. Greg was disappointed but guessed there was more to come.

'Welcome aboard, Greg,' Hammick said in his thick Merseyside accent.

Cheers and general pleased noises reverberated around the room. Greg took the moment to have a quick word with the man in front of him.

'Speaking of members,' Greg looked downward at Hammick's crotch that had grown a skyward-pointing mound that poked above the waistband of his shorts. 'I thought you were supposed to be straight.'

Hammick's face was open and innocent as Greg pinched the erection, right at the top.

'I never thought it could be this way,' Hammick said, wantonly.

Greg took hold of the eager length eyeing the thick outline it made underneath the material. 'Is it your first time?' he asked, thinking back to the way Matt had acted when they had slept together.

'No.' Hammick took in a sharp breath as Greg wanked him. 'But you're the best I've had so far.'

'*Non, non, non!*' Grenet's attention had returned to the centre of the circle. He wagged a disapproving finger at Greg. 'None of that please, Greg. You are a winner today, after all.'

'He means I have to do all the work.' Hammick dropped to his knees and unzipped Greg's fly. 'But don't worry,' he reassured. 'I think I will be enjoying this as much as you will.'

As Greg looked downward he knew that what Hammick had just said couldn't possibly be true. The young man prostrate in front of him, dressed as he was in football gear, just looked too good for him not to be enjoying the proceedings more. The bright green of the Portham shirt, the parts of Hammick's arms and the mid-section of his legs that were exposed and that seemed much sexier than if they were fully uncovered, the way Hammick's cock was stiff in his shorts, all made for a view that just got to Greg deep down. He felt his heartbeat increase with excitement as Hammick's hand slid inside his trousers and took hold of his hard-on. At first, he was just fondled and squeezed. Sometimes the hand would stroke along the insides of his thigh, sometimes it would take hold of his balls and play with them, but he was never actually taken fully out. Greg pulsated with need as Hammick explored his crotch, finding an entrance at the leg of his boxer shorts so that at last their skin made unrestricted contact. The angle was awkward as Hammick repositioned his grip. Greg's penis pointed downward across his left thigh, although somehow the increased pressure upon it enhanced the pleasure as the wrist action began once more. Gradually a steady rhythm was built up. Greg could sense he had become wet, the sticky patch upon the palm he felt on him adding to the ease with which they rubbed together. The sensations Greg felt were so, so good and quickly, far too quickly, he perceived a rearing orgasm.

'Come on, Hammick,' Grenet's voice interrupted the events. 'You know that's not what we're here for.'

The noise broke Greg's concentration and the build-up subsided. He had almost forgotten he was being watched.

'Sorry, sir. I was getting carried away.' Hammick began fiddling with Greg's belt.

'Now apologise to our new recruit,' Grenet ordered.

Hammick did as he was told, then pulled down Greg's trousers and boxer shorts simultaneously. 'Now for your real reward.'

Greg felt suddenly naked. His throbbing manhood stood out at the bottom of his shirt-tails for all to see.

'Nice one, Greggy,' Charmers shouted, sounding pleased. 'Now let's see what you can do with it.'

Some of the other men also shouted encouragement. Greg stopped feeling embarrassed and began to enjoy being watched. Being in a state that was usually reserved for private moments but was now being seen by many felt forbidden and dirty. He had always dreamed that the teasing and games that went on between men, the slaps on the bum and dick tweaks in the showers, the freedom and unselfconsciousness of being naked together, would take another more physical turn. That team-mates and men he had played against surrounded him made it seem as if those dreams were now coming true.

Hammick brushed his cheek against Greg's penis. As contact was made a bridge of dribbling pre-come arced from the knob end to Hammick's face. Greg shivered at the sight of his sticky erection alongside such a handsome guy and wondered how good it would look to the men around him. Eager for the touch of Hammick's wet mouth, he placed his hand on the young striker's jawline and stroked a thumb over and around his soft, ready lips before he inserted. Hammick rolled his tongue around the digit and pushed his head forward taking it in as far as it would go. The warm, slippery touch of the saliva-dampened flesh was exquisite and Greg was restless to have it placed elsewhere upon his body. Leading Hammick forward, he pushed downward opening the young man's lower jaw.

Greg withdrew his thumb allowing Hammick to open wide. He traced his glans slowly down Hammick's cheekbone, savouring the moment before letting himself rest on the tip of the outstretched tongue. His penis bounced a little as the blood pulsed through it. Hammick steadied it with one hand before closing his lips over the end. The feeling of the encircling moist heat was overwhelming. Greg wondered how many blow-jobs the striker had given before. The mouth was certainly active and fervent, although he hadn't been taken in particularly far. He pushed ahead with his hips slightly and Hammick made a disapproving grunting noise before letting Greg's cock slip out of him.

'Relax,' Greg reassured. 'I won't hurt you.'

'I know.' Hammick took the freed muscle into his hand, and began playing with it, dragging Greg's foreskin up and over the top. 'It's just that I'm quite new to this. Take it steady, all right?'

Greg nodded. He knew what Hammick's fears were as a newcomer to oral sex, but felt sure he would help the man enjoy it soon enough.

Hammick stuck his tongue out once more, running up the side of Greg's shaft, then paying particular attention to the greasy mess at the end. He dribbled a little, wiping his pouted lips up and down first one side then the other, then concentrating at the top. The technique produced its desired effects.

'Who taught you that?' Greg panted. 'Your girlfriend?'

Several of the other men laughed at the joke. Greg thrilled again at the naughty, taboo pleasure of being watched while he was being eaten. He began to feel quite damp, his own juices having mixed with Hammick's spit to make a sheen that was pleasantly cool in the open air. Wanting the sensation all over his crotch he positioned himself so that he stood almost directly over the man in front of him. The young man's hot breath beat out readily on to his testicles. The cue obviously taken, the licking began with long slow forceful strokes that started at the base of Greg's arse and dragged right the way up his groin. Hammick took his time, as if to make Greg relish every second of it, but was as ardent at his careful munching as a hungry dog at his bowl. Greg's horniness level rose at the sight of someone enjoying his body so much. As Hammick began a soft toothless chewing of his balls, he couldn't help but move his fingers over his expectant cock. He was surprised as Hammick moved the hand away.

'No,' he said. 'Let me take care of it.'

Hammick shifted around taking Greg's prick-end into his mouth once again. Showing he meant business, this time there was no tender but earnest mouthing and instead he went straight for the action Greg needed: hard, relentless head. At first Hammick gagged slightly at his attempts to accept the penis further into him, making uncomfortable wordless noises that made Greg feel like pulling out. But after a little perseverance soon he was sliding up and down Greg's pole in a piston-like manner, quickly becoming able to take in the cock as far as it would go. Several times Greg felt the grabbing at his buttocks that meant he would be dragged towards Hammick's face, the younger man looking upward, nose buried in pubic hair as he struggled to swallow the entirety of the length. The noises Hammick made were no longer of discomfort but of desirous requitement, of sheer passionate enjoyment at sucking. Before long, Greg knew he was near his peak again, his out-of-breath grunts becoming louder with every movement Hammick made. It was at the point before he lost himself completely that he heard Grenet speak once more.

'Do you, Greg Christopher Williams, pledge allegiance to the Secret League?' he demanded.

At that moment, Greg would have agreed to almost anything to be left alone so he could shoot. He answered with a loud affirmative response.

'Do you swear to bide by our traditions, be respectful of our history, take part in our rituals?'

'Yes.' Once more Greg replied, not caring what he was letting himself in for, with Hammick still chugging rapidly back and forth along his bits.

'Do you promise to keep us hidden and to be loyal to us above all?'

'Oh yes, yes! My God, yes!'

Unable to hold back any longer Greg let the first eruption of his orgasm go. The jerk was so violent that he sprang out of Hammick's mouth, the spurt of hot white globules spraying across Hammick's face like thrown whipped cream. He shot again and again, wanking himself off with abandon into Hammick's greedy orifice, some of the come flying past

Hammick's lips, the rest streaming across his cheeks and forehead, dripping down on to his neck and shirt. He shuddered with each blissful wave, found himself a million miles away with every glorious throb. There were no people around him during that orgasm. The world barely existed and all that mattered at that moment was his cock and Hammick's face, one of history's all-time perfect matches. The moment was meant to be, but it was also unfortunately transient and eventually, as Greg's body calmed, his mind came back to earth and slid into the warm, duvet-like comfort of afterglow.

Down at Greg's slowly deflating penis, Hammick licked, desperate to taste the last few drops. It was a messy but beautiful sight: a devastatingly handsome man with his face and shirt splashed with jism. Greg picked up one of the more sizeable blobs with his index finger and tongued it to see what he was missing.

'I never tasted spunk before,' Hammick said, somewhat absent with delight.

'What do you think?' Greg asked.

'Sweet.' Hammick closed his eyes and swallowed visibly. 'Oh, it was so, so sweet.'

Greg sensed movement at his shoulder. It was Grenet with an outstretched hand.

'Welcome my friend. You're a fully fledged member now.'

They shook hands as below them Hammick took off his shirt and began to dry himself with it.

'Guess we won't be seeing that in your football tips video, eh, Hammick?' Charmers laughed as he approached. He gave the striker a soft boot to the thigh before he too took Greg by the hand and shook firmly.

'Don't you be too concerned, though Greggy,' Charmers continued. 'Weston'll win every cup match we're in. We'll stay in the driving seat from now on.'

As approving cheers and discouraging groans rumbled around the room, Greg eyed Hammick's ruddy, still shiny face, and the hearty erection that jutted out between his outstretched legs. He thought of the salty, manly taste on his tongue and knew that losing wouldn't actually be as bad an outcome as Charmers thought.

Recovering from the fun he had had with Hammick, Greg spent the next half an hour or so in the position of voyeur, taking time to watch the various antics that went on unabashed around the room. He found it hard to believe what he was seeing most of the time. Members of his own team, men whom he had only recently met, with their erect cocks pointing out of their trousers or jeans, being sucked off by fully kitted Portham players. Greg loved the shamelessness of it all, how no one seemed to care who saw what was done to them or done by them, even to the point where they revelled in being seen as they performed. The sight of so many sexually aroused men, with their shorts filled with the evidence of their lusts or perhaps with their shirt adorned by a dribble of come, was truly wonderful. He chatted with the other men as they too rested. They seemed as happy to see what was going on as he was, making jokes about the size of the cocks of those having sex around them, or about the volume of the loads they had seen ejected. Greg remained horny despite Hammick's earlier efforts, and gradually began to wonder if and when he would get another turn. Eventually, Grenet interrupted his viewing, tapping him on the shoulder from behind.

'Ready for round two?' Under one arm, Grenet had the Portham midfielder Greg had seen greedily eating away at Charmers' cock not fifteen minutes previously. 'This is Doug,' Grenet squeezed the man with a shaky grip.

'Yeah, I know.' Greg recognised the man as Douglas Collins, not only from the game they had played earlier in the day, but from his various appearances in the media. In his thirties, Collins had been in the public eye a long time, and was considered a fine, dependable player. Collins was a small, slight man. Pale-skinned, he had dark hair and green irises that betrayed his Irish origins. He had what looked like a good three days' worth of stubble growth that directed Greg's look to focus on his attractive, gleaming eyes.

'Pleased to meet you properly at last.' Greg stuck out his hand by way of greeting. He was pleased with Doug's arrival, having seen what Collins had been capable of with Charmers and prepared for some similar action himself.

'And Hammick,' Grenet began wryly. At Grenet's other side, Greg's choice from earlier stood shuffling his stockinged feet with his usual, nervy embarrassment. 'I think you have met, no?'

The four men laughed.

'Looks like I've been selected this time.' Greg beamed at the young striker who was biting his lip as if unsure of himself.

'Don't look so scared,' Greg reassured. 'I'm glad you did.' Then, taking Collins by the hand he continued, 'I'm glad you both did.'

Grenet turned, headed off elsewhere. 'I'll leave you to it. No need for any more of my help here, I think.'

Greg licked his lips, then placed them directly on to Collins' own. The midfielder was instantly responsive, invading Greg's mouth with an amorous snake-like tongue. Greg enjoyed the graze of Collins' beard against him. It was not as sharp as freshly shaved or newly grown facial hair, instead it gave a little under the pressure of their skins together, brushing up to him with enough force to add that pleasing extra something to their kiss. Here is a man, the sensation said to him, a hairy, testosterone-filled man. Greg was immediately thrilled and his penis reacted accordingly. He clasped Collins fervently in his arms, then slid a hand up the leg of the midfielder's shorts at the back so he could get a decent handful of the man's arse. The buttock he grasped was furry and although in proportion to Collins' slight frame, was toned and filled Greg's palm with firmness. He took big pinches as they snogged with each other, sometimes simply holding one cheek so that his fingers rested up Collins' heat-filled crack. Greg toyed with the rug of pubic hairs that had grown up the split, fingering around until he found the space that contained the creases of skin surrounding Collins' anus. He tickled the circle of puckered folds a little before penetrating, causing Collins to wriggle in his grasp. He found he entered easily and soon he had two digits inside the tight orifice and was stimulating at a brisk speed.

'Fucking hell, you don't mess about,' Collins growled.

'Did you want me to?' Greg asked, giving a significant jut forward with his hand at the same time. Collins' expression of rapture and a brief appreciative tightening of the muscles around Greg's fingers gave him the answer he expected.

'That looks nice.' The two men were interrupted by Hammick who had moved to stand directly next to them. 'Any chance I can get in on the action?'

'Enthusiastic, isn't he?' Collins grinned at Greg, then turned to the third of their party. 'What's up Hammick? All those women we see you linked with in the papers not treating you right?'

Hammick shrugged shyly. Collins put an arm around the striker and edged him forward, then spoke, once more as if only to Greg.

'It's his age. Can't get enough of it when you're that young,' he ribbed.

'Says you,' Hammick said, rising to the bait at last. 'Time hasn't slowed you down, has it, granddad?'

He reached across and flicked at Collins' erect prick with a fingertip, causing the midfielder to wince visibly.

'Hey, you two. Play nicely,' Greg intervened. Although he was enjoying the kidding and physical play he was ready to step the action up a gear. 'Or I'll make the third man.'

He leaned towards Hammick, placing their foreheads

together. He liked seeing such a beautiful face so close up and he teased it, fluttering his eyelashes against it and rubbing his nose upon Hammick's own before lunging for the full kiss.

Hammick was regarded by many fans as a player who had a great future ahead of him, although his notorious technical expertise was considered marred by an overzealousness that was put down to his young age. He kissed, Greg thought, like he played football, eagerly but with a mechanical rather than spontaneous approach, needing the right coaching and more first-hand experience to attain brilliance. As the more seasoned man in the sphere of gay love, Greg felt it was his duty to offer some advice.

'Take it easy, fella.' He patted Hammick on the jawline. 'Relax a little. It's not a race.'

Hammick looked downward, a reddening coming to his face as Greg lunged again. This time the connection really had something. Hammick's jaw had loosened and his movements had slowed, becoming powerful and driven rather than rushed.

'Mmmm, that's better,' Greg knew Hammick would make as great a fuck as he would a footballer one day. 'Now you two, why don't you make it up between you.'

Collins and Hammick smiled at each other before they too brought their lips together. Greg marvelled at the clash of the two sexy men, one older and stubbly, the other young, smooth and boyish. It was so near to him he could see every little motion, every brush of one man's lips against the other, every tender nibble of flesh. By the time Collins and Hammick began simply licking each other's tongues right in front of him, Greg found himself unable to do anything but join in. He placed a hand behind both of the footballers' necks and held them in position while their mouths softly munched together. The sensation of being facially linked with more than one man, of having not one, but two tongues wriggling over his own was fantastic. The three gradually built up a pattern of action, two of them pairing off together while the third watched, then all of them joining in at the same time. Greg moved his hands downward and repeated the move he had performed on Collins alone previously, slipping his grasp up the back legs of both men's shorts. Simultaneously, he poked around the split of their arses, discovering their respective anuses almost at the same time. He slid his fingers upward. Collins was loosened, his pube-circled hole ready and waiting for action, whereas Hammick was tight, practically closed off, and Greg had to stroke around a while before he could feel any give at all.

'Hey,' he whispered to the younger man. 'Don't be scared. Let yourself go a little. You'll love it.'

He kissed Hammick directly all the while pressing hard with his middle finger until the timid chute relented. Hammick let out a loud utterance of pain and pleasure mixed, closing his eyes, then biting his bottom lip as Greg drove in further. The fit was very tight and Greg wondered whether anyone else had been up there before. But as Hammick began pushing backward to take in more, an expression of bliss on his face, Greg knew, whether Hammick was an arse-virgin or not, that his actions were not going unappreciated. Now Greg had a man on each hand and he could feel them squeezing against his digits heartily. He finger-fucked in and out as the three of them kissed, and soon satisfied, primal noises could be heard with every move inward. Greg looked down, ready to see what was happening at crotch level. Next to the mound sticking out from his own trousers were the lumps between Hammick's and Collins' legs that were sometimes rubbing together, sometimes knocking into himself. Having more room to manoeuvre in their loose, lustrous shorts, both his compatriots' pricks had raised almost fully up and outward, making tent-like shapes in front of them and causing their meaty testicles to become outlined at the inside leg where the material had rucked upward. Collins' thick length had a notable curve to it. Its owner was obviously very horny as a spot of pre-come had seeped through at the tip to cause a dark wet patch to show through the green Portham shorts. Hammick's cock was a little longer than his team-mate's and very straight. It jumped visibly up and down with Hammick's excitement. Greg removed his fingers from the footballer's passages so he could take hold of the two protuberances. Hammick and Collins moaned in gratitude as Greg gripped hard then began to wank. He felt right down to the bases so that the material of the men's shorts were tight against them, then pulled right up again, knowing how much friction would be caused by the bunched-up clothing. In return, Collins placed his hands on Greg's balls while Hammick traced his fingertips along the erection above. The action quickly became a tangle of hands, forearms and penises. Greg loved the feeling of men at every angle, of an overwhelming maleness engulfing him and soon he found himself tugging at his belt to expose himself fully.

'Get 'em out,' he said, pulling his pants down to the floor.

'But the rules,' Hammick began. 'We've gone too far already.'

'Fuck the rules,' Greg was near overcome by desire. 'I want to see 'em.'

Hammick looked at Collins as if for guidance. After a couple of seconds, Collins nodded and the two lowered their shorts. Greg moved in close once more, his left thigh pressing against Collins' slim but hirsute right leg and his right thigh against Hammick's well-developed quadriceps. Bared, Collins' genitals were as furry as the rest of him, with a curly dark mop covering his balls and crotch and continuing upward to his belly. In comparision, Hammick had a real textbook prick. Perfectly proportioned, the cock ran straight up and down as if someone had sculpted it. The trilogy of trembling man-meat made for a great view for Greg. He put his hands between both men's thighs and enjoyed juggling four balls for a while instead of the usual two.

'Listen,' Collins interjected with a horny intake of breath. 'If anybody notices, we could get into quite a lot of trouble for this.'

Greg looked around. At that moment there were no onlookers. The rest of the men were involved in a grouping a good few metres away. Had it been down to his decision, he would have risked continuing, but sensing both Collins' and Hammick's worries, he decided he should relent.

'OK then, fellas. Let's get down to what you're here for.'

Hammick and Collins stepped out of their shorts then squatted, their legs spreading and causing their thighs to thicken and their rock-hard members raising the hems of their footballs shirts. They sat either side of Greg and as their faces edged forward he could feel the steamy buffeting of their hot breath on his crotch.

'Who's first?' Greg asked, ready to be gobbled.

'He's had a go already.' Collins nodded at his team-mate. 'I think it's my turn.'

He placed the grip of his thumb and forefinger on Greg's prick, stuck out his tongue and rested Greg's swollen helmet upon it. Greg shivered at the touch. Not an hour before he had been sucked off by one man and now here was another, equally enthusiastic for him. He felt the pair of succulent lips close on to him and then slide forward. A ripple of warmth ran over him as the mouth enclosed. He put his hand on the back of Collins' head, not to force him downward, but to emphasise the feeling of entering someone's body in such a manner. He ran his fingers through Collins' hair, stroked the man's face as the sucking continued. He watched as Collins pulled completely off, licking with a frantic tongue as the excess of his saliva dribbled down his chin and shirt in clear, shiny bubbles and strands. Collins made wordless, sexual noises as he performed, making animal-like pants every time he rubbed his pout against the end of the length or pressed it hard against his face. Greg noticed how much Collins was enjoying the experience. Some men just love eating pricks, Greg thought, and Collins was one of them, a really dirty man-muncher and one up there with the best of them. Greg could have taken what Collins was doing to him for the rest of the night, but eventually the midfielder stopped to point Greg's erection towards the third of their party.

'Your turn,' he said, pushing the younger man's head forward with his free hand.

'Hey, hey, Greggy!' Having been so engrossed in his entertainment, Greg hadn't noticed that he had got an audience. It was Charmers, having broken away from the other, larger group to watch the new boy's second stint. In only his shirt, the rest of his clothing having been discarded elsewhere, Charmers stood yanking at himself, his hairy balls jiggling as he did so.

'Looks good,' he shouted. 'Having fun?'

'You bet.' As Greg spoke, Hammick moved around slightly, kneeling so his buttocks rested upon his calves. 'Want to join in?'

Charmers shook his head. 'Nah, mate. I'll leave it to you. Don't mind if I carry on appreciating the view though, do you?'

'It's your loss.' Greg gave an encouraging nod to Hammick who was wearing a timid but ardent look of anticipation on his face. The signal given, he pounced, taking Greg inside him with one swoop. He kept the dick there for some time, his tongue undulating as he gulped and swallowed.

Understanding how ravenous Hammick was for him, with much willpower Greg slipped himself backward and out. Hammick's juicy lips smacked together as he exited. Immediately, Hammick dashed at the unrestrained cock. Remembering a trick that had been played on himself not so long ago, Greg waggled just out of the young striker's reach, placing one hand on the man's forehead so that despite his struggles he just couldn't regain a hold. Hammick reached for the thing with his hands, but Greg simply hit the clutches away. At that moment Hammick looked so sexy in his need, trying impatiently to fill his mouth once more, his tongue out-stretched and his head dashing this way and that. Greg kept him in his frantic state for quite a while, but eventually the sight of someone so anxious to get some prick was too much and Greg was unable to keep his own needs at bay any longer.

'Come on then.' Greg indicated to Collins who had been masturbating with abandon while he waited. 'Time to get the full squad on the pitch.'

Greg's hard-on throbbed as the two men placed their mouths on either side of his shaft and began moving up and down it with their tongues. They french-kissed his purple helmet together, their hands between their legs jerking ener-getically. Before long, Greg had reached his peak. He squirted again and again, Hammick and Collins desperately grabbing for him, vying to get his hot jism in their mouths or on their faces. His orgasm subsiding, he watched as his lovers brought themselves off, the fluid splashing out from their shaking fists and on to their legs and shirts. They spurted out so far as to hit each other, and their kit and exposed flesh became covered in streaks and blobs of white cream.

'Fucking hell, boys.' Charmers flicked his hand as he approached so the sticky mess that had collected on his fingers after his own orgasm splattered off him on to the ground. 'You three are something else.'

'We aim to please,' Greg laughed, pulling up his trousers.

'No regrets about coming along tonight, then?'

'You've got to be joking! And miss these two?' Greg nodded down at Hammick and Collins who were still messy with juice. 'My only regret is that I didn't get initiated earlier. I hate to think what I missed at the play-offs!'

Eight

The morning after the quarter-final, Greg rose early. He bought several papers from his local newsagent, not just his usual daily, wanting to see what the pundits thought about him and thinking that he would keep the articles as a souvenir of his career. Back at his flat, he was pleased with what had been written about him. Though, as Trevor Brown had said, many articles talked as much about his tumble as the good football he had played, the write-ups were largely encouraging and excited about the promising new talent on the scene. Some even had pictures of him after the second goal he had scored. Looking at those photos really brought it all home. He had made it at last, reached the point in his life where he was doing exactly what he always wanted to do at the highest level possible. It was an enviable position, he knew. Alongside the good press and support he had received that day, there would no doubt be jealous criticism and digs in the future. But he realised taking the rough with the smooth would be all part of the job, and in those early hours of the day after his first cup game he felt confident in his capacity to do just that.

Greg was eating breakfast when his phone rang. He answered quickly, not expecting and not usually receiving calls at such an early hour on a Sunday morning.

'Hi Greg! Simon here!'

Greg recognised the voice as that of Simon Baker, the publicity agent Trevor Brown had advised him to take on.

'Listen, I know it's early, I know it's your day off, but I'm wondering how interested you'd be in taking advantage of your first flurry of fame.'

Greg was as suspicious as he was curious. He was aware

of the benefits of self-promotion in football but didn't want his life taken over by work outside the game.

'It depends. What do you want me to do.'

'It's just a little interview. For one of the sports magazines. They want to find out more about you, get some history, that sort of thing. It's for the fans, Greg.'

Greg knew Baker was more interested in the fame and fortunes of Weston City than the spreading of information to the club's fans, but intrigued by the possibilities his new career could bring he decided to give the interview a go.

'OK. How about some details?'

Enthusiastic, Baker told Greg more about the magazine, the time Greg would meet his interviewer, the restaurant they would meet at and general advice on what to say. Having not really had such interest in him when he played for Middleton, Greg became quite excited, and he found he enjoyed the day much more than he had initially expected. The journalist he spoke to was enquiring but not prying, and the overall experience felt like an introduction to a refreshing new area of his job.

The next few weeks were somewhat of a blur for Greg. Weston's demanding exercise and practice schedule continued as did Greg's first venture into the public eye. As a new and important signing to one of Britain's top clubs, he found people taking a great fascination in who he was and requests for him to do publicity work were frequent. Baker said it was to do with his 'star qualities': basically that he was young, handsome and gifted. He accepted some of the offers that came his way, his face adorning the front covers of a couple of glossy monthlies and a weekend supplement during that initial period. He even appeared on a chat show, which went smoothly, although being in front of a studio audience caused him nerves that playing in front of fans in a stadium never did. Soon enough companies were after him to endorse their products and he eventually chose a contract with a sports gear manufacturer. He appreciated the extra money that the work brought in. The amount was far more than he had ever dreamed of earning, but he decided to restrict his participation in anything outside football itself, wanting to keep his feet on the ground and not run himself into it.

Before long, people were stopping Greg in the street, sometimes asking for autographs, sometimes just wanting to chat about the last game he had played. Most were friendly and supportive and Greg didn't mind the intrusions into his life. He could remember a time when he was just a fan like them, and how the men he watched on the pitch meant so much to him and how he would have done anything to get to talk to them or have them sign their name on a programme or a piece of paper. Without letting himself become egotistical, he began to recognise his status as a hero, and recognising the important relationship between heroes and their fans, he always made sure he gave time to those who called his name outside the actual matches.

On the whole Greg felt on top of the world during that initial period at Weston. His ambitions were at last being realised and most days he just walked on air, overjoyed at how lucky he had been. Being a footballer seemed like the greatest job on earth. The extra cash he was earning had bought him more than a new flat: he had bought new furniture and clothes, and set up a financial plan that would see that he and his mother would be secure until doomsday. But the economic advantages of his profession had always been secondary to Greg. He didn't play football to make a living, even though it did bring in a good one. He did it for exactly the same reasons he slept with men. He just loved to do it. It permeated every iota of his being to the point that he knew it was something that he was simply born to do.

There was hard work, of course. Training did appear, as he had initially thought, to demand slightly more of him than it had done at Middleton. But the extra strain, and the fact that he was pushed to finding capabilities within himself that he never knew he had, even the routine of it all, thrilled him. It posed the challenge he had been waiting for all his life and he meant to meet and defeat it with determination.

What made things even better at Weston was how readily his team-mates accepted him, and in return how much he liked their company. He had his favourites there, of course. Jameson, City's goalkeeper, was a tall and attractive man with a slow, self-effacing wit, who Greg went out with several times for a drink in the more exclusive bars in town. Charmers was a real lad. His near-ugly looks, and the beginnings of a beer-belly that no amount of exercise appeared to shift, matched well his raucous but unavoidably appealing nature. He was forever playing practical jokes at the expense of his friends. The first time Greg found himself on the receiving end of Charmers' humour was also an event that he found erotic in the extreme. It was mid-week, and the day's training had gone well. Charmers was in his usual high spirits, teasing and ridiculing the team and Kenner as they returned to the changing-rooms. He was a funny man, and the boys were in a good mood because of him, egging him on, fueling him with material for his pranks. For some reason that day, perhaps because he was still relatively new, Greg became the focus of the midfielder's attentions and as he entered the showers to wash himself, he was hit with one of the man's genial insults.

'Here he comes.' Charmers laughed as Greg found a spare shower nozzle. 'Hey, watch yourself, Willy. There's a lot of water and soap about in here. You might slip and fall over.'

The shower corridor was packed with naked footballers and they roared with laughter, less at the inventiveness of Charmers' gag and more at his intention to humiliate the new boy.

'Good one, mate,' Greg shouted back sarcastically, a jet of

hot water pummelling his back. 'Who writes your lines? Help the Aged?'

The men around laughed once more. Sharp intakes of breath could be heard. Greg had obviously incurred Charmers' wrath and he knew he had a fight on his hands.

Charmers hit him with a barrage of good-natured but derogatory comments. Greg couldn't help but laugh. Charmers was a quick and funny man and Greg just had to like him even when he was being made the butt of his jokes. Greg hit back with some good returns though, and the men around him seemed to be hanging on every word of the verbal battle to see who would win.

Having cleaned himself, Greg made to leave the showers. In a jokey show of aggression, he deliberately walked up to Charmers at the end of the corridor, and standing right next to him, gave him a fake hostile stare. Charmers nodded arrogantly, then looked Greg up and down, an encouraging rumble from the rest of the team echoing along the tiled walls. He let his gaze rest at Greg's crotch.

'Oh,' he began mock-innocently. 'They call you Willy because of your surname!'

Greg balked as the men's noise boomed out once again. He wasn't the best-hung man in the world, but he had a substantial length and one that he was proud of. Though he felt a little offended, the situation had begun to arouse him. Standing there naked, Charmers looking directly at his prick like that was very titillating. He looked back into the showers at the giggling men, their muscular bodies wet with water and shiny and foamy with soap, hands rubbing their skin, feeling up their arses and around their genitals. That Charmers was staring at his member in front of all them, combined with the fact that he knew from his experiences at the Secret League that Charmers was probably enjoying his view a lot more than he was letting on, turned him on even more.

Greg panned down Charmers' body. It wasn't in the fantastic shape a lot of his team-mates' were. The man was around five foot eight, and his torso carried on it an extra layer, most notably around his stomach. Greg couldn't deny that it gave Charmers a sexy edge, adding to his true, down-the-pub-at-lunchtime, kebab-and-chips manful aura and right at that moment he wanted to run his hands over it, kiss it and take it into his arms. Knowing of the restrictions on his behaviour caused by his audience, he simply let his eyes rest on Charmers' packet. Charmers had a rather stubby dick buried in a big bush of dark pubes that also covered his testicles. It was attractive, suckable even, but in terms of size it just didn't compare to Greg's own.

Greg tilted his head, self-satisfied. 'You know what they say, mate. People in glass houses . . .'

He turned as his team-mates blared out once more. He didn't get too far away from the corridor however, feeling a foot hooking his leg after his first couple of steps. Not expecting the move and unable to keep himself upright, he fell head first into the large laundry basket kept in the changing room for the team's used and dirty kit. He became buried in clothing and a strong pungent smell of men's sweat on socks, shirts and shorts filled his nostrils.

'Enjoy your trip, Willy?' Greg could hear Charmers right behind him as he struggled to set himself upright once more. He had managed to get his feet back on the ground when he felt someone grab him from behind.

'It's not the size, babe, it's what you do with it.' It was Charmers, having taken hold of Greg in a mighty bear hug. Their wet bodies pressed together and Greg could feel Charmers' cock and balls squirming against his arse. Charmers began pretending to roger Greg, much to the amusement of those around them. He leaned over and whispered into Greg's ear so that no one else could hear him. 'And I'd really fucking love to show you what I can do with mine.'

Greg was laughing at both himself and at Charmers' antics, but he also felt very, very turned on by it all. He could sense the blood rushing to his member and, not wanting to be caught in such an embarrassing state in front of most of his team, he struggled free.

'I'll get you for this.' He grinned at his friend, quickly heading for a towel to cover up his half-kindled state.

'I fucking hope so.' Charmers winked back. At that moment the man looked very sexy, blokey and cocky, a real rough treasure and Greg would have loved to take things further had the situation allowed. As it was he had to wait until he was back home at his flat where, hours later, still excited by what had happened, he had a fantastic session of self-stimulation. He just couldn't get the feeling of Charmers behind him, of the scents of the used kit, the sensation of being watched by so many men out of his mind. He imagined that he and Charmers had just continued what they had started and he had been buggered over the laundry basket in front of his entire team. It was a truly great wank, almost as good as if his fantasies had actually happened and afterward he lay on his sofa, spent, happy and sleepy and glad of having had such a good day.

The event didn't pass unnoticed by those who had seen it either. Soon enough Greg had been given the team nickname of 'Tripping Willy' that was quickly shortened to 'Trip', and when he found himself turning his head to answer that very moniker without thinking about it, he knew he had found a club that suited him to a tee. The team was a good one and that they gelled so well off the pitch, Greg knew from experience, meant they would have the trust and co-operation needed to really play on it.

Of all the people at Weston Greg liked it was Leon Grenet who became his closest friend. The two saw each other frequently after work, Grenet showing his new chum what Weston had to offer. He introduced him to the best places to go at night, took him to shows and the theatre and invited him to meals to meet his own already established social circle. Greg was glad of having someone like that around. Moving to a new city could be very difficult, especially a big city like Weston and not knowing anyone there could make one feel very lonely. But thanks to Grenet, he was rarely by himself and never short of things to do, and his transition into a place he didn't know was as smooth as his move into his new job.

Sometimes Greg and Grenet would sleep together after a night out, mutually enjoying the access to an attractive face and well-toned body. Both men knew the relationship wouldn't advance to a romantic level and they simply appreciated the intimacy they had achieved, and the physical delights it offered. From time to time Greg would quiz Grenet about the Secret League. Greg knew Grenet must be quite highly involved, having both initiated him and facilitated his introduction ceremony. But whenever Greg pried too far, Grenet would simply clam up, changing the subject or becoming silent. The most Greg could get out of the man was just how hush-hush the clandestine society was, hinting that they were involved in much bigger things than the sexual adventures of footballers and that Grenet's reticence was caused by his beliefs that outsiders were desperate to find out more. Talking about the League in public, even in the privacy of their own homes, Grenet said, could have lead to their discovery, and damaging repercussions for them and the other men involved. Greg took Grenet's fears with a large pinch of salt, thinking that his team-mate was just trying to make the League sound more important than it actually was. At the same time he enjoyed all the furtiveness. It made his involvement seem mysterious, possibly even dangerous, and all the sexier for being so. If he felt lucky at becoming a top division footballer, he felt equally lucky that it brought access to such fantastic group sex play, and in the run-up to the semi-final he found himself itching for the match ahead, not only for the opportunity to play important, high quality football, but for the horny goings-on it would bring in its wake.

Nine

One of the early pieces of promotional work Greg agreed to do was the opening of a new sports shop in Weston city centre. Up to that point he had not done too much public appearance work, but despite that he wasn't too worried. Baker and the other boys on the team had told him more or less what to expect. The morning would consist of a lot of standing around, signing footballs and shirts, and having a couple of photos done for the local newspaper. It would all be easy, undemanding stuff. He arrived as requested at nine-thirty in the morning. He had been told to go to the back entrance of the shop to avoid too much attention gathering at the front and after parking up, he went to knock on the exit door.

Before long, a flustered-looking man in a suit opened up, then took Greg's hand and shook it furiously.

'Ah, Mr Williams! Glad you could make it. I'm Kevin Barrow, branch manager. I've been speaking with your agent a lot lately.'

'I bet you have. He's quite a man isn't he?'

Greg stepped inside as Barrow began laughing.

'Yes, I suppose you could say that. Friendly, but very persistent. Anyway, he managed to help me get you here so he must be doing something right.'

Barrow led Greg down the corridor past a couple of doors marked STAFF and STOCK-ROOM into the actual shop itself.

'Well here it is.' Barrow waved an outstretched arm as he spoke. The shop was filled with trainers, shirts and equipment: the usual accoutrements of a high-street sports store. Greg noticed that the shutters were down on the front windows and entrance although he could hear the noise of shoppers outside going about their daily business. 'I expect you've opened a million of these things, haven't you?' Barrow said.

'No, actually. This is my first.'

'Really? Well I'm sure you'll find it all straightforward. And there's always me to turn to if you have any trouble.'

Barrow mopped his brow with a handkerchief. Greg could see how damp the man's forehead was: Barrow was actually more worried than he was letting on, and Greg wondered whether he had turned up late.

'Now this is our staff.' Several shop assistants were scattered around the shop floor, all in the prerequisite uniform of a dark blue Sportmaster polo shirt, tracksuit bottoms and trainers. Barrow directed Greg's attention to all of them in turn as he said their names. 'This is Mary, this is Karen, that's Kirk, James and Stuart.'

Greg gave a nod towards all of them, letting his gaze rest a while on Stuart who was particularly pleasing on the eye. Stuart was a real regular-guy-on-the-street type, not classically handsome, but still attractive. He was pale skinned, his hair was gelled into a spiky style, and he grinned back with a sexy white-toothed smile as Greg looked at him.

'That's the introductions over. We'll keep the staffroom empty for a bit while you get changed. The curtains are closed so there won't be anyone looking in.'

Barrow pointed Greg towards the corridor they had just come down.

'Changed?' Greg had no idea what the man meant.

'Yes, into your kit.' To Barrow it was obviously all straightforward. 'In your car is it? Well, it'll not take two minutes to put on.'

'But I haven't brought a kit. I didn't know I was supposed to.'

Greg hadn't been asked to bring anything but himself. Whether it was Baker's mistake or Barrow's didn't matter. It was the increasingly distraught branch manager who had to deal with the aftermath.

Barrow wrung his hands with barely hidden frustration, obviously hating the fact that things weren't going exactly to plan.

'There must be something in the stock-room you can wear. After all, this is Sportsmaster.' Barrow chuckled nervously. 'Stuart! Give Mr Williams a hand, will you? Try and find a City kit in his size. The new design preferably. And be quick about it.'

'Okay, Mr Barrow.' Stuart sprang into action. 'I'll see what I can do.'

Greg felt extremely grateful for the choice of aid and turned to Barrow to proffer a few words of reassurance.

'Don't worry, Kevin,' he said as he headed back down the corridor. 'I'm sure we'll find something that'll fit.'

The stock-room was filled with unopened plastic bags full of clothes and shelves full of trainers. As Greg entered, Stuart was bent over with his head in one of the large boxes of football shirts. Greg took some time to appreciate the view before he spoke, noticing how appealing Stuart's arse looked from that particular angle. Stuart was slim, but he was evidently quite active and his buttocks curved with a perfect roundness beneath the loose material of his tracksuit. Greg felt randy. He knew exactly what he wanted to do to that peach in front of him, but also knew he had to test the waters first before he took any action.

'This your new job?' he asked the seemingly headless body.

'Yeah. Just for the spring and summer, like. I'm off to Uni in the autumn to study P.E.'

'Oh right. I thought you looked in good shape.'

'Thanks. I get quite a lot of exercise. I play five-a-side with some mates on Sundays and go to the gym in the week. I like to have a nice trim body.'

Greg could see how true that was. 'Don't we all?' he teased. The assistant chuckled.

Greg went further into the room to get closer to Stuart, knowing how sexy invasions of proximity could be if they didn't seem threatening.

'You know, I just can't believe I'm here with you today.' Stuart raised his voice over the rustling of clothing packages.

'Really?' Greg said. 'Are you a fan?'

Stuart turned around. He looked surprised to see Greg right behind him. Then, showing that Greg's closeness was not a problem, he flashed his bright teeth, returning his attentions to the box in front of him. The peach rose and waggled into view again.

'Only the greatest fan Weston City has ever known. I go to every match. Even the away ones.'

'That's what I like to hear. What do you think of their new striker?' Greg joked.

Stuart laughed. Having found what he had been looking for he stood up once more, a shirt in Weston's new, sky-blue colours in one hand. He looked directly into Greg's eyes as he continued. 'I think it was a good move. I like . . .'

He paused, and Greg was expectant to see what the assistant would say next. Intriguingly, the young man cast his eyes downward.

'I like the way you play, Greg,' he said before handing the shirt over. 'This should be okay.' Stuart made to leave but Greg stopped him.

'Wait,' he exclaimed, with not a little anxiousness. 'I mean, just till I see if it fits. If it doesn't I can't imagine me being able to find another one.'

'I was just going to give you some privacy.' Stuart shrugged.

'Don't bother. I'm sure you've seen it all before.' Greg smiled as he unbuttoned his shirt. He knew he looked good as he undressed. The life of a footballer with its regular exercise programmes and the need for a good diet meant that Greg's body was in excellent shape. He enjoyed exposing his sinewy torso and the furtive glances the action caused Stuart to make at him. By this time he was certain that the shop-worker was interested in giving more than just the usual admiration he received from fans. Stuart's embarrassed shuffles, the way he watched Greg, but at the same time was trying not to, made his hidden intentions clear.

As Greg slipped on the Weston shirt, he already had in mind a next move.

'Like a glove,' he said, brushing himself down and staring directly at the man in front of him. 'Now for the rest of it.'

Greg took off his shoes and socks, undid his belt and whipped off his trousers and pants simultaneously. Being an attacker meant that his thigh, buttock and calf muscles received a lot of exercise to provide kicking strength and he knew his legs looked as good as his upper body. Stuart's magnetised stare told him that the time he had put in at the gym had not gone unappreciated. Being looked at like that, doing an impromptu striptease for a horny, nervous audience of one was such a thrill he couldn't help but get semi-hard. He scratched himself, as if unaware of anything out of the ordinary going on, allowing his thickening prick to bounce against his hand as he did so, lifting up his balls as if he had an itch between his legs, all the time aware of how good the mock self-play must look.

'Any chance you can help me out with what else I need?' he asked, raising the direction of Stuart's gaze once more.

Stuart appeared unsure of himself, but at the same time in no hurry to make an exit. He was obviously interested in what was on offer to him, but not entirely certain how to react.

'Erm – some shorts. I'll get you some shorts.'

He moved to stand directly opposite Greg, not too distant from him but not too close either.

'How big . . . I mean, what size are you?' he gulped. He looked directly into Greg's eyes, half as if he was enjoying what he saw and half as if he was too scared to look anywhere else.

'Take a guess.' Greg nodded downward, causing Stuart to move his eyes tentatively in the same direction, pausing at the waistline but unable to stop himself from looking lower.

Greg's penis had reached quite an angle now, not as elevated as when it reached maximum hardness, but noticeably aroused and it had started to pulse a little at the stronger beats of Greg's heart.

'Er, well, I'm sure I can find something for you.' Stuart turned around. 'They're around here somewhere.'

He bent over. Greg wasn't sure if the shorts were actually in the particular box the assistant was looking in or whether Stuart just wanted to make himself appear as inviting as he possibly could. Either way the view was terrific, two faultlessly spherical bubbles of flesh beneath satiny tracksuit material less than a foot away from his quivering cock. It was too much for him to resist – the trainers, the white socks pulled up and over the bottom of the tracksuit legs – and Greg felt his hard-on fill to its ultimate, belly-level height. The game had gone on too long now and Greg was ready to score the clincher.

'Oh, screw the shorts, Stuart,' he said, moving forward. 'I don't think I'll be needing them for a while.'

He placed his cock directly along the ridge between Stuart's elevated cheeks and sighed at the initial breakthrough contact. Greg waited a moment, relishing the first touch of another body against the underside of his erection, pressing backward against his balls, then gently began squirming around with his hips. He leaned over, working both hands along Stuart's hard back muscles, right up to the armpits, which were hot and quite damp. He slipped his fingers up the sleeves of Stuart's shirt and felt around at the wetness that coated the skin and hairs.

'You're hot,' he said, rubbing the sweat back and forth.

'I – I don't do this very often,' explained Stuart.

'Like fuck you don't.' Greg sniffed at his fingers. The scent was fresh and full-bodied, salty, meaty and unmistakably manly. Turned on by the testosterone in his nostrils, Greg pressed his chest against Stuart's body, and placed his mouth at the nape of Stuart's neck where the shaved slope of his hairstyle diminished into bare skin. He loved that part of a man's body, especially if the hair was short, and he brushed his lips against the sharp but yielding spikes before taking a bite of the taut skin.

'Ow!' exclaimed the man in his arms.

'Sorry. Getting carried away.'

'No, no.' Stuart sounded almost totally lost in sensual pleasure. 'I liked it.'

Greg bit once more, never one to hold back on a request. He let the first chomp down linger, before he chewed tenderly then let the wetness of his lips enclose the area. He could feel Stuart writhe beneath him, the tight backside against his crotch squirming in response. Stuart turned his face to the left and, reaching forward, Greg kissed him. It was an awkward but ardent move. He couldn't get round far enough to meet Stuart's mouth entirely and instead settled for half the lips and a wriggling outstretched tongue. He smooched Stuart's face, eyelids and ears. That both men strained to make the connection turned Greg on greatly. They were both so desperate to kiss that they settled for the rapid licking of the bits of each other's face they could reach, their greedy tongues clashing together in a violent, spit-ridden war of muscle. Greg increased the intensity of his hip movements, moving from the basic caressing of Stuart's split cheeks with his member to more prodding and intruding thrusts. He moved his hands down Stuart's upper body and put them inside the assistant's shirt to get an unrestricted feel of his skin. As he had imagined, the young man's body was fit and trim. He fingered Stuart's belly-button, rubbing the rest of Stuart's flat stomach with his hand as it rose and fell with each breath. Moving upward he discovered a well-defined but not huge pair of pectorals. He squeezed them with passion, before tweaking their small perky, nipples with thumb and forefinger. Stuart blurted out an expletive that had obviously been far too long withheld.

'If you only knew how many times I dreamed of this. A professional footballer at my arse . . .' Stuart's voice wobbled with sheer ecstasy.

'It's not all I'm going to get at.' Greg took a firm hold of Stuart's crotch, the bulging contents of the youthful lunchbox filling his hands without trouble.

'Big fella, I see,' Greg said as he sorted out the man's genitals, taking the thick solid member into his right hand and the bulbous, swollen bollocks into his left. The cock he held felt huge. Even taking into account the clothing around it, it was perhaps three inches in circumference and a good eight or nine in length. He began dragging his fingers along it from the base upward, appreciating the rustle and texture of the material that covered it as he did so. Stuart groaned with euphoria when Greg reached the head then pinched it at the point that would cause most effect. He gripped it once more, giving it a good hard squeeze before starting to properly pull on it, fondling the hefty balls with his other hand and sometimes moving his caresses along Stuart's trembling, muscular thighs.

'We can't do this,' Stuart eventually said, unconvincingly. 'We haven't time. What about the opening of the shop?'

'I'll have to be politely late.' Greg put his hands down Stuart's tracksuit bottoms. He wasn't exactly bothered too much about what he had arrived at Sportsmaster to do at that point. 'Besides, I'd rather open you up any day.'

Stuart swore once more at the skin-to-skin contact and Greg played with him briefly before turning him around. He pulled at the elasticated waistband around Stuart's midriff, stretching it outward then over the large, erect manhood.

'No underwear,' he noticed aloud as Stuart bounced into the open.

'I like the feel of it like that.'

'I bet you do.' Greg could see Stuart wasn't as innocent as he made out. 'I bet you like the feel of this as well.'

Liberated, the cock more than lived up to Greg's imaginings of it. It was circumcised so that its deep pink gobstopper of a round head was fully revealed. It was as huge as Greg had estimated, being one of those dicks Greg could have sucked forever, just getting off on the chunky size chugging into his gullet. Standing to attention, it looked lewd and irresistible and Greg could hold his fingers back no longer. He spat on his hand for lubrication, then took hold of the cock once more. Greg loved the sight of another man's genitals in his clutches. There was something so forbidden, so immediate and erotic about it. And the actual feel of what a man carried between his legs! The rasping hairs on loose testicular skin contrasting with the smooth hardness and heat of a pulsating erection all created a barrage of sensation that made Greg's heart pound with lust.

He stopped wanking briefly to move his own length next to Stuart's, then positioned the pricks together, one on top of the other. He took hold of Stuart's right hand then linked it with his own around their joined bodies.

'What do you think of that?' he asked, initiating the repeated jerking of the mutual grasp.

'I . . . I like the way you play,' Stuart replied, referring to the comment he had made earlier.

Greg smiled, then lunged with a savage kiss. The full-on collision of the two men's faces felt explosive. He pushed the entirety of his tongue into Stuart's mouth, licked and bit the man's lips, chin and jawline. Greg was horny as hell now and his actions became forceful, almost unconscious, almost uncontrolled as he thought of nothing else but physical satisfaction. He dragged his love-partner into an energetic, tussling embrace. He just couldn't get enough of the body in his arms as they kissed furiously, the unyielding back and shoulder muscles, the hot pumped-up dick against his belly and the fleshy feel of gorgeous buttocks in his hands. If he could have absorbed Stuart into his clinch he would have. As it was, the two pressed together tightly, wriggling against each other like caught fish in a basket.

Eventually Greg reached a point where he could contain himself no longer.

'I've got to have you, Stuart,' he begged. 'I can't stand it any longer. I've got to put it inside.'

'Oh, Greg!' Stuart, breathless, sounded more than ready. 'I want it. Please. I've got to get fucked.'

Stuart turned around. Leaning over, he placed a hand on each half of his rump and parted them, revealing the glorious hidden area for Greg's perusal.

Short curly hairs encircled Stuart's hole and drew a line to the balls that dangled invitingly between his thighs. The anus itself was like a dark, welcoming slit. It was vertical, about one and a half inches long and had the customary wrinkles of pink skin surrounding it. Greg found himself fingering it almost immediately, relishing the spectacle of his digits disappearing up the chute, the furrows that clamped against him and the tight pressing muscles of the rectum that seemed to invite more and more of him inside. He slipped back and forth slowly a few times to the sound of Stuart's appreciative moans until he felt the passage give a little.

'Are you ready for it?' he asked, desperately hoping that the moment had arrived.

'Yes. Oh, yes.' Stuart sounded as if he would do anything to get some cock inside him. 'But I want to watch you as you do me.'

Stuart picked up a large box of clothes and placed it on top of one of a similar size. His movements were constricted by his tracksuit bottoms, so sitting down on his makeshift platform he pulled them off, leaving one trainer on his right foot and just a white, slightly grubby sock on his left. As Stuart raised his legs, Greg wondered if the man knew how sexy he looked like that, partially clothed, his sporty footwear haphazard and somehow incongruous with his nudity but being all the more arousing for it.

'I'm ready now.' Stuart had placed one hand behind the bend of each knee. His arsehole winked at Greg as if to indicate its willing state.

Feeling all fingers and thumbs in frantic anticipation, Greg took his wallet from his trouser pocket, found the emergency condom he kept in one of its compartments and quickly but carefully rolled it on to his now ultra-sensitive pecker. He lifted Stuart's calves onto his shoulders so they could rest there, then positioned his rubber-covered erection where his fingers had just exited. His bell-end was on fire as it rested against Stuart's entrance and the sensation of the passage opening up and closing around him was heavenly as he pushed forward. Fully inserted, he put more of his body weight on to the man underneath him so that their faces were only millimetres apart. Greg thrilled at seeing Stuart's simul- taneously pained and enraptured expression so close up, those man-on-the-street features branded with a look of such need. He kissed Stuart again and felt his rectum-bound hard- on surge and pound with readiness. He was almost at the point of climax already. But he knew he couldn't come. Not yet. He had other duties to perform.

'Do it, football star,' Stuart urged. 'Put one in the net for me.'

Greg did as he was told, pulling back with his hips, then pushing forward, enjoying the fully enclosed snugness against his cock as he did so. He thought he would ejaculate almost straight away, but knowing with concentration he could restrain it and realising the release would be so much better if he waited, he held back, and instead increased the power of his thrusts until he pounded fully out and fully in with repeated deep rams. He fucked faster and faster, Stuart seemingly capable and wanting to take more and more, bouncing and groaning underneath him with every bang. He didn't know how Stuart could take such a pummelling but looking downward at the assistant's fevered wanking, hearing his moans and phrases of encouragement, he knew he was doing exactly what was required.

Greg began to feel like some kind of beast. All thoughts were subsumed by desire and everything became focused out except the end of his cock and the machine-like motion that was producing such joy in his body. Before long, Stuart's love-noises became frequent and uncontrolled and Greg knew the man didn't have much staying power left in him. More than ready for his own release, he tilted his upper body back again, priming himself for something that he knew would make his own time that bit stronger. Licking backward against one of the calves at his neck, he moved to brush his cheek against the top of Stuart's sock. Not missing a beat of his hips, he turned his head into the instep and inhaled. As he had hoped, Stuart's nervous, excited feet had become as sweaty as his armpits and the smell was rank and pungent. Obviously understanding the hint, Stuart moved his foot around to cover Greg's face. Greg began taking regular, deep sniffs and managed to taste a patch of the dampened, aromatic material before he finally started to blow. With the first explosion at his crotch, he bit down on Stuart's big toe, sucking it as the eruptions wracked his body. The flavour was fantastic, as was the way he felt his muscles tense, then relax repeatedly, shaking him so that he fucked almost without effort. He felt his own spunk filling the condom, then as Stuart too began to shoot, the spasming rectum around him squashed the hot liquid against his used, pleasured dick. Greg watched as Stuart below him, eyes closed, brought himself off in his own hands, that huge thing of his firing over and over again like a cannon, balls bobbling away, the jets of cream streaming in long streaks across his shirt. Greg stayed inside until Stuart had let loose his final drop, opened his eyes and given him a big grin of contentment. The two men kissed, Greg moving his fingers over the warm wet patches Stuart had made as they did so. There was something about seeing another man's load like that that made him just have to touch it, and as he exited Stuart's body he licked his fingers clean with relish.

Greg had barely had time to pull off his rubber when there was a knock at the door.

'Mr Williams? Stuart? Are you two OK in there?' It was Mr Barrow and he had a rather distraught tone to his voice.

Hurriedly the two men began dressing, Stuart finally finding a pair of appropriate shorts, then taking off his sticky shirt, hiding it and replacing it with a spare.

'Everything's fine, Mr Barrow. Just getting changed now.' Greg checked his watch. It was ten-twenty. The opening was in ten minutes' time.

'You made me forget where I was for a while,' he told Stuart. 'Do you know how long we've been in here?'

'Yeah,' Stuart chuckled. 'It happens when you're having fun.'

Soon enough, Greg was kitted up and prepared to allay Mr Barrow's worries once more.

'Sorry about that,' he explained as he left the stock-room. 'Me and him. Just getting acquainted. We've got a lot in common.'

'Really?' Barrows looked surprised. He gave Stuart a

pleased, congratulatory nod. 'Hear that, Stuart. That's quite a compliment.' And then he turned back to Greg. 'Well, if he works as hard as you do on the pitch.'

Greg headed off into the store, prepared to greet his public. 'Oh, he's a hard worker all right, Mr Barrows,' he called behind him. 'You've got one that can take the pace there and no mistake.'

The morning went quickly and though there were many people after his attention or his signature, Greg enjoyed himself. He and Stuart exchanged many friendly, understanding glances throughout the time he spent in the shop and he liked the fact that they shared a mutual secret that no one else around them knew about. Before he left he took Stuart's address and phone number with the intention of getting a Weston publicity agent to sort him out with future season tickets in return for, as Greg told Mr Barrow, the great help he had been in the stockroom. Barrow was delighted at the news and told Stuart in front of the other workers what a bright future he had ahead of him. Greg agreed that the outlook was rosy for the young assistant, but for entirely different reasons. He liked Stuart and realised that one day he would make a great catch for someone. As he made his final farewell handshakes to the Sportmaster staff, Greg had it in the back of his mind to ask Grenet whether the Secret League had a sub-division for fans, as Stuart could be such a potential treasure to them.

Later that evening, as the fulfilling radiance of Greg's morning encounter subsided, the nagging awareness of something missing in his life returned. Greg found himself sat in his flat, mobile in hand, uneasily weighing up the consequences of a call he was going to make. Eventually, he decided, it was inevitable. He was just destined to try one more time. He dialled and a woman with a northern accent answered.

'Oh, hi, Sarah. It's Greg.' Greg was trying to sound like nothing was wrong, like he had not made similar stabs at making contact many times over the past few weeks to no avail. 'Is Matt around?'

'Yeah, I'll just get him for you. How are you, while I'm on the phone?'

The two exchanged pleasantries and caught up as much as their acquaintance would allow. Greg liked Sarah. She was a good woman and they got on well. He believed that she had nothing to do with Matt's sudden change in demeanour as she seemed so unaware of anything going on. But no matter what he thought of her as a person, his conviction that she would be wrong for Matt in the long run was cast-iron strong and as he heard her leave the phone, he just knew he would do almost anything to replace her position in Matt's life.

Greg heard voices, no exact words, but anxious concerned tones in the distance on the end of the line. Before long, Sarah returned with an apology.

'Er . . . sorry, Greg. I thought Matt was here, but he must have just popped out for something. I never heard him leave.'

The excuse sounded unconvincing, but Greg had heard similar lines from Matt's mother and father several times before.

'It's OK, Sarah,' he sighed. 'It's not urgent. It's just that I've not heard from him in a while. Can you get him to call me back?'

'Yeah. I'll try.'

'Are you sure you've got the number there?'

Greg knew he was clutching at straws, but he clutched at them anyway.

'It's here on the pad.' Sarah read the number aloud. 'OK, then? I'll make sure he knows you called. And I'll be seeing you soon. Take care.'

They said goodbye.

Greg felt tearful at the rebuff. He lay back on his sofa, staring at the ceiling, frustrated and angry. He knew as soon as he made the breakthrough contact Matt would be incapable of doing anything but responding, but the way his lover was acting just made the re-establishing of those links simply seem impossible.

Over the next few weeks there followed a period of unease for Greg. He was giving one hundred per cent at training sessions and yet his performances during actual matches seemed lacking. He became aware of amateurish mistakes he kept making, bad passes that gave possession to the other side and missed goals he should have easily scored. One time, without thinking, he foolishly overreached while attempting to tackle, inflaming his thigh muscle so that he had to spend the rest of the match on the sidelines cursing himself. More than once Brown, during his post-match talk, singled Greg out and like an angry teacher with a bad student reprimanded him for the things he had done or not done during the previous ninety minutes. Dead-cert wins ended up being draws or losses and Greg knew that although he couldn't blame himself entirely for Weston's poor run, his wayward efforts had definitely contributed. Soon enough the press he received turned sour, disappointed that the promise he had shown earlier on in the season seemed to have disappeared, that the thrilling playing and great competitions they had expected just hadn't come to pass. Luckily the pundits realised that Greg did have it in him, but for some reason he wasn't achieving what he was capable of and they began to question why. Was he unhappy with the move to Weston? With his team-mates? With his pay? Or couldn't he handle the sudden increase in his fame? The world wanted an explanation but at that point only Greg himself knew the truth and he wasn't prepared to share it.

It was after another goalless draw when Brown arranged a meeting, asking Greg to turn up at his office so just the two of them could speak together. Greg feared a heavy one-on-one confrontation, as in that match he had made some very silly errors, but at the same time he welcomed the chance to speak intimately with Brown. After all, the manager only wanted what was best for his team and no matter what he said or how angrily he said it, somewhere in there would be good advice and Greg felt he could do with the help.

It didn't take long for Brown to answer the knock on his door. Greg entered and sat down, expecting the worst.

'All right, new boy. What's all this about?' Brown sounded determined, but surprisingly not annoyed.

Greg leaned forward in his chair, and rubbed his hands over his face. He knew exactly what was affecting his abilities.

'It's – It's difficult.' Greg was aware how distant and evasive he sounded, but he couldn't help himself. It was a hard, complicated and painful subject to touch upon.

'Baseline, Greg,' Brown obviously wanted to attack the problem practically. 'Are you happy here?'

'Yes, of course.' That was something Greg had no doubt about. He thought back to the early matches with City, not two months earlier, how well they had gone and how glad he had been to be finally at the top. He was more than happy as a Weston team-member and it was only recently that things had started to go wrong.

'Well, is it me? Someone on the team? Found something in your contract that you're not happy with?'

'No, it's none of those things. It's nothing to do with Weston at all.'

'That's a relief.' Suddenly, Brown looked shocked. 'It's not the booze, is it?'

Greg laughed, shook his head.

'Thank God for that.' As a player himself, back in the eighties, Brown's team-mate and friend Steve Anderson had been a star player. But Anderson's fondness for alcohol eventually led him to ruin and he and Brown's tumultuous relationship had hit the headlines many times, with Brown attempting to help his friend into rehab, only to find him up to his old tricks mere days afterward. 'It's not drugs, I know that's not your scene. It's got to be the private life.'

Brown had hit the nail on the head and Greg knew he couldn't hide it. 'Well, yeah. It's something outside the game. Something I just can't get out of my mind.'

Brown gave a half-smile. He looked fatherly and understanding.

'Listen, I'm not going to pry. What happens when you leave the pitch in that respect is entirely up to you. And I know you're a reticent man: I read the interviews. You're happy enough to talk about the game, but when it comes to yourself, that's something else. That's fine with me. I like a man with secrets. And I can tell if I'm on at you any longer I'm just going to make you uncomfortable. It's a sore point, ain't it, this matter of yours?'

Greg nodded.

'Besides, I'm no agony aunt, so I'm not sure what I'd have to say would be of any use anyway.' Brown paused, and his next words took on a thoughtful air as if they revealed more about himself than he intended. 'I suppose you could say when it comes to matters of the heart, I'm not a fountain of knowledge. After all, my age and I'm still a single man.'

He chuckled, despite the slight sadness in his tone.

'What I'm trying to say is I know you have it in you. one of the brightest hopes I've ever seen and you could be one of the greatest players this country has ever known. I don't think anyone, not even the press, can doubt you're talented. But at the You're moment you're just pissing it all away. And it's up to you to turn things around.'

The importance of what Brown was saying was having its effect on Greg. The compliments had felt like a true, substantial boost to his ego. Here was Trevor Brown, a living legend, telling him that he was capable of achieving similar if not greater heights than he had. And though, deep down, Greg had known already what to do, having things spelled out like that him by someone else made him face up to it outright. It was up to him to sort himself out, and with Brown behind him, he knew that he could do it.

'Listen, I'm giving you some time off. Not too much, mind. We're not letting you get out of touch. Just a couple of days to see what you can do about getting that head of yours cleared.'

'Thanks, boss.' It sounded like a good idea. The time since his introduction to Weston had been a rush of hard work and it did seem like time to have a proper rest, rather than one that had an interview or a public appearance scheduled into it. 'I think I need it.'

'Well, use it to your best advantage. Because when you're back I want you up to standard. The cup semi is not long away and I want Weston, all of Weston, to be able to perform at their best by the time that match comes around.'

'I can do it, boss.'

'I'm sure you can. Now skedaddle out of here. I've got some reporters to talk to and they can be pretty slippery when they're trying to be critical.'

Greg made an exit, not exactly elated, but definitely in better spirits than when he left the field at the end of his last match. Brown had ignited a spark within him, boosted the conviction that he had the capacity to change his life. Grateful of the time he had been given to perform exactly that task, he headed outside to his car, knowing the solution to his problems were but a motorway drive away.

Ten

After packing a sports bag with some overnight things, Greg set off on the journey to his home town. He had warned his mother on the phone of his arrival, assuring her that no, nothing was wrong and that he was just using his well earned break time to do some visiting.

He arrived a couple of hours later. It was mid-evening and he was surprised to find several cars waiting outside the house taking up the space where he usually parked. Pulling up further down the street, he took his bag from the boot only to find people were shouting out his name.

'Greg! Greg! Over here, Willy!'

The flash of cameras told Greg that the journalists were after him again.

'Greg, we've heard you're not happy at Weston. Is it true?' A reporter had sprinted to Greg's side and was hurrying to keep up with him.

'No, no, of course not.' Greg was angry at the invasion of his and Lila's privacy but he wanted to put paid to rumours if he could.

'What's the break for? Is Trevor Brown rethinking your transfer?'

'Listen, mate.' Greg stopped at the gate to the pathway of his mother's house. 'I'm just visiting my Mum. There's no trouble at City, there's no problems caused by the move and I'm not dating anyone from a soap opera. Now give it a rest will you? In fact you might as well get off now, because you won't be getting anything out of me tonight.'

As the questions and clicking of cameras continued, Greg closed the gate behind him and walked up the pathway. His mother answered the door before he had a chance to press the bell.

'They've been here for hours!' she exclaimed as she ushered him in. 'Get in here before they eat you alive.'

He slipped inside. Before he had chance to realise what she was up to, his mother rushed past him, a bucket in her hand.

'Mum, no!' he shouted after her. Lila ran into the garden in her slippers then hurled the water she was carrying at the confused and surprised journalists.

'Go on! Get out of it!' she cried as they scurried away. 'And don't come back, you little blighters. You're not welcome!'

'I can't believe you just did that!' Greg couldn't stop himself from laughing at the sight of this feisty mother in cardigan and glasses behaving in such an unexpected manner. She looked more like she should be somewhere playing bingo than taking direct action to reclaim her privacy.

'Well, bloody cheek! You might be famous but we can't have them hassling you like that, can we? On your time off as well.'

Lila closed the door behind her, gave her son a hug and an affectionate peck on the cheek.

'It's nice to know you can still take care of yourself.' Greg followed his mother down the corridor into the kitchen.

'And don't you forget it. Right, cup of tea do you? There's biccies in the barrel if your special diet will allow it.'

Greg seated himself at the table, after taking a couple of chocolate digestives from the tin on the side. His mother peered out of the window as she filled the kettle at the sink.

'It looks like they got the message, anyway. Don't mess with Lila Williams. You've not got what it takes.'

'That's true enough.' Greg smirked.

'What I want to know is how they knew you'd be here. How they found out so fast you were taking time off.'

'That's a point. I told Trevor I was coming, just to let him know where I'd be, but nobody else.'

'Sounds like someone's pulling a fast one. You'd better watch who you're talking to.'

'It's hard at the top.' Greg decided not to let the press bother him. He had other things on his mind. But his mother appeared to have a bee in her bonnet about the disturbance.

'Tell me about it. It's not the first time they've been round like that, you know,' she continued.

'Really?' Greg knew that Lila had had some interest in her lately but not realised it was anything as intrusive as what he'd just seen happen.

'Oh yes!' Lila poured hot water into the teapot. 'It's been more focused recently. They're not here all the time or anything like that. But they've a tendency to appear sometimes after a match. I think they're after a special angle, want to know my opinion or something. I suppose it's to be expected with all the exposure you get.'

'Oh Lila, you shouldn't have to put up with them in your life. Not because of me. It's not right.'

Lila sighed. 'I know what you're getting at duck, and the answer is still no. I'm happy here and I'm staying and that's that. Beside, like you said, I can take care of myself.'

'Well you just let me know if it starts to bother you. I'm in a position where something can be done about it.'

It was becoming more and more important to Greg that his mother moved out of the area.

'I will, I will. I promise.' Lila poured the drinks and passed one to her son. 'Hey, look at this. I've been sorting out some jumble for the local fair.'

She went over to the corner of the room, rustled in a black bin-liner full of discarded objects.

'I don't think there's anything you'd want here. But there are a lot of memories. Remember this?'

Lila pulled out an old T-shirt with the name of a band

Greg liked as a teenager on the front. As Lila had suggested, seeing it again instantly brought back a flood of recollections. He remembered where he had bought the shirt. It was at a gig the band had played a good five years earlier. He and Matt had gone to see them, drinking a lot more lager than they had meant to in the process. They missed the last bus home and ended up staying out way past the time that they had both told their parents they would return. He remembered the scolding Lila had given him, and the subsequent grounding that followed, but also how it had all seemed worth it for having had such a great time with Matt.

'What's wrong?' Lila had obviously cottoned on to Greg's distant thoughts. 'I knew there was something when you said you were coming across. Well, let's have it out, love. There's no use keeping it inside if it's getting you down.'

She too sat down at the table, caressing one of Greg's shoulders with her hand. Greg knew it was time to reveal all and he did exactly that, telling his mother how he felt about Matt and what had happened the night he had heard about the marriage. He told her how he knew Matt felt the same way he did, how he couldn't understand what had gone wrong between them, and how Matt was keeping him at arm's length. At first Lila just listened without interrupting with advice. Greg was appreciative of the sympathetic ear. He realised how much he had needed someone to tell all his troubles to and in the process of doing so, how the simple act of talking and revealing his problems made him feel better about them and more able to cope.

Eventually, he had talked himself out and it was time for Lila to make her response. She smiled and took hold of Greg's hand as she began to speak. 'To tell you the truth, love. I'm surprised.'

Greg looked confused, before his mother explained.

'Surprised it took you this bloody long to get to this point. I could see it years ago, how you two felt for each other. And honestly sometimes I thought I'd have to bang your heads together to make you realise it.'

'Was it that obvious?' Greg shrugged.

'Obvious? It was like Romeo and Julian around here until you moved out. But like typical men, you just couldn't admit it to yourselves, could you?'

'Not until it was too late.' Greg felt suddenly despondent.

'Too late? It's not too late! It's never too late for a love like yours, Greg. Emotions like that can overcome anything. It's just sometimes they need a helping hand.'

Lila rose, taking the cups to the sink to rinse them out.

'What are you saying?'

'I think you know what you have to do,' his mother replied, turning on the taps. 'What you came here for. I can kid myself all I want, but I know it wasn't only to see me.'

'Yeah, I must confess. I did have an ulterior motive. To see Matt face to face at last, I mean.'

'I think it's the only thing you can do. Once he sees you, he'll know what's what. But I don't think it's a good idea to do it tonight.'

'Why not?' Greg, deciding to make himself useful, picked up a tea-towel.

'It's getting late. You're tired, I can tell. Bags under those eyes like a bloodhound. You'll be in a much better state to face it all in the morning. Besides, I was wrong about those reporters. They're still out there. And you don't want them tagging along with you on a trip as important as you've got to make.'

Suddenly distracted, Lila banged on the kitchen window furiously. 'Hey you!' Having caught the pressman's attention, she raised two fingers to him in salute, then mouthed an expletive, much to the amusement of Greg, who shook with laughter at her side.

His mother was right, he realised. Though he did feel relieved and more positive, he was tired and needed a good night's rest before he tackled anything else. And leading the tabloids to Matt's when what he had intended was a quiet, intimate and very significant discussion between them would be a very bad idea. No, as Lila had suggested he would leave everything till the morning. It would all be clearer then, including, he hoped, the end of his mother's pathway.

In the morning, Greg rose refreshed. He felt like he had had a great night's sleep and that he was more than prepared for the events the day had to throw at him.

After showering, shaving and dressing he went downstairs to find Lila frying breakfast.

'Don't look at the papers, love,' she said over the sizzles. 'They'll only annoy you.'

'Oh, God.' Greg thought of his mother's water-throwing antics and was suddenly hit by their newsworthiness. 'There's nothing on you in there?'

'No, not at all.' Lila put a couple of plates on the table. 'I must have scared them too much. It's all about you, I'm afraid. Page four, I think it is. Big photo as well.'

Greg flicked through the newspaper quickly.

'Now don't you take any notice of it,' his mother warned. 'You know what these idiots are like.'

Greg found the piece. There was no mention of Lila or of buckets of water. Instead it was all about himself, starting with a large photograph of him arriving at his mother's street. He looked flustered and a little upset. He knew his appearance was caused by the unexpected discovery of would-be interviewers on Lila's doorstep, but as he carried on to the article beneath, he discovered the story was trying to argue it was a result of his dissatisfaction with Weston. The rest of the article had twisted recent events just as much. It had pinned the reason for the holiday he had taken on a supposed clash of opinion between him and Trevor Brown and speculated on the possibility that Greg would not be staying long at Weston.

It even tried to put forward that he didn't get on with the rest of the team, citing name-calling and antagonism between him and Charmers as evidence. But what got at him most was the paragraph that attacked him personally, that tried to insinuate that the initial demonstration of his talents was a fluke and that Weston's recent run of bad luck was a direct result of his inability to play at such a high level. Greg couldn't take the pace either on or off the pitch, the writer of the article argued. Whether he had got the wrong end of the stick or whether it was just an attempt at muck-raking didn't matter much to Greg. It had the same effect. His blood was boiling.

'What? That's libellous!' He threw the paper on the table in anger.

'Now don't worry about it. I'm sure they're only trying to wind you up.' Lila chomped on a piece of toast. 'Perhaps it was me. Perhaps they're trying to get back at you because I was so nasty to them.'

'Well it's working. I'm furious.'

'I know, love. It's terrible what they said. But try not to let it get to you too much. They only do stuff like that to sell papers.'

Greg sat down. He knew his mother was right but for some reason, the story had really angered him.

'Oh dear!' Lila began serving up. 'You've a face like murder now. Next time I'm hiding that rag before you've a chance to get to it. Brown or red?'

She held up two bottles of sauce, one in each hand, and Greg plumped for red.

'I tell you what, though,' Lila continued. 'If you think of the tosspot who wrote that and the things he said about you when you're on the pitch next Saturday, you'll be playing like your arse is on fire. Goals everywhere, just out of sheer unadulterated fury.'

It was good advice and Greg couldn't avoid it. Why should he let what some no-good Fleet Street hack makes up about him get him down? He knew he could do it, and what was more now he felt he had something to prove. He would show exactly what he had in him the very next chance he got.

'Thanks Mum.' Greg leaned over the table to kiss his mother on the cheek as she placed a grease-filled plate in front of him.

'It's only what you usually get,' she said, somewhat puzzled.

'No, I mean, for putting up with me when I'm grumpy.'

Lila burst into laughter. 'Oh Greg! This morning was nothing. I lived with you when you were a teenager, remember?'

Greg grinned. His mood had turned around completely and he felt a renewed confidence as he tucked into his breakfast. He couldn't wait to return to Weston. He felt like it was him against the world now, and he knew exactly who was going to win.

Before long, Greg heard the ring of his mobile. He had left it in the hallway as he had walked in the house and he got up from the table to answer the call.

'See who that is before you take it,' his mother warned. 'It's been a busy enough morning already. We don't want any more trouble.'

'Don't I always?' Greg checked the display. He recognised the number as Trevor Brown's and, bemused at why the man should be ringing him so early, he pressed the talk button.

'Listen, Greg.' Brown sounded irritated. 'I've seen the papers, and I'm just ringing to tell you to take no notice of them. You know and I know things are fine between us and Weston has not been reconsidering your contract.'

'Yeah, Trevor,' Greg interrupted. 'I'm OK about it.'

'Good on you, mate! That's what I like to hear. Fighting spirit! Now there's just one other thing. I know we sorted out this break, and I still think it's a good idea . . .'

'Ye-es.' Greg guessed there was something forbidding on the horizon.

'And it's up to you, no pressure at all, but I figure if you were to make it back here this afternoon for a couple of hours, it would show those bastards where we're really at. You working hard on the pitch, me cheering you on at the sidelines. Still take the holiday you need, just postpone it for a week or two until this has all died down. What do you think?'

Greg didn't know how to answer. If he left Middleton that morning it wouldn't give him a chance to meet up with Matt and that was an opportunity he knew they both needed. But he also knew that his position at Weston, still in its early days, was a fragile one, and he had to do what he could to provide it with stability. Returning to training sooner than planned would mean that he could show the press, the public, Brown and his team-mates that he was dedicated. He could show them what he was made of. Deciding impulsively that his hiatus, and Matt, could be put off till later as Brown had suggested, he agreed to drive back to Weston as soon as he had finished breakfast.

'Brilliant!' Brown was elated. 'I'll get in touch with Baker, get a couple of the friendlier journos there, see what we can do about damage limitation.'

The decision Greg had made was difficult and he only hoped he had made a good one. He did feel optimistic again about his career, if not about his relationship with Matt and he made his goodbyes feeling somewhat uncertain of himself.

His mother was equally doubtful when he returned to the table. Couldn't he hang on a couple of hours at least, just to pop round to Matt's and say hello? But Greg knew that he couldn't. What he had to talk over with Matt would take longer than the time of a brief visit, and he didn't want to end up trying to rush off having opened up a major can of emotional worms with the man. No, when he did meet up with Matt, and he assured Lila that it would happen very, very soon, it would be a long visit for an intimate and considered period so they could take as long as they needed to sort everything out between them.

Greg left mid-morning, convinced he had done the right thing.

The afternoon's practice went well. Brown was pleased to see him and the boys on the team showed understanding and sympathy. Greg trained hard, and certain of the next day's papers ran more complimentary coverage of his return, dismissing the stories from earlier in the week as rumours and conjecture. By the time the semi-final arrived Greg was in good spirits. Despite being aware that not everyone who would be at the game was convinced of what he could do, and the build-'em-up, knock-'em-down contingent of the sports press was eager to see him fail, what had changed was what mattered most. Once more, inside him, Greg knew that he had what it took to succeed.

'Penforth Rovers, lads.' Trevor Brown began his pre-match pep talk sternly, like a sergeant major briefing his troops before war. 'They're a formidable side, they're a popular side and they've had a great season so far. You know we've not been doing too well lately, you know the sensible money is on them. But there's been some turnaround recently, some fantastic skills being shown in training that they're not going to be aware of. You lot have got it. When you do it right, you're a very special side, one of the greatest teams I've ever had the honour to work with. And today you're going out there and you're going to show the entire world what I mean. And if you don't there'll be me to answer to.'

'Spanked botties all round if we lose, then, Trev?' joked Charmers as the team began to make their way out.

'Other way around, mate.' Brown winked. 'That's what you get if you win!'

Out on the pitch, Greg became aware of an atmosphere he had never experienced before. Weston's fans, though displaying a certain amount of zeal for their team, seemed wary in their encouragements especially when compared to the cockiness of the Rovers' audience. Every time a Weston player got the ball, cheers were muted, rather than spirited, as if the onlookers were on the edge of their seats and silent with anticipation, waiting to see whether their beloved boys would fail again or make their long-awaited come-back. The uneasy air didn't help Weston's gameplay much. Though Greg felt he was trying in a way that he had not managed for quite a while, errors caused by his team's caginess saw them concede a goal seconds before the half-time whistle blew.

Back in the changing rooms, Brown gave his team a heavy admonishing. City weren't playing as the force they could. They weren't working together and they were heading for another forfeited game. Greg knew that Brown was right and a disappointment welled within him. He thought back to what had happened after the last cup match, the fantastic sex he had experienced as a result of City's success and knew that he had to be involved in that again. Weston had to win the semi, he decided, as he wasn't prepared to forgo what the Secret League had to offer the winners for anything. Suddenly, as Brown wrapped up his speech, an idea popped into Greg's head. He grabbed hold of Grenet, before the man had chance to leave.

'Think of tonight,' he said forcefully. 'Think of what we could be missing out on.'

Grenet nodded, as if his reserve had been renewed.

'Thank you, *mon chère*,' he said, grateful. 'Sometimes you can lose sight of the things that are important.'

At that moment, Charmers brushed past the two men. Grenet stopped him, whispered something into his ear. A look of realisation came to Charmers' face.

'Damn right,' Charmers assented. 'I'm not missing that for the world. I'll tell the others.'

Before the second half had started, all members of the League had been reminded of what was at stake. The game resumed with Weston playing with replenished vigour and Greg knew his little ploy had done the trick. He himself couldn't stop fantasising about the cocks, balls and arses that would be his were his team to win, but instead of getting in the way of his playing, his imaginings gave his game a new edge. Every time he needed to pass or to avoid a tackle, he simply thought about a blow-job or a fuck with the opposition and the ball did exactly what he wanted it to. Soon City began to play as if they were parts of the same body. They gained chances, good chances, and were playing at last as Brown had told them they could. And then, before they had been back on the pitch fifteen minutes, Weston had equalised with a header from Greg. The crowd went crazy. City were back in the game at last!

For the next half an hour, Greg felt truly wonderful. Weston played like a well-oiled machine, with streamlined passes and some expressive, imaginative technique, and, best of all, displaying the almost intuitive co-operation that good football so desperately requires. It became a closely fought match, but Greg was determined that he had to put his team in the lead. During the closing moments of the match, the fans were yelling for City as never before, overjoyed to see the return of such great playing. Spurred on by the sound, Greg followed Grenet deep into Penforth's half. Dodging a midfielder, he found a space. It wasn't a good one: his shot was obscured, but time was running out and he was anxious to take the chance. He called Grenet's name and met the ball from his team-mate's pass. Before any of Portham's defence could steal it back, before Greg had an opportunity to think twice, he had lobbed the ball with a defiant move into the top corner. It was a fantastic shot, curving with absolute precision past the reach of Penforth's leaping goalkeeper. Greg fell to his knees with rapture, punching the air with his fist as the resonating yell of Weston's fans thundered around the stadium. He and his team-mates had done it, turned around their fortunes within a single half of one game. Greg felt triumphant as he was roughly embraced and kissed by his colleagues. City were going ahead to the final, and as important, they would be continuing as victors at that night's League meeting.

The next few hours went by in a crazy celebratory haze. Greg was on the top of the world as he showered and changed, singing along and mucking around with the other players in a mood so good that he never wanted to leave the stadium. It was only after Grenet made a mysterious comment about time moving on that he finally began to make a move, returning home excited about what lay ahead.

It was not until late evening that he received the call on his door buzzer. He answered it, finding Grenet's face distorted in the intercom's black-and-white screen.

'*C'est moi.*' The Frenchman's voice crackled through the speaker. 'Meet me downstairs. And bring your car keys.'

Greg obeyed, feeling as much of the tremble of butterflies in his stomach as he had done before the match that afternoon.

He found Grenet outside, leaning against his sports car. 'Are you parked near?' Grenet asked, aloof.

Greg pointed across the road.

'Get in. I shall lead the way.'

'Ever heard of car pooling?' Greg joked. Solemnly Grenet shook his head and tutted as he climbed into the driver's seat of his convertible. Feeling scolded, Greg went to his own car and, as Grenet set off, began following closely behind.

The drive took about thirty minutes though Greg was aware that the trip could have been much shorter. For some reason, be it to make the journey more mysterious or to confuse Greg's sense of direction, Grenet took many detours, first around various back streets of Weston's city centre, and then on the outskirts through suburbs and areas that could just as easily have been avoided by taking the main roads. Finally, they had reached one of the green areas of dense forest that lay between Weston and its nearest neighbouring city, and Grenet pulled up in a lay-by that Greg presumed to be on the edge of a large country park.

'Erm, where the hell are we?' he asked as he got out of his car.

Grenet was fiddling in his car boot. Greg felt slightly scared by what was ahead but knowing the joys of what had happened at the last League meeting allowed the fear simply to raise his anticipation to new heights.

'Sh! You don't need to know that, my friend. You just need to enjoy what's to come.' Grenet took out a large sports bag.

'What's in there?' Greg questioned as Grenet began leading him into the woods.

'You're too impatient.' Grenet sounded authoritarian. 'Now keep quiet until we arrive.'

Unlike the car trip, the walk into the woods was direct and focused. Almost immediately Greg could see a light through the trees shining in the twilight. It was obviously from an artificial source and Greg knew that it could only mean one thing; other people were around. As they got closer, Grenet opened his bag and took out a large torch. He flashed a couple of short beams ahead, then two long ones, still not paying too much attention to the man at his side. Greg felt like asking what it was all about but sensing Grenet's formal attitude decided he would be better off letting everything pan out unhindered.

Soon enough the trees opened into a small circular clearing. There was woodchip underfoot and a portable lantern placed on one of the picnic benches, the light Greg had seen previously, broke the increasing shade. As at his first League meeting, some of the faces of the men standing around Greg knew well as members of his own term. Charmers was there again, with that ever-cheeky grin, as was Weston's goalie and a couple of their defenders. Again as last time, the team they had opposed and won against had a number of their players scattered around. Dressed in the kit they had worn during the game, they appeared slightly nervous as Greg and Grenet arrived, obviously, like Greg, not fully aware of what the night had in store.

'Hello, and welcome to the festivities, my friends.' Grenet threw his bag on to the nearest table with a thud, the group positioning themselves around him as he did so. 'Now, no initiates this time. We're all old . . .' Grenet stopped as if remembering himself, and looked over to Greg. 'Or relatively old hands to this, so I don't see why we don't get straight down to business.'

He unzipped his bag and delved inside.

'Once more, commiserations to the losers.' He pulled out one of the largest dildos Greg had ever seen. It was matt black and remarkably lifelike. Shadows contoured over its veins and underneath its helmet as Grenet placed it next to the lantern on the table. On sight of its size a number of semi-sadistic laughs and good-humoured but self-pitying groans ran through the clearing. 'And congratulations to us, the winners.' Grenet now had a massive, pale butt-plug in his hands. With a click, he switched it on and it began its electric hum loudly as the members of Weston gave a hearty cheer for themselves.

'Now, rules as usual.' Grenet carried on emptying the bag, taking from it a collection of vibrators, love balls and other sex toys, all of differing shapes, sizes and varieties. 'First goal-scorer takes on an opposing member of the defence. So that's you, Mr Williams, and, of course, our butterfinged friend Mr Salford.'

Grenet pointed at Greg and Henry Salford, the Penforth goalkeeper.

'I'm providing the entertainments again?' Greg asked, knowing his happy grin would betray just how much he enjoyed his last tenure in the spotlight.

'Ever thought of becoming a stripogram, Trip?' Charmers shouted across, as sarcastic as ever.

'Nah.' Greg shook his head. 'There'd be too many calls to your place.' He made his way over to Grenet's bench, the sound of manly laughter all around him. 'It's my birthday, again, honest!' he mocked as Salford swaggered over to join him. Salford was a very sexy man with a large build well suited to his position on the pitch. He had long, dark brown hair and a thick moustache that crossed a friendly, open face. Greg was glad of the selection. Had he been given a choice he would have picked the hunk that stood in front of him without thinking twice.

'Better get your trousers down now, Charmers,' Greg teased. 'Looks like you're in for a good time.'

Charmers grabbed his crotch and gave it a good shake as the League members laughed once more.

'Right,' Salford clapped his gloved hands together. 'Where do you want me?'

Where don't I want you? Greg thought to himself. 'How's about knelt on the bench?'

'Whatever you want.' Salford did as he was told, kneeling on all fours with his hands on the wooden tabletop and his knees on the plank-like seats. The large taut globes of his butt spread to fill his black shorts. The backs of his thick thigh muscles extended impressively and were covered with short curls of leg hair. His thick wool socks were slightly muddy, as were his huge, size-twelve football boots that pointed groundwards. Greg thrilled at the thought of having such an attractive man as his plaything, ready to perform any action that took his fancy.

'Let's get you out into the open.' Greg slid his hand up Salford's shirt to feel around for the waistband of his shorts. Finding a good grip he slowly eased them downward, Salford's great glutes gradually appearing to the cheers of the small crowd around them. Exposed, Salford's arse was a treat. The hairs that coated his legs continued over his cheeks and led up to make a furry coating at his crack. Salford's large balls dangled down between his thighs and, wanting to complete the picture, Greg reached below them to pull back Salford's great rod. Salford had a semi-erection already and it pressed downward against his leg as Greg positioned it into place.

'That's a sight for sore eyes,' Greg murmured, in awe of the impact the naked man's crotch had on him.

'He'll have a sore arse in a minute,' Charmers chuckled, his hands fiddling away in his pockets.

'Don't forget the protection,' Grenet warned over the League's raucous noises. Greg, realising what Grenet meant, picked up one pair of the rubber gloves that had been taken out with the sex toys and put them on. He didn't mind that such an action would mean less skin to skin contact. There was something about the texture of rubber enclosing his hands, the thwack and squeak of putting the gloves on, that was freakish and sexual.

Salford turned his head, looking slightly concerned.

'Take it easy on us, will you, mate? I mean pick a small one to start off with. I'm not so used to this.'

'About once a year, isn't it?' Greg joked, referring to the way Penforth always seemed to get knocked out of the cup at semi-final stage. 'How about this one?'

Greg picked up a white, pen-shaped vibrator of around seven inches long and five inches in circumference. Salford winced when he saw it but Greg wouldn't give him any more leeway than he already had.

'You're just chicken,' he mocked. 'Don't forget who won

today. And don't worry either. I'll soon get you loosened up.'

Greg picked up a pump of lubrication and pressed down three times. The clear, slimy liquid squirted out into his palm with an almost body-function-like squelching noise. He put his hand up the split of Salford's arse, so that most of the gel would squeeze up there, then began massaging the man in front of him, not only around the anus but all over his backside. Greg loved to see a big backside greased up like that, the skin all shiny, the hairs matting together with gunk. Framed by a football shirt and shorts, it just looked all the more ripe for the taking.

Greg parted the hoop of pubes that surrounded Salford's pucker and found an inviting dark star pursing in and out at him. He stroked it gently at first, causing Salford to sigh with pleasure, then ran his fingertips round and around its tiny creases of sensitive skin knowing the teasing, tickling sensations the movement would bring. He took another big squirt of lube into his palm, then rubbed it over the fingers of his right hand. He began to apply pressure initially with his index finger, finding Salford's arse nice and tight, but gradually giving way to the pushing of his slippery digit. Fully inserted, he found Salford squeezing away at him and groaning as heartily as an unfit man on a ten mile jog.

'You OK?' Greg wondered whether the man was up to what he wanted to do to him.

'Ooh, yeah. It takes its time, that's all.'

'Ready for another one?' Greg asked, gliding his free hand over one of Salford's glistening meaty buttocks.

'Give it your best shot, striker.'

With that encouragement, Greg quickly manoeuvred a second finger up Salford's clenching hole. Penetration had become much easier: Salford's rectum was gradually relaxing under the duress of the foreign bodies within it. Soon Greg had slipped in a third and was slowly but surely dragging his hand back and forth up the airtight chute. Salford had built up a regular rhythm, pushing backwards with the weight of his body to meet Greg's every stroke upward. Eventually he made it obvious that he was ready for more.

'You're in position now. It's time to score,' he groaned.

With a soft 'schlump', Greg removed his hand from Salford's body. The anus, now slightly loosened and increased in size, was reddened from the abrasions against it. It looked like a waiting target, just begging to be shot at and pierced by some scalding hot arrow. Greg would have given anything to get his prick inside it, but knowing that the League's regulations were pretty strict on any activities apart from the ones ordained for that particular meeting, he decided that he had better not try. His horny member was vehement against the inside of his trousers, almost angrily aroused at the actions its owner was performing. Greg wondered just how much he could get away with and, turned on enough to risk disapproval, he wiped his sticky glove on Salford's shirt so that he could undo his trousers. His shaft pulsated as its constriction was suddenly removed and he let it twang onto Salford's arse with a tender slap. The feel of slicked-up skin on his cock after it had spent so long hard within his clothing was acute and delightful, and he began gliding his inflated knob over Salford's shimmering buns wantonly.

'Get on with it!' Charmers shouted from the sidelines. Greg turned to find the men around him were still watching intently, and that some, like the ever dick-hungry Charmers, were masturbating readily as they looked on.

'Sorry, mate.' Greg picked up his weapon of choice and rubbered it quickly. 'I shan't keep you waiting any longer.'

He switched the vibrator on, and found the rest of the League quietened as if in wonder of its persistent but gentle buzzing sound.

'Come on, Willy,' Salford purred enthusiastically. 'Give it all you've got.'

The love machine quivering in his hand, Greg squatted down so he could get a better take on its journey inward. With Salford's arse at the level of his face, the heated scent of the goalkeeper, the sweat on his balls and arse that had mixed with the vaguely perfumed lube, presented itself to Greg's nostrils and he clutched at his erection, taking in deep hearty breaths. He set the vibrator to its lowest setting and began pressing it against Salford's ring, staring merely inches away as the man's bum-lips opened up and began moulding themselves around the trembling plastic. Salford made a deep pained mewl.

'Too big?' Greg asked, concerned that he was causing too much pain.

'N-no,' Salford stammered. 'That's – just right.'

Greg drove the thing right up to the hilt, so that his fingertips gripped barely the last half-inch at the edges of Salford's entrance.

'Now take it out again,' Salford pleaded.

'Hey! Who's in charge here?' Greg kidded. Salford turned his head back and looked towards the man at his bottom.

'Please, Greg,' he gasped, slowly. 'I'll do anything if you do.'

Enjoying having someone at his mercy like that, Greg did as he was told. Millimetre by millimetre he withdrew the surrogate shaft, not fully, leaving the pointed end inside Salford so that the man's hole remained stretched.

'Do you want me to turn things up a little?' he asked, fiddling with the vibrator's controls. The only answer he received was a satisfied 'mmm' as the battery-operated tool increased the rapidity of its shakes. When it reached full speed, Greg pushed it upward once more, only this time didn't wait for the entreaty to remove it, instead bringing it out almost straight away. He began to build up a regular fucking motion. The fake cock looked so good hammering in and out of Salford that Greg couldn't help but fiddle with himself at the same time. As before, Salford began thrusting backwards every time Greg shoved his hand upward and soon the pumping movements were as hard and fast as full sexual penetration. Before long Greg could feel the thickening in his penis that was the sign that his time was near.

He stood up once more, ready to present Salford with a final gift. Guessing what Greg was up to Salford looked back once more.

'I want to feel it,' he begged, wriggling on the vibrator with abandon. 'I want your hot load all over my hairy arse.'

Greg was more than ready to oblige. By that point, his fist was flying up and down his cock, and aiming carefully, he let himself explode. He entered a glorious reverie as the first milky stream spurted out of him and flew right across Salford's furry spread cheeks. His head spun as another, then another jet arced out of him and through the air, coating the jiggling bottom with creamy liquid. Not wanting to waste a drop, he wiped himself over Salford's backside as the throbs lessened, his oozing penis smearing all over the curvy expanses of flesh until Greg knew his balls were well and truly emptied.

Almost without Greg noticing, Salford had stopped moving. Greg finally took his hand off the vibrator and Salford turned over, not removing the length from himself, just lying back on the tabletop so that his manhood flopped against his belly. His meat was sticky with gunk at the head and he had a spray of sperm all over his shirt.

'Looks like you enjoyed yourself as much as I did,' Greg panted, trying to get his breath back.

Salford at last slid the dildo from within himself, then held it up like a trophy. 'I think I probably enjoyed it more.'

'Nothing ventured, nothing gained.' Greg pulled up his trousers once more as the general mumble of voices around him signified that the fun for the rest of the crowd was just beginning.

'Stick around.' Salford sat up, squirmed his shorts upward, then reached for the large black dildo Grenet had pulled out of his bag. 'I might well be graduating later.'

'Can't wait till next year, then?' Greg chuckled as he re-buckled his belt.

'Right now I don't feel like I can wait ten minutes.'

Salford took hold of Greg's hand and gave it a caring, grateful squeeze. He looked directly into Greg's eyes. 'You know where I am if you want me.'

Greg gave Salford a brief kiss. He had enjoyed penetrating the man greatly and did intend to return later for a second stint, but at that moment what he had in mind was tasting some of the other goodies on offer.

Somewhat sore from his orgasm, initially Greg restricted himself to the role of voyeur, watching along with a couple of other guys as Grenet inserted a series of diamond-shaped butt-plugs into Adam McGrath, the skinny ginger-haired Penforth centre-forward. Grenet stripped the man completely naked before he started, and laid him on his back on the table where Salford and Greg had fucked. McGrath's skin was pale in the lantern-light as he held open his arse. Clearly overheated by the events of the evening he came before the second plug was inside him. Charmers, who was looking on and in typical derogatory spirits, taunted the man about his longevity but, despite that, McGrath remained in position covered in his own cream and begging Grenet to give him more. Greg was amazed as Grenet continued. McGrath quickly became erect again, and he wanked until the fourth, almost fist-sized lump of plastic was in him, and he came again, so that his belly and chest were well and truly glazed with the contents of his sack.

'What do you think of that, eh, Charmers?' he panted, avenged as Grenet removed the plug once more.

'My hat's off to you.' Charmers nodded deferentially.

'And your pants!' Greg interjected, playfully tweaking at Charmers' solid, dripping member.

It was after that incident that Greg felt like helping out himself a bit more. Collecting the whopping double-ended dildo and two of the Penforth team-members who had not yet received their forfeit he found a grassy patch near the bushes that seemed just perfect for what he had in mind. He ordered his new-found friends to take off their shorts, enjoying the view as their freed, hairy parts dangled semi-erect in anticipation, then got them to kneel down on the ground facing away from each other. He lubed them up quickly, eager to get something inside them. The dildo was maybe fifteen inches long, pink, and had a realistic fat-headed cock-shape at each end. He eased it first into one man alone, then, when a decent length had entered, directed it into the other. Taking a thigh of each man, he shuffled the two backward, closer to each other, until their buttocks touched and the artificial phallus had all but disappeared from view. The sex-play looked so dirty that Greg had to release his aching prick once more. He allowed one of the men to wank him off a little, and the other to fondle his balls. He even took sneaky feels of their dicks as their arses bounced and slapped against each other. But he didn't come for a second time that night until he was back with Salford, introducing the man to the huge black plastic member and the joys of heavy-duty rectum stretching.

Greg left the park around midnight, shagged out in more ways than one. The action had more or less finished by that time, although two or three men remained and he could have stopped there longer had his tender penis allowed it. As he made his way back to the car, he marvelled at the things that had gone on that night. He was satisfied, pleased and amused by another successful League gathering and excited by the prospect of what would happen after the final. His mouth literally watered at his imaginings and he drove away thankful that Weston were a good enough team to make it through to the end of the cup final.

Eleven

Greg finally managed to get the break from training Brown had promised him. He made the trip to Middleton in the morning of his day off. He had not informed his mother of his return, knowing that a visit with her could add hours to his journey and every spare moment he had he wanted to spend on the task he had in mind.

Feeling cautious as a result of the media's recent increase in interest in him, he parked his car in the car park of the Black Bull. It was a good few minutes' walk away from his intended destination but he knew the sight of a flash car on the street where he used to live would be a sure-fire sign to any journalists that he was back in town. He could not chance a repeat of the incidents caused by his last visit, not with the day being so important, and as an extra precaution he had dressed down especially for the occasion. Some old, worn-out jeans, grubby white trainers, a tired cap and a two-day unshaven face made for a passable disguise. He half-fancied himself as he checked his appearance in the reflection of his car door. He looked like a real diamond in the rough, the kind of guy he used to see in Middleton's town centre on nights out at the weekend, desperately trying to pull the local women. It was an amusing change from the usual, well-dressed, smooth look he usually went for and he hoped it would work well as camouflage. He knew he had not made himself invisible. If anyone were to look too hard they would make out who he was. But what he wore was enough to provide the degree of anonymity he needed, and during the brisk walk to Matt's parents' house he found that no one gave him even a second glance.

Greg took off his sunglasses as he knocked on the door of

the house, nervously checking around one last time to make sure he had not been followed. It was Sarah, Matt's fiancée, who opened the door. She seemed quite distraught and, crying, threw her arms around Greg as soon as she saw his face.

'Oh, Greg!' she sobbed. 'I'm so glad you're here.'

'What's happened?' Even though Sarah was in actuality Greg's competition, he still liked her and cared about her enough to not want to see her in such a state. 'Come on, you can tell me.'

Sarah removed herself from Greg's arms and began wiping her face with a ragged tissue.

'It's Matt.' Sarah blew her nose hard. 'He's gone. We had an argument and now I don't know where he is.'

'Oh, Sarah, I am sorry.' Despite Greg's feelings for Matt, what he told the woman was true and he rubbed her shoulder with true sympathy. 'Listen, any chance I can come in and talk it over. I might be able to help. And not that I'm trying to worry you any further, but I'm in hiding at the moment.'

'The papers!' Sarah looked over Greg's shoulder with suddenly aware shock. 'Of course. You'd better come in.'

Shutting the door behind them, Sarah led him down the hallway. In the kitchen she explained further. The row had been over nothing, she said. One of her aunties hadn't received an invitation to the wedding, whether someone had forgotten to send one or whether it was the post that had lost it she didn't know, but it had led to a disagreement that had escalated out of all proportions, and had ended with Matt storming out on her.

'And that was last night?' Greg asked over a hot cup of tea.

Sarah nodded.

'No mention at all of where he was headed?'

'No, there was nothing. No contact from him since either.

Matt's parents are out looking for him. I'm manning the phones just in case he rings here.' Sarah paused as if thinking for a second. 'You know, the worst thing was he wasn't angry with me, I could tell. It was like he was shouting at himself, frustrated with himself for something.'

'It's just nerves,' Greg said, wondering how much Sarah had cottoned on to. 'The stress of getting everything organised. It's no easy ride.'

Sarah looked directly at Greg, speaking as if the words of reassurance he had just uttered had barely been registered. 'Me and Matt, we've been together a long, long time now. I know him better than I've known anyone, perhaps better than he knows himself. There are things that I don't think he's realised yet. And I think that part of me, most of me, in fact has been pushing him into this wedding to make him come to terms with himself. I knew it would take something big for him to change. And I do love him, but –'

She broke off, trying to find the right words. 'But more than that I want to see him happy. Maybe, and don't you dare tell a soul this, maybe I want that even more than I want us to be married.'

'Are you having second thoughts?' Greg asked.

'No.' Sarah now sounded focused. 'It's more like my first thoughts are coming closer and closer to the surface, that I'm finally discovering a truth that I've known all along. Oh, Greg, do I sound like a wicked person for doing all this, causing so much trouble to so many people?'

Greg laughed. 'Of course not!'

'A fool then? Am I an idiot for trying to help out in such a bizarre manner?'

'No! Not at all. I think you were right. He needed someone like you to do something so caring no matter what the trouble. We all end up complicating things at some time or other when really they're all just very straightforward.'

Greg sensed a clearing of the situation that existed between Matt, Sarah and himself, and the atmosphere seemed positive and relaxed.

'You think everything will sort out, then?' Even Sarah seemed more hopeful, having stopped her tears.

'I'm sure of it. You're a brave girl, Sarah. And a kind, kind friend for acting in the way you have.'

Sarah smiled the first smile Greg had seen her manage since he had arrived. Then, suddenly her mouth popped open with remembrance.

'That was it!' She pointed as if the memory had appeared in front of her in the air. 'There was something strange Matt said just before he left yesterday. I don't know if it would mean anything to you.'

'What was it?' Greg knew the next important thing on the agenda would be to actually find Matt again.

'Something about – I know! He said he was leaving to put his feet on solid ground. He just kind of muttered it, almost as if he wasn't even talking to me. Does it ring any bells?'

'Loud enough to shake the belfry.' Greg knew exactly what Matt had meant, and he stood up to put on his jacket. 'Listen, Sarah, would it be okay if I went to talk to him alone for a while?'

'I'd like to come with you if I could.'

'I'll have him back by this afternoon, I promise. And I'll ring you if there's anything, if there's the slightest thing wrong.'

Greg was practically out of the door when Sarah agreed. 'Well, if you think that it's best.'

'Thanks, love. And chin up. Everything's going to be fine.'

Sarah nodded as Greg left the room and gave him a warm smile that showed she felt reassured.

Fosthorpe was a seaside town a mere twenty miles away from Middleton. Too small to compete with the larger resorts further north up the coast, its tourist trade had declined over the past few years but it remained a picturesque if quiet place to spend some time. Greg arrived there not forty minutes after leaving Sarah. He had realised the 'solid ground' Matt had mentioned referred to a spot the two of them used to visit when in their teens, when they needed a break from the confines of their home town, catching the coach at the weekend to go surfing or swimming or sometimes simply to watch the sea.

Greg left his car on the seafront, in one of the spaces at the top of the large concrete walls that provided a barrier between the sea at high tide and the small row of gift shops and amusement arcades that comprised Fosthorpe's small entertainment sector. The bay itself was really quite lovely. It arced out for several miles beneath imposing cliffs into the sea mists like a backdrop to a beautiful, romantic dream. Greg gazed across it appreciating the view and simultaneously keeping his eyes peeled for a part of it that he remembered from not too long ago in his past. He spotted the cove quickly and, spying a lone figure within it, sped off along the beach to meet his quarry.

'Find what you were looking for?' Greg had crept up behind Matt who was standing on a large outcrop of dark grey rocks staring out at the waves. He turned on hearing Greg's voice.

'What are you doing here?' Matt still seemed angry with him.

'I'm looking for you. Finally. I'm here to find you.'

'Took your time, didn't you?' Matt looked away once more. 'I thought you'd given up on your old life now that you've hit the big time.'

'What do you mean?' Greg moved closer. He figured Matt was trying his hardest to get a rise out of him, but he knew to react angrily would only cause more trouble. 'I've been busy because of work, much busier than I was at Middleton, but I always have time for you, Matt, when you need me, you know that.'

'Well it doesn't feel that way. That last phone call we had. You were more concerned about where your sofa was going than you were about talking to me. And the way you ran off the last morning I saw you. After all we'd been through that night, after all we'd done.'

Greg remembered he did have to leave early that morning. He had not felt that anything had been rushed at all, but perhaps in Matt's sensitive state his departure had all appeared premature. And the following weeks he had just been too preoccupied to make a visit or a proper phone call. It was possible that such behaviour would seem cold, even if it was just an unintentional by-product of his new, activity-filled life.

'Matt, I'm sorry. Really sorry. It's just a misunderstanding. I thought things were fine between us until recently. And with the move, my new job and so on –'

'Some things got pushed aside?' Matt asked sarcastically.

'No.' Greg sounded determined as he too climbed the rocks. 'You're the world to me, Matt. I would never hurt you knowingly, not in a million years.'

Matt said nothing, sighed and shook his head, still avoiding eye contact. Greg stood at the side of his friend. Matt's face looked tired and Greg realised he must have slept, uncomfortably, in his car the previous night. His eyes had a pinkish tinge signifying that he had been crying. Somehow, despite his distraught appearance, Matt looked all the more attractive to Greg. There was a vulnerability, a need, just below all Matt's masculine bravado that showed on his face, and Greg knew he would simply have to respond to it.

'Have you worked out how I knew you would be here?' he asked, trying to find a chink in Matt's macho armour.

Matt shrugged as if uninterested.

'It was what you said to Sarah. About wanting to find solid ground.'

Matt flicked a quick glance over and encouraged, Greg continued.

'You can't have thought I'd forgotten. That time one spring when we came out here swimming and we got the time of the tides wrong. The sea came in too fast and we ended up stuck here on the beach for hours, waiting for it to go out again.'

Matt smiled, puffed out a laugh.

'It was a good job we'd left our clothes up here wasn't it? It became pretty cold after a while.'

Matt rubbed his chin, thoughtfully. Greg knew that he had realised he was referring to the way that they had ended up cuddling together for warmth. Greg could see he was breaking through to his friend at last.

'And after that, any time anything would go wrong back home, and we'd come around here to get away, it'd be this spot we'd make our way to. The solid ground in the middle of everything crashing about around us.

'And I guess what I'm trying to say to you is that we've got a past together. We've got history. And when we've worked things out between us we've got one hell of a future as well.'

Greg watched as Matt finally turned around to face him properly.

'Why do you always have to be the one that's right?' he smiled, showing his forgiveness. 'C'mere, mate. Let me make it up to you for acting so stupid.' Matt opened his big arms and the two men hugged each other hard.

'You're not stupid, Matt,' Greg whispered to his friend. 'You must never think that you're stupid.'

Greg lessened his grip a little but found that Matt kept his arms firmly locked.

'I've been thinking a lot lately, Greg. About us. I think that part of my troubles recently, part of my anger has been caused by frustration more than anything.'

'What are you saying?' Greg had guessed what Matt was about to ask for but he wanted to hear him say it.

'I want to do it again, Greg. Just one more time. With you.'

The sound of Matt's words, rasped in his deep, growly, northern accent made Greg shiver with happiness and excitement. He thought briefly of Sarah, and that to have sex with Matt once more didn't seem like a betrayal of her as, from what she had said earlier, it was what she had realised was best for Matt in the long run.

'I'd love to. I'd really, really love to.' Greg took Matt by the hand and began leading him back down the rocks. 'And I think I've got the perfect location. Follow me.'

Greg headed off round the corner, back on to the pebbly beach and into a small alcove.

'How about here?' he said, enthusiastic.

'Isn't it a bit conspicuous?' Matt, troubled, looked behind him down the beach.

'This is Fosthorpe, remember?'

It was another quiet day for the town. Greg could see a couple of dots far in the distance that were probably people, but he wasn't particularly worried about being seen.

'And besides, if anyone does turn up, we can go further inside where it's darker. Pretend we're getting changed into swimming trunks or something.'

'OK.' Matt was breathless already. He signified his agreement with a series of brief kisses over Greg's face and lips. 'I'm so horny Greg. I'm so fucking horny for you.'

Greg felt himself being pressed against the rocky wall of the alcove under the strong caresses of his lover. Worried that Matt's eagerness might mean things would be over too quickly he decided he should slow things down a little.

'No, wait,' he said in between the barrage of Matt's kisses. 'I want to see you.'

Matt looked perplexed until Greg explained. 'All of you. I want to see all of you. Take off your shirt. Go on. Do it for me.'

Matt smirked and began fiddling at the collar of his shirt. 'I hope you're going to do the same.'

'Of course,' Greg agreed. 'Eventually.'

Matt moved back a yard or so. He looked great as his expansive chest peeped out of his unbuttoned clothing then was brought into the open, his brawny shoulders and almost perfectly round deltoids extending as he revealed his naked torso. He bunched up his shirt into a ball, then threw it further into the cave. He put his hands on his waist and Greg could see how the crotch of his blue denim jeans had become a sexy, crammed mound poking outward. He looked directly at it, saw it jump a couple of times under his gaze before he carried on with his encouragements.

'And the rest,' he told his lover.

Matt sat on a large rock behind him, took off his large boots and socks, then slowly eased off his jeans. His legs were broad and chunky and coated in dark hair. Matt stood there in his white Y-fronts, mouth open and a yearning expression on his face. His underwear was well and truly filled. His cock pressed upward against his lower belly and it made a truncheon-like contour under the material. His balls filled a soft, touchable bump between his thighs.

'Go on, mate. I've seen it before, remember.' Greg had seen the man in such a state before but he wanted to see him again, fully naked and in surroundings that were so attractive and filled with such good memories for the both of them.

Matt slipped off his pants so that his hairy basket was liberated. He stepped forward and began to kiss Greg wantonly.

'What about me? I thought you wanted to see me strip as well,' Greg whispered in one of Matt's rare pauses.

'I like the look of you like that. Leave it on for me a while. Please.'

Greg had forgotten he was still in his 'disguise'. He wondered briefly if Matt, like himself, had a tendency to go for the rougher type of man, then lost himself in the pleasure of having such a beautiful specimen of masculinity in his arms. He ran his hands down Matt's broad, hard back, took hold of the man's firm round buttocks, one in each hand, and squeezed them. He pulled Matt towards him so that their genital areas rubbed together, loving having his friend completely nude and writhing upon him. He could feel Matt's dense member hot against his jeans and breaking away he looked downward. There it was, just as he remembered it. Huge and fat, its skin brown and contrasting with the paler colouring of the rest of Matt's body, its foreskin high, running almost to the tip so that only a small circle of his friend's purple bell-end poked through. It was a really impressive, beautiful penis, and Matt was a beautiful man, but as Greg lunged to kiss his friend once more he knew that physical attraction wasn't all that was going on between them. Matt's touches, the pressure of his body upon Greg's didn't merely turn Greg on, they seemed to reach some inner, hidden realm within him that no one had even begun to approach before. Greg was in paradise right at that moment, before their love-making had barely started, and he knew, with the distant sound of the waves in his ears, that something truly incredible was happening between the two of them.

'Take me, Greg. Please. I want to feel it up me again.' Matt's dusky eyes were watery as he made his earnest plea and Greg wondered if the man was about to cry with want or with happiness. He became convinced that Matt felt as strongly as he did and was enjoying himself as much as he was, but he wasn't ready to penetrate him just yet.

'Help me out, Matt.' Greg wanted their bodies to touch as closely as their spirits were. 'Undress me.'

With heavy, anxious fingers, Matt fiddled at Greg's shirt, quickly removing it before starting work on his jeans. Soon they were off too and Matt was squatting to undo Greg's laces and take off his trainers. Their clothes in a pile at the side of them, the two men looked each other up and down tentatively, as if their very stares might break the moment, before they grabbed at one another again, their mouths locking and fighting together unrestrained. Matt's skin felt great rubbing upon Greg's own. The hard muscles he grabbed at and Matt's powerful manhandling had soon raised his arousal even higher, and he could feel a gummy patch at their bellies where their dicks had begun to leak in pleasure. He put his hand between Matt's legs and fondled the man's warm hairy bollocks, jiggling them before moving his clutches upward to take hold of his friend's piece. He tossed it a few times, the thing almost jumping out of his hand it was so filled and its throbs were so strong. He put his own cock just underneath it and grasped it so that he could wank them both at the same time. Matt was drizzling pre-come readily and it smeared all over Greg's length making his skin and its thick blue vein shiny. Greg worried once more that Matt was just too near his time and, wanting to introduce some delaying tactics, he pulled away.

'You've never tasted cock before, have you?' he asked.

Matt looked down, almost embarrassed. 'But I'd love to, Greg.'

'And I'd love to be your first.' Greg placed both his hands on Matt's massive shoulders and pushed him downward, not forcing the man, it was more like he was directing where he should go. Matt kissed him all over on his way down, on his chest and nipples, and all over his abdomen, until he knelt with his face at the level of Greg's erection.

'What do you want me to do?' he asked, taking the thing into his fingers.

'Lick the end. You know, right at the bit that feels best.'

Matt did as he was told, his tongue rasping along the underside of Greg's glans. Greg gasped at the touch, and even more so as he saw his hunky lover begin to taste his piss-slit, obviously enjoying the flavour of the ooze that seeped from it.

'Now put me in your mouth and hold it there a while.'

Again, Matt obeyed, taking only the very end of Greg into his lips.

'Go on,' Greg encouraged. 'Do it like you want to.'

Gingerly, Matt took more of Greg inside him. He slid halfway down the pole, then back up quickly. Greg sprang away from his hold and Matt laughed at his own ineptitude before leaping back upon it. Learning from his mistakes, this time when he reversed he managed to keep the thing within him, sliding back down it slowly but surely. He quickly became adept at his devouring, growing faster in the speed he moved his neck, and able to take more and more of the cock into him. Greg speedily became lost in the joys of introducing his friend to sucking meat and was extremely horny by the time Matt stopped.

'How was that for a first attempt?' he asked. His chin was covered in dribble, as was Greg's dick that rested on his neck.

'Are you sure it was a first attempt?' Greg sighed.

Feeling that he had spread out their time together enough, Greg began making moves to take the sex to the next stage. He grabbed Matt's elbow and raised him to a standing position so they could embrace once more. This time, he introduced his middle finger into their french-kiss, waggling it between both their tongues, letting Matt suck it until it was coated with saliva. Removing it from his friend's mouth, he placed his hands once more at Matt's behind, speedily finding the man's anus before his digit had time to dry. He poked at it a couple of times before it relaxed, opening enough for him to penetrate. Matt grimaced at the insertion, but his moan of approval signalled that he wanted more. Greg frigged his friend a few times before putting another couple of fingers inside, the rectum gradually stretching and becoming more welcoming.

'Oh, Greg,' Matt puffed. He took hold of Greg's dick with both hands and gripped it tightly. 'Now this. Fill me with your cock.'

Greg smiled to show his approval as he slid his hand from his friend. 'I'll do anything you want,' he said, knowing at that moment that he would truly do anything Matt asked.

'Come over here.' Matt stepped over the pebbled sand of the alcove floor, back to where he had sat earlier to remove his boots. He bent over the large rock placing his hands upon it to provide some stability. 'Take me from behind.'

Matt's arse curved so attractively in that particular position that Greg just had to bend over to kiss it. He bit and sucked first at one hairless buttock then the other, and then opened them to gain a better view of Matt's desperate hole. The furrowed inlet fluctuated at him and he spat at it before pushing his face right inward to take a full and proper taste. Greg lapped a couple of times from the base of Matt's balls to the base of his spine slowly, then sticking his tongue out as far as it would go, directed it up the musky passage. He began to face-fuck his friend, delighted at the forbidden, rare smells, the way the rectum clasped his tongue so tightly, the sweat-and saliva-dampened buttocks that rubbed against his cheeks. But despite his enjoyment of the butt-munching, he found himself unable to provide Matt with such sensations for too long, wanting desperately to replace his mouth with his penis just as much as Matt had begged him to.

Hastily finding his jeans he searched in the pockets for a condom. Matt turned his head behind him to watch Greg rubber up. Matt looked happy and lusty. He reached behind him for Greg's protected dick and aimed it between his bum cheeks. The journey upward took a couple of attempts, Greg's bell-end rubbing upward or just below the tight passage, but finally the mark was hit. Greg found his eyes closing with sheer joy as the man beneath him opened up around him and gripped more and more of him until he was fully inside.

'That's it, Greg,' Matt murmured, their bodies pressed firmly together. 'That's what I've been wanting. So much you wouldn't believe.'

Greg looked downward. Only the very root of his engorged member protruded out of his friend's arse. It was shiny, and just above his bush he could see the ring of rubber that was the base of his condom. He began to fuck, watching as his thing poked in and out of the man in front of him. Matt groaned with every thrust, sounding like he was at the true heights of rapture. Greg nibbled at the man's neck as he screwed, then let his hands wander over the muscular body he was inside, his rambling touches stopping briefly to tweak Matt's nipples before he moved them to take hold of his friend's chunky legs. Increasing the speed of his ruts, he began yanking Matt backwards at the same time so their bodies slapped together with ferocity.

'Oh, Greg! Greg!' Matt cried out his lover's name repeatedly like a mantra. 'That's how I wanted it. Oh, it feels so good!'

Guessing Matt was as close to orgasm as he was Greg grabbed hold of his friend's mammoth erection as he shagged, making the man moan even louder. It was extremely hard now and its end dripped with goo. Greg looked down the beach as he began to wank again. The setting was so idyllic and picturesque, their coupling so perfect and so highly erotic. Greg felt completely enclosed by Matt, not just how the man's arse encompassed his dick as they fucked, but totally lost in the man's body, as if Matt's very soul had closed around his own and they had made a true and deep contact with each other. Feeling warm inside, and very, very loved, he began to come off. It wasn't just pleasure as his body convulsed on top of Matt's, his dick jerking away frantically inside his friend, it was something much, much more. He felt Matt come almost simultaneously, the monster prick in his fist pumping away, its load hot and slimy upon his fingers. Matt's rectum speedily contracted and relaxed around him, milking the last of his oats from him as their excited, relieved grunts echoed around the cavern. It had been a truly mind-blowing experience and Greg was more than disappointed when he had to finally withdraw.

Matt turned and sat on the rock. His tool remained erect and dribbled from the end as he shifted around. He was sweaty and his cheeks were flushed with blood.

'That was amazing.' He sounded as absent as Greg felt. 'Even better than last time.'

Greg planted a tender kiss on the man's lips. 'I know,' he said, half-wondering what would happen next between them.

Deciding they needed to rest a while before moving on, the two men found a sandy patch next to the inner wall of the cave and sat down, Greg taking his friend underneath his arm. It was a delicate and close time between them. They remained together for a good while, only re-dressing gradu- ally. Somehow they had not noticed the cold when they were making love but now Fosthorpe's beach seemed quite cool and when their clothing didn't seem enough, they warmed each other with their body heat. They talked and talked, Greg feeling that they were as close again as they had ever been, that there was a warmth and understanding there even when they were silent that meant, as Greg had thought, that something much greater than their bodies had made contact. Greg could have stayed there for much longer than he did but the upcoming final and, more alarmingly, the wrath of Trevor Brown began pressing upon him.

'Are you sure you understand?' he asked, rising to his feet after explaining himself for the umpteenth time. 'I'm not rushing off or running away from you. It's the match. It's a big one. And I always like to feel prepared for those.'

'Yeah, I know.' Matt stood up as well. 'I'm not so paranoid now.'

The two began walking back up the beach towards where Greg had parked up. They had not got far when it became obvious that Matt had something to reveal.

'What I said – about it being one last time between me and you –' he began.

'Go on,' Greg encouraged.

'That's what I intended. Just to get it out of my system.'

Yeah, right. Fat chance, thought Greg. But he remained silent.

'And I'm thinking that maybe – maybe the marriage should still go ahead. I know there are strong feelings between us but –'

'OK. If that's what you really think,' Greg interrupted. It seemed like Matt was trying to convince himself more than anyone else.

'Will you still be there for me? I mean, as best man and everything?'

'Yes, of course. I'll be there for you whatever happens. And don't you forget it.' Greg had begun to understand Matt's thinking just the way Sarah had. It was up to Matt himself to come to terms with his true potential and he would keep putting it off, making excuses until he was ready to take the big step. Greg was confident that it would happen though. And soon. It was simply a case of waiting for the day to roll around.

'You ought to get back to Sarah. Or give her a call at least,' Greg said as he got into his car. 'She was pretty worried.'

'Yeah. I'll set off straight away. I feel a lot better now anyway.' Matt leaned towards the driver's window.

I bet you do, thought Greg. 'That's good. Now don't let yourself get wound up again. There's no trouble we can't see through together.'

Matt paused, thinking and then, as if he had come to a realisation, said, 'I know that.'

Greg raised himself out of his seat a little, leaned across and kissed Matt on his stubbly cheek.

'I'm looking forward to your stag night,' he shouted as he reversed.

'Oh, right. Is it all in hand?' Matt asked innocently.

'It will be.' Greg laughed, causing a bemused look to appear on his poor friend's face. 'You can count on that!'

Twelve

The rest of the afternoon was taken up by a hard but exhilarating training session. Since he had been absent that morning, Greg stayed on into mid-evening to both show his willingness and determination and to demonstrate to himself that he really meant business. He felt good afterward, having pushed himself just enough, and in his mind he was positive about all aspects of his life, not only the upcoming match but the future he knew he had with Matt.

He arrived back at his flat around eight o'clock, tired but with that invigorating rush that comes after good exercise. He found a couple of messages waiting for him on his answer machine. One was from his mother, hoping that he would call back later and the other was from Grenet. He hadn't been in long when his phone rang once more.

'Psst, can you keep a secret?' It was Leon again.

Greg laughed as he said hello. He knew League business was never conducted over the phone and presumed Grenet was joking around about something completely different.

'Are you up for it tonight?' Grenet husked.

'You know me, mate. Up for it anytime.'

'Good, good. That's what I wanted to hear. We're having a little party this evening, you and me. To calm our pre-match nerves.'

'We are? What about the ban?' Greg was slightly concerned. In an attempt to keep his team ultra-fit during the run-up to the final, Trevor Brown had prohibited the consumption of alcohol until after the actual game.

'Fuck it. No one need ever know. Come on, I know how worked up you've been lately. It'll do you good to get away from it all for a while. You'll play better in the long run if you do, trust me.'

Greg had been in similar situations with Grenet before. When Leon wanted a night on the town there was little chance of getting out of it. The man was just too persistent, too persuasive. But the prospect of an impromptu knees-up had never before arisen at such an important point in the footballing calendar. To go out for a night's drinking risked not only being unfit to play in the final, but if he and Grenet were discovered the possibility that Brown might fine them, or even suspend them from playing. More than that, Greg knew an excursion with Grenet meant that the focus of the evening would be on one thing; sex and lots of it. He pondered briefly about Matt, about whether some good playing around would feel like betraying his true love. Then, deciding that if Matt could convince himself he was getting married in a couple of weeks, he was entitled to a little fun in compensation, he threw caution to the wind and agreed to Grenet's impish plan.

'Wonderful! You'll not regret it, my friend, I assure you. I've ordered the limousine. It should arrive about nine.'

'Limousine?' Greg interrupted, startled.

'My treat. I intend to make tonight a night to remember.'

'Sounds ominous. Where are we going?'

'Ah. Another surprise. The driver will take good care of you, however. And I'll meet you when you get there. *D'accord?*'

It all seemed a bit of a rush to Greg, but Grenet wasn't about to explain further.

'*À ce soir, mon petit,*' he chuckled, hanging up before Greg had a chance to ask any more questions.

Not knowing whether he had made the right decision, but deciding to keep to it anyway, Greg began to get ready. Even though he had not been told where he would end up that night, he guessed that if he was arriving in a limo it must be somewhere flash, and what he wore should be in accordance with that. He put on an expensive dressy suit he had bought only the week before, and checked himself in the full-length mirror he had in the wardrobe in his bedroom. His clothes were dark and stylish: shiny black shoes, a striking large belt-buckle and the collars of his purple shirt were open and crept out over his jacket in a sexy, casual manner. The look was a million miles away from the local-lad, dressed-down disguise he had worn to meet Matt that morning. Now he was smooth, suave and dashing, and he had the air of sophistication and money about him.

Greg's intercom buzzer sounded bang on nine o'clock. He answered, then made his way downstairs to find a large black car parked outside. Despite having had several months as a top-class football player, he had not yet become accustomed to all the luxuries his income could bring. In his mind, he was still the person who learned his trade kicking cans around on the streets of Middleton as a kid and things like good clothes and posh cars still had the heady effect on him that they would have on any average person. He eyed his driver who was standing outside the car holding open one of the side doors. The man was dressed in a dark uniform. He had Nordic features: golden-brown skin, icy blue eyes and a strong, dimpled chin. Underneath the driver's cap, Greg could see some closely cut dark-blond hair. He was certainly an attractive man and he smiled heartily as Greg approached.

'Good evening sir!' he beamed.

'Cheers.' Having never been inside a limousine before Greg was unsure how to react to being waited on in such a manner. He got in the car and found the seating area spacious and plush, being made of oxblood leather with matching carpet. The windows were darkened so that he could look out but no one could see in. There was a drinks cabinet built into the back seat and feeling that he should take full advantage of the facilities, he poured himself a shot of whisky into a cut-glass tumbler as the car set off.

'You know where we're headed, then?' Greg asked, taking his first warming sip.

'Yes, sir. Mr Grenet briefed me well on the events of the evening.' The driver had a cockney accent that Greg found rather sexy.

'You know more than me, then. I haven't a clue where I'm going to end up. Any chance of letting the secret slip?'

'I'm sorry sir, no can do. But don't get too concerned. Mr Grenet chose me especially to take good care of you and any needs you might have.'

In the rear-view mirror, Greg caught a glance of the driver's wry grin as he spoke. He had begun to suspect some kind of a set-up, one of Grenet's little mysterious tricks. He began to wonder just how far the handsome driver would go to look after him. He had to admit to himself, he was getting off on the deferential treatment: being called 'sir' and having someone there to work specifically for him. That his servant was so attractive and apparently so eager to please simply made the situation all the more erotic. Greg asked a question, hoping that it would provoke an appropriate response.

'So what exactly did Mr Grenet tell you about me?'

'Oh, lots of things.' The driver turned. He seemed to be taking the same maze of streets that Grenet had led Greg down before the League's last meeting. 'That you'd be a very good man to work for. Not afraid to take charge. That's what I like in my employers. And he did comment upon how good-looking you were, although I must say, in the flesh you exceed all my expectations. Much better than even what you look like on the telly, if you don't mind me saying.'

It wasn't a very subtle way for the driver to show his intentions but it had worked. Greg had received the hidden message loud and clear.

'Well, thanks, mate.'

'Call me Barnes, sir.' The driver raised his hand to his cap in salute.

'And you can call me Greg.' Greg finished his whisky, put his glass back in the cabinet.

'I'd rather call you sir, sir. If that's all right with you.'

Greg was liking how things were turning very, very much. There was a kinky air to the proceedings that he wanted to play along with, and he thought well before making his next move.

Noticing that Barnes kept looking at something in the cockpit as well as what was ahead on the road, he decided to find out what it was.

'It's my monitor, sir,' Barnes replied to his enquiry. 'Do you see that little camera in the back there?'

Greg spotted a small spy-cam embedded in the car's roof.

'It's what we use to keep an eye on any trouble. Some of our clientele can often get quite drunk, or rowdy and all sorts of things can happen back there.'

Greg eased himself back into his seat. He stretched his arms out and spread his thighs wide open.

'So you've got a good view of me there, then?' he asked, knowing full well the answer. He had a semi-erection already, and he looked downward to find it raising up at the front of his trousers.

'Oh yes, sir. Very good.'

'And how would you like it if I started doing this?'

Greg took a handful of his own packet and gave it a hearty squeeze.

'I'd like it a lot sir. I'd like that one hell of a lot. Should I pull over now?'

Aware of the dangers he might cause, but too tempted by the chance to tease the poor driver, Greg answered in the negative.

'But you be careful there,' he warned, shaking his now fully pumped up thing like a cautionary finger. 'Keep your eyes on the road as much as you can.'

Greg unzipped his fly and inserted his hand within the newly opened hole, his steaming rigid cock beating against his eager grasp. He began moving his palm up and down himself, so that though his action couldn't be seen directly it was obvious that he was masturbating. He was horny as anything, not only from being watched by Barnes, but also from wanking off on the move, where other cars and people were so nearby and yet had no idea what he was doing.

He pulled out his dick through the opening of his trousers and lifted up his balls so that the entirety of his genitals was on display.

'What do you think of that then, Barnes?' he asked waggling his stiffness wantonly.

'Excellent, sir. A really beautiful piece, if you can excuse my forwardness. It's making my mouth water just looking at it.'

Greg eased his trousers off. His buttocks, lightly covered with sweat, were sticky against the car's upholstery. He liked the squirmy, almost human feeling against his skin. He was jerking quite readily now, his thumb and forefinger going up and down his purple head like a man shaking a dice. Every now and then he would just let himself throb against his belly, stroking his splayed inner thighs to give Barnes a good unhindered view of his sex organs. He found his balls quickly became moist and he had to peel their loose skin off his seat with a rasp every time he picked them up.

'Is it too hot in there, sir? Should I perhaps open the sunroof?' Barnes asked, obviously having noted the problem.

Greg heard Barnes flick a switch and the square in the roof above him slid slowly open.

'Ah, that's nice.' A cool breeze blew into the car gently

tickling around Greg's exposed genitals and legs. 'And it gives me an idea. You can pull over now, when you find somewhere suitable.'

Barnes drove for maybe a minute more, eventually turning down a dead end that looked like some kind of loading bay.

'There won't be too many people around here.' Barnes had removed his gaze from his screen and now looked directly upon Greg. 'Like I said before,' he smiled. 'Much better than on the television.'

Greg edged forward and stuck his head into the cockpit.

'How's your gearstick, driver?' he asked, reaching over to grab at Barnes' crotch. Barnes was hard, very hard, his dick and balls pressing tightly against his thigh.

'It's rather restricted, sir. If you could be so kind as to –'

Greg opened up Barnes' trousers to let the man burst out. The cock was chunky and short, almost beer-can-size in thickness. It was covered in thick ropy veins and was circumcised, and its round red head was full and appetising as an oversized cherry.

'I wouldn't mind a ride on that.' Greg tugged at the shaft a couple of times causing Barnes to murmur appreciatively.

'Mmm. Anything you want, sir. Anything you want.' Barnes began rocking his hips back and forth so that he screwed Greg's curled fingers gently. 'Now, sir. You said you had something in mind?'

'That's right. Open the sunroof fully, will you?'

Barnes did as he was told. Greg stood up so that his upper body stuck out of the top of the car. They were parked out of the way, but in the distance at the other end of the street he could make out a few people and the noises of those who, like him were out for a good time. He looked downward. Having cottoned on to what Greg wanted Barnes had eased himself back through the dividing window, his head inches away from Greg's erection.

'Now suck me off, Barnes. And you can wank at the same

time if you like. But pay most of your attention to me.' Greg made himself sound like a disgruntled employer both knowing that Barnes would enjoy it, and also getting off on having someone to boss around himself.

'It'll be my pleasure, sir. Anything else and you can just ask.'

The next noise Barnes made was a slurp as his mouth closed around Greg's prick. A ripple of familiar but always welcome pleasure went through Greg. Barnes looked very sexy right at that moment, his body and neck reaching desperately to get some man-meat inside his lips, his gorgeous tanned face with his cheeks sucked inward bobbing up and down to satisfy his master. That Barnes was in uniform made him look even better. The peak of his cap that came down almost to brow level, the collar of his crisp white shirt complete with black tie and jacket, just emphasised his masculinity, and gave the proceedings the air of rank and subordination that made Greg's cock pulsate with arousal. He leaned to one side to see what was happening further inside the car. As he had guessed, Barnes was furiously yanking away at himself with a leather-gloved hand like there was no tomorrow.

'Hey, not so fast.' Greg slapped Barnes on the jawline until he stopped playing with himself. 'That's better,' he praised. 'Now keep still and I'll take the strain off your neck awhile.'

Greg placed a hand behind the driver's head, stroking the man's prickly but soft, recently cut hair as he did so. He quickly took another look around the street, liking the fact that he was getting blown practically in the open air. He steadied himself on the roof and, controlling the direction of his solid rod with his free hand, began moving in and out of Barnes' mouth, watching as his erection made the classic sausage-shaped indentations in the man's cheek, then pressing himself against the wet roughness of his writhing tongue. He found he could slide all the way back without problem.

Barnes looked particularly sexy having swallowed the whole of Greg's piece, his nose and lips pressing against Greg's bush and balls, and his hot desperate breaths beating into his crotch. Several times Greg stayed in like that just appreciating the view. But he preferred it when there was motion, when he was making the repetitive movements with his lower body and Barnes strained backward, frantic to have his throat pounded.

Quickly, Greg reached a steady pace. He knew that the sex wasn't something either of them wanted to take much time over; it was just a quick explosive fuck and he was nearly ready for it to end.

'You – can – do – it – again, now – Barnes,' he struggled to say, his attentions elsewhere. 'Masturbate – I want to see you – shoot all over your – uniform.'

Barnes moaned gratefully. Still pumping away, Greg watched as his driver seized his own cock and balls and began jacking off wildly. Almost immediately, he saw the stumpy dick jump then start to spray its sticky, white fluids like a garden sprinkler gone haywire, shooting globules and jets all over Barnes' clothes right up to his chest. Barnes' gloves became covered in yoghurt-like dribbles, and it was the sight of hands in black leather, coated in creamy trickles that finally helped bring Greg off. He withdrew as soon as he felt the final stiffenings within, changing to manual self-stimulation as his dick flew out of Barnes' mouth. He shivered with wobbly legs at the first throb and juddered again and again as he wanked. His spunk showered Barnes' manly, tanned face with a thick spew and he wiped his helmet over the shiny sticky skin as his orgasm finally weakened.

Spent, Greg checked outside a final time. Although he could still see and hear evidence of people out and about not so far away, nobody had caught on to the fact they were there and had been doing what they were doing. He fell back into his seat, thighs shaky with released tension.

'That was one smooth journey, Barnes. You pass my driving test any day,' he joked.

'All part of the service, sir.' Barnes was wiping his face with his handkerchief. He looked very appealing all messy like that and Greg would have stuck around for another go had other things not been pressing on his mind.

'Now about this night out,' he said, pulling up his trousers.

'Way ahead of you, Mr Williams.' Having cleaned himself off, Barnes started up his engine and drove away.

A few minutes later they were in Weston's city centre. Barnes pulled in at the side of a club Greg had not seen before.

'This is a new one on me,' he said, eyeing the brightly illuminated sign as he got out of the car.

'Rockwells, sir. It's only recently opened. And rather exclusive as well.' Barnes closed the passenger door as Greg began taking some notes from his wallet.

'Oh no, Mr Williams.' Barnes waved a flat palm at Greg in refusal. 'I think you've tipped me quite heavily enough already.'

Ignoring the man, Greg forced a sizeable gratuity into his hand.

'You'll be around when I leave, won't you?' he requested. He didn't know what the night had in store and Barnes seemed like a good choice for backup or even better for reinforcements.

'Thank you, Mr Williams.' Barnes nodded, playing the subservient role as ever. 'I'll make sure I won't be too far away.'

Greg set off as Barnes drove away to find a parking space. He headed towards the large awning that ran down the steps of Rockwells' entranceway. A long queue was waiting along the street and he eyed it quickly to see if he could spot Grenet.

'Mr Williams!'

Greg turned to see who had called his name. It was one of the bulky, rough-looking bouncers. He waved Greg towards him.

'We were told you were coming. It's OK. You don't have to wait. Mr Grenet has already arrived.'

The bouncer unclipped the velvet rope barrier and ushered Greg inward through a side door.

Inside, Greg found the club to be very unlike most of the other night-spots he knew. The place was brightly lit and the music, although loud, was not deafening and was jazzy and relaxing rather than dancy and upbeat. Decorated in a baroque style, its high ceiling was held up by thick mock-marble pillars. Silver and gold cherubim statuettes were dotted around the walls and old-master-style artwork completed the over-the-top theme. The club was gauche and funny: Greg liked it and looked around for other extravagant details as he waited at the bar.

'Trip! Up here!'

Just as he had paid for his first drink, Greg heard a familiar voice trying to get his attention. He spotted Grenet up on the balcony waving at him with a happy grin on his face. Greg quickly made his way upstairs.

'So you like the limousine, my friend!' Grenet asked, taking a hearty swig from a glass of champagne.

'I liked what was inside it better.' Greg chuckled, planting a play punch directly upon Grenet's shoulder.

'He's good at his job, no? I make sure he's behind the wheel every trip I take. Better than the taxi, any day.'

The balcony was home to several tables that provided a respite for clubbers who wanted to get away from the bustle down below. At the side of Grenet sat three attractive young men and Greg found himself catching their stares as he and Grenet spoke. The men were dressed in highly fashionable, up-to-the-minute clothing, all had good bodies and all were extremely handsome. Greg recognised their faces and though he couldn't place the men was pretty sure he didn't know them personally.

'I see your interest in my friends,' Grenet said, obviously having cottoned on to Greg's diverted attentions. 'Let me introduce you, although I'm sure you should know each other by sight already. Greg this is Tony, Joe and Ben.'

Greg held out his hand to all three men. 'I feel like I know you guys from somewhere.'

The boys laughed. '1, 2, 3?' said Joe. 'You know –' He sang the first line of the chorus to a song that had been at number one a couple of weeks earlier. 'You put the love in me –'

'Oh yeah!' The penny had dropped. 1, 2, 3 were the newest boy band to hit the heights of success. Greg remembered publicity events in the local news. The boys were doing a national tour and had played Weston the day before. 'You'll have to excuse my ignorance. I've been a bit busy lately.'

Greg found an empty chair and sat down next to Ben, the cheeky-faced, most boyish-looking member of the group.

'Well, we know who you are all right,' Ben said. 'In fact, Leon's been telling us quite a lot about you.'

Greg thought back to what Barnes had told him earlier on, about what Grenet had revealed about Greg's "needs" for the evening.

'You just can't stop talking lately, can you?' he teased his friend.

Grenet settled himself at the opposite side of the table.

'I have a very active mouth, I have been told,' he said, winking and slipping an arm around Tony in a very friendly manner.

'Don't worry. From what I've heard, there's nothing bad to be said.' Joe leaned forward. He was the most manly-featured of the group, being the oldest at twenty-two and wearing both a goatee and a pierced eyebrow.

'That's nice to hear.' Greg could sense some strong undercurrents to the conversation and he was more than willing to be dragged under. 'But it means I'm the only one left in the dark. Up until thirty seconds ago, I didn't even know your names. Anybody want to help me out further?'

Joe and Ben gave each other shifty but good-humoured looks. Ben picked up the bottle of champagne the group had been sharing and poured out a glass for Greg, the pert bicep that extended out of his sleeveless shirt curling up into a lickable tennis ball shape as he moved.

'Why don't you sink the rest of that pint and have a drink with us? Consider yourself 1, 2, 3's new-found friend.'

Greg downed the remains of his lager and took a sip of the drink he had been given. It was sweet and expensive-tasting, and very fizzy.

'I think I'm going to enjoy myself tonight,' he said feeling the buzz of alcohol inside him.

'I'll drink to that,' Joe said, raising his glass in a toast.

A few drinks later, Greg, Joe and Ben were calling it a night. They left Grenet and Tony in the club, the two men enjoying drinking, dancing and each other's company too much to take off elsewhere.

Greg had given Barnes a warning call on his mobile before leaving the club and, outside, he found his limousine waiting as requested.

'Travelling in style, eh, Greg?' Joe asked as he entered the car. With Ben and Greg on the backseat already, he headed for the seat facing opposite until Greg indicated otherwise.

'Room enough here for three.' Greg patted the leather at the side of him and Joe moved across. 'Bit of a squeeze but I think we can manage.'

There was actually plenty of space in the back, but Greg spread his legs widely to feel the warm body heat of the two men next to him.

'Right,' Joe clapped his hands together as if ready to

organise the remainder of the night's events. 'Where are we off to now?'

'It's pretty cosy in here,' Greg suggested. 'How about we just drive around a little?'

'Sounds good to me.' Joe nodded heartily. Greg let his stare linger a while over the young man's face. Joe was often named as most 1, 2, 3 fans' favourite member of the band and, at that moment, his good looks didn't disappoint. He was definitely well-groomed and looked-after. His light-brown hair was coiffured into a gel-covered, spiky style and the square of facial hair around his mouth was carefully shaven and designed. But despite such preening Joe retained a glint of wildness in his green eyes: it exuded a defiant and raw sexuality that made Greg's stomach quiver with desire to the point where he could barely wait to get the action started.

'Get the picture, Barnes?' Greg asked, trying to hint to his driver to keep an eye on what was happening on the back seat on his monitor.

'I think I see, sir.' Barnes set off. Greg saw him flicking at the appropriate switch before the car had even reached the end of the road.

Greg now turned to the man on his right. In complete contrast to Joe, Ben was fresh faced, but at that moment his usual impudent features were conveying shyness. He kept avoiding Greg's eyes, but Greg continued to stare at the man's almost girlishly pretty face. Ben's dark hair was ruffled into a relaxed style and his pale, milky skin was impeccably clear and smooth. Greg leaned across to place a soft peck on his cheek. Somewhat to the footballer's surprise, Ben shrank away slightly.

'W-what about him?' Ben pointed towards the front of the car.

'Barnes? Oh, he won't mind. But we can put the screen up if you like.'

Greg pressed the button in the door that made the

dividing window between the back of the car and the cockpit slide upward. Made of the same darkened one-way glass as the windows, it seemed as if Barnes would not be able to see what was going on behind him. But Greg knew to his secret satisfaction that thanks to a small television screen the driver would be enjoying every single second.

'Feel better?' he asked Ben.

The young man nodded, then looked downward a couple of times timidly before presenting Greg with a long, open and enthusiastic kiss. 'You could say that,' Ben said, licking his lips as they parted.

'Now me.' Joe hooked his arm around Greg's neck and dragged him inward. The headlock felt dominating and sexy and Joe's kiss was as forceful with rough, almost brutish lips, bites and a penetrating, powerful tongue.

Greg felt dizzy with lust as he pulled away. 'They get it wrong when they call you a boy band, don't they?' He repositioned himself in his seat. 'No doubt about it. You two are real men.'

Proving their worth once more, Ben and Joe lunged for Greg simultaneously. All three men's mouths met with a supple clashing, their lips and tongues extended and writhing together in a fleshy, saliva-coated tussle. Greg focused his attention on first one man then the other. He would bring his partners together in front of him to enjoy the rare pleasure of seeing up close two men engaged in intimate sexual activity before joining in himself once more. It was highly erotic snogging two beautiful men at once, and all the more so knowing that Barnes was watching him do it.

'Come on then, mate.' Joe eased himself backward with an amiable but self-satisfied look on his face. 'I've seen his,' he said and nodded towards Ben, 'plenty of times. Let's have a look at what you've got to offer.'

'What's in it for me if I show you?' Greg wanted to put up a face of bravado to rival Joe's cockiness.

'Depends on what it's like.' The man was remaining smug.

'I can cope with that. Here you go then, boys. Get a load of this.'

Greg eased his trousers and underwear down allowing his cock to rear up between his naked legs. 'What do you think?'

'Not bad.' Joe was grinning at Greg's prick like the cat that had got the cream. 'Not bad at all.'

'Now, how about you two?' Greg tugged on the end of his piece as he spoke. 'Let's see what I'm up against. Come on, Ben. You first.'

Ben giggled nervously before he slid open his belt and slipped off his expensive designer jeans and pants. 'OK,' he said with obvious relief. 'I've done it.'

The naked skin of Ben's lower body was as pale as that of his face and his dick was the same shade, sticking upward and trembling slightly both with excitement and the vibrations of the car. It was a slim but lengthy piece with a foreskin that didn't roll back at all, instead staying tightly over the head, creating flaps of skin right at the end. Ben's balls were hairless and Greg noticed that the pubic area above was closely cropped so that only a small patch of fuzz remained.

'You shave,' he exclaimed. 'Nice touch.'

'My turn.' Joe jumped up. He loosened his clothes in a half-standing position so that Greg caught a glimpse of his tight curved cheeks before he sat down once more. As Joe took hold of his shaft at the base and began displaying it like a trophy, Greg realised where the man got his self-confidence. Joe's prick was a monster, perhaps ten inches long and impressively thick. It grew pinker towards its bulbous, already sticky end, was speckled with tiny bumps and its thick blue vein split into three separate strands halfway up the length.

'Do I win?' Joe said, egotistically.

'I'll see what you can do with it first,' Greg replied, taking hold of it with his left hand. He could barely get a full grip around it, but it felt good as he began squeezing: it was as hot as an oven and as full as if he had taken hold of the wrong end of a baseball bat. Joe laid his head back, surrendering to the pleasure of the massage. Greg reached out with his free hand to Ben, finding the young man's boner jumping into his palm as soon as he needed it.

'Down, boy,' he joked, starting to pull. 'Now how's about me?'

Taking the cue, Joe and Ben's hands snaked over Greg's thighs to meet at his crotch, Joe caressing and juggling Greg's testicles, while Ben wanked above. The three hard cocks being jerked off in a row looked fantastic to Greg, and that he held and was being held by two men turned him on greatly. Quickly the mutual beating became unfocused, hands, forearms and penises banging into each other as the three men grew frantic with need. Greg found himself near orgasm barely minutes after the session had started, but before it was too late, Ben revealed he had other plans.

'Feel like taking this back to our place?' he panted, taking hold of Greg's wrist to slow his yanking down.

Somewhat disappointed at the thought of losing his audience in Barnes, but intrigued at what may lie elsewhere, Greg agreed. The three restored themselves to a semblance of order while Greg found out from his driver their whereabouts. Luckily enough, they were mere streets away from the band's hotel and within five minutes they had arrived there.

Greg told Barnes to stay around, generously tipping the driver for his continued loyalty. He followed the boys inside the lobby, becoming immediately impressed by the extravagant, classy décor of the place. All dark marble and gold, the hotel was as lavish as Rockwells had been earlier that night.

'Is this what happens when you get to number one?' he asked, as he entered the lift behind them.

'Yeah.' Joe performed his manly headlock on the footballer once more as the doors slid shut. 'And this.'

They began canoodling and fondling, Ben joining in from the side until the elevator had reached the penthouse floor.

'Didn't get caught,' Ben said as they headed down the hall, spinning his door key on one finger.

'Better luck next time,' Greg joked, receiving a stinging slap on his behind from Joe for his cheek.

The boys' room was huge, almost apartment-sized and Greg was awed as he entered. A large window provided an outstanding view of the city's skyline as a backdrop and the furnishings were stylish and expensive-looking. Greg wasn't given too much time to linger, however, being dragged by Ben towards a side door before he could settle down.

'Now this,' said the increasingly less bashful young man, 'is one of the real perks of the job.'

He flicked a light-switch as he entered the room, revealing a sumptuous en-suite jacuzzi. The bathtub was immense and Ben turned it on immediately, causing the water to bubble and fizz. Greg rolled his sleeve up and, sitting on the side of the tub, put in his hand.

'Mmm. Nice. Hot already, as well. Isn't that a bit costly?'

'Record company's paying for it.' Joe shrugged. 'Now are we going to stand here chatting about bills all night or are we getting in?'

Greg took off his jacket and began unbuttoning his shirt. 'Does that answer your question?' he asked.

His new friends followed his lead by stripping down as well, their clothes mixing in a messy pile on the floor. Greg appreciated the chance to view Ben and Joe's bodies in greater detail. Joe was the larger of the two, although not the taller, being not much over five and a half feet but with a meaty, chiselled body adorned with fine hairs on the chest. His serpent-like penis was semi-hard and bouncing around between his developed thighs as he undressed. Ben was similarly exercised but his body was fit and lean, like an athlete's, and his smooth chalky skin made him look like an ancient Greek relief come to life.

Greg was the first in the pool, sitting between two jets that pummelled his buttocks and thighs. The water pounded all over his body, massaging him, tickling up between his legs and undulating beneath his balls and dick.

'Come on, guys,' he encouraged. 'The water's great!'

The two men joined him, sitting either side, one under each of his arms. They began their three-way kissing once more. Greg felt a wandering, prickly sensation at his knees. At first he couldn't tell whether it was simply the force of the water, but then as the touches continued rising higher up his legs, he knew it was Ben and Joe feeling him up again. Although it was only two men that caressed him it felt like many more as the jacuzzi bubbled away. He quickly found his partners' cocks to reciprocate the hand-jobbing. He was falling fast into the enveloping ecstasy of it all when Joe lifted himself up and out of the water. The pop star moved to sit on the side of the bath, his nude, concrete-solid thing pressing against his belly as he dangled his feet in the pool.

'I want to know what it feels like,' he challenged, idly fiddling with his enormous tail-end.

'What's that?' Greg suspected what Joe meant but he wanted to hear him say it.

'What every gay man in the world wants. A footballer's mouth on his cock.'

'I'll see what I can do.' Greg put his head between Joe's thighs and breathed a hot blast of air on to the furry bollocks in front of him. 'Is this what you had in mind?'

'More like this.' Joe pushed his penis downward and began wiping it over Greg's face. It was wet from the water and its red bulb was gooey. Greg felt some ooze smear across his forehead and cheeks. Needing it to invade him immediately, Greg opened his mouth wide. It filled him, flexing up against his palate and prodding the inside of his cheeks as he began to suck. With every move down he tried to swallow more of it. He found he could only manage three quarters of it and almost gagged every time Joe's head jammed into his tonsils but at the same time he loved the way it crammed him so well.

'You're certainly a big fella,' he said, taking a break, the huge thing twanging out of his lips as he began to speak.

'Big enough for two, I think.' Obviously tired of just watching, Ben had moved across the jacuzzi. He pushed Joe's legs open wider so that he could be accommodated within them as well as Greg. It was a tight squeeze but a pleasant, sexy one and the men's wet bodies quickly became entangled and pressed close together.

Greg and Ben began sharing the cock in front of them, ravenously attacking it like starved beasts. They lapped at the bell-end heartily, their tongues colliding in their desperate mouthing. They began to masturbate each other at the same time, their arms splashing the water furiously as they wanked. Before long, Joe's moans grew very loud and he signalled that his orgasm was imminent.

'I'm ready!' he cried, arching his neck backwards. 'Oh guys, am I ready!'

Greg watched as Ben speedily inserted Joe between his gums, drinking the first few loads with hearty gulps. The men swapped over, a hot spray managing to target Greg's face directly before he got the pulsating thing within his lips once more. Joe was throbbing so hard it was difficult to keep hold of him and his cock beat a staccato rhythm in Greg's mouth as he guzzled the salty fluids down.

Having finished off Joe, Greg turned his attentions to Ben. He kissed the man and jerked him with abandon. Ben's mouth was slimy with come and it was the sexy taste and slippery writhing that finally brought Greg off, his contractions under the water soon joined by Ben's own.

Greg was in a daze for the first few moments afterward. He lay his head on Joe's thigh until he began to come round.

'Are you OK?' Greg opened his eyes to find Ben beaming at him.

'Yeah,' Greg replied, groggy from joy. 'I think you two just put the love in me.'

Joe leaped up and, unashamed of his nakedness, began one of his band's choreographed dance steps.

'1, 2, 3,' he rapped, self-satisfied, 'is the place to be. 1, 2, 3 is the place to be!'

Greg couldn't help but laugh as he got out of the tub.

'Listen, guys.' He began picking up a towel from the rail. 'Sorry to do a hit and run on you like this, but I'd better leave. I've got training tomorrow, unfortunately. But how does next time you're in town sound?'

Joe changed his dance step. 'Will-y is the place to be. Will-y is the place to be,' he sang, showing his consent.

'You're a fool.' Greg placed a peck on the man's cheek. Finding his jacket he took his mobile from an inner pocket and made a quick call to Barnes. After brief but amorous goodbyes to the band he met his driver downstairs. Barnes was rather disappointed that Greg was too exhausted for a re-run of their drive earlier that evening but Greg promised that he would keep the man in mind the next time he wanted to travel somewhere in style. Greg made it home late, much later than he had wanted to, and sank quickly into bed hoping he wouldn't feel too bad in the morning.

Thirteen

The next day Greg awoke to the sound of his alarm buzzing at the usual early time. His head was cloudy and painful from the effects of a small hangover, but what was causing him the most problem was that he was tired from staying up so late. Knowing he couldn't ring in sick like other people, he rose more or less immediately, the idea in his mind that caffeine, a good breakfast and paracetamol would sort him out in time for practice.

He had just switched on his kettle when the phone rang.

'Get the TV on. Now.' It was Trevor Brown on the end of the line and he sounded angry. Greg did as he was told, turning on the small portable television set he kept on the kitchen worktop. His heart sank like a stone as he clicked channels, finding the sports section of the news on one of them.

'. . . pictures of Leon Grenet and Greg Williams obviously enjoying themselves during a night on the town hit the papers today,' the newsreader reported. There was a photograph of Greg and Grenet, drinks in hand, behind him. 'Merely days before the Weston City strikers are due to play in the cup final and breaking manager Trevor Brown's veto on alcohol. Journalists say the footballers' antics show disrespect both for the game and their team, but it remains to be seen how fans, and Brown, will react.'

'Shit, Trevor.' Greg knew he was in real trouble. 'I'm sorry. Listen, I didn't even have that much to drink –'

'That's not the point. Rules are rules. You know what I said. No booze till after the final. Or else.'

Or else. Brown had threatened suspension as the ultimate

punishment for going against his training plan and Greg
steeled himself for the worst.

'So what are you going to do?' he asked. Saturday's match
would be the most important and the most significant game
Greg had ever played and perhaps would ever play. He felt
like he had taken a full punch to the stomach just thinking
that Brown might stop him from being there.

Brown sighed. 'I've thought it over. Spoken to Leon
already. The good news is that I'm giving you a second
chance –'

Greg yelled out with elation.

'– but don't expect your pay-packet to be so large the next
time it arrives.'

Greg didn't mind about the fine. He was simply relieved
that he would still be playing for the cup. 'Thanks, boss. You
don't know what this means to me,' he said, thrilled to bits.

'Yeah, well.' Brown still sounded stern. 'If it happens again,
and it better not happen again, I won't be so good about it,
do you hear me?'

'Yes, boss.'

'And there's another bloody press conference this afternoon because of what you two have been up to. I want you
deferential and regretful and ready to make it up to the
punters out there.'

Greg didn't need Brown's prompting. He knew he had
done wrong, no matter how much he had enjoyed himself.

'I'll see you at the practice later on, boss. And thanks
again.'

With a grumpy growl, Brown hung up.

The day and those that followed it were not easy ones.
Media coverage of the final was almost omnipresent and Greg
could barely turn on the television without seeing an advert
for the game or some programme about it. Both he and
Grenet took a lot of criticism during that run up, but they
fought it off well, managing to show their willingness and

ability, and the appropriate shame for going against Brown's outlines for the team, and they came out the other side relatively unscathed. By the time the day of the final had arrived, popular opinion seemed to have turned once more behind Greg. People were eager to see what he could do when the real pressure was on, and hoped, like many classic players before him, that what he would achieve would be spectacular.

The game was to be played against Darley Rangers at the famous Bredbury Stadium. Darley were a great team. Fit, coasting on an excellent run of wins and having some of the best players in the world on their side. Greg knew the match wouldn't be easily won. His tension reached its peak in the changing-rooms as he listened to Trevor Brown's pre-game speech, and he barely took notice of what his manager was saying, taking in only the odd words of positive encouragement and tactical advice. He so desperately wanted Weston to win, not only for the glory of the cup, but for what the Secret League had to offer with it. Greg felt very nervous as he at last went out on to the pitch, but at the same time was determined to weigh the outcome in his team's favour.

Darley had won the kick-off and they managed to keep possession of the ball for the opening minutes. But Weston pressed them well. Greg had never seen the crowd so fired up and the fact that millions more were watching in their homes or were in the pub egging him on galvanised him, and before long he had taken the ball. He and Grenet made headway into Darley's midfield, then onwards and it was only a contentious tackle that stopped Greg from shooting. The challenge went by uncarded by the referee, though to Greg and the many booing City fans it was obviously a deliberate foul. The game restarted with Darley blocking too well for Greg to take advantage of the invasion he and Grenet had made into enemy territory and he ended up losing the ball. Greg didn't feel disappointed by the event. Far from it: he felt encouraged. The way he had played and interacted with Grenet and the other members of his team had been precise and focused. City were no longer playing good football, they were playing great football, Greg realised, and with that thought something within him clicked. Weston were in with more than a chance at the final, they were going to win it hands down. And within ten minutes of battling between the two teams, Weston were back in charge. Charmers thundered towards Greg with the ball at his feet. Receiving an excellent pass forwards, Greg sped towards the goal, deftly avoided a challenge and, with his first proper shot that day, wellied the ball past the outstretched goalkeeper.

Greg could feel the cheers of the crowd vibrating within his belly as Weston celebrated their early lead. He was ecstatic as his team-mates piled onto him, their kisses moistening his cheeks and lips, knowing that as long as City continued to play as they had done so far the game was theirs.

The rest of the first half saw both teams demonstrating some excellent gameplay. Only an unfortunate error from a Weston defender led to Darley equalising seconds before the half-time whistle blew.

Inside the changing-rooms, Brown's mid-match talk was spirited and congratulatory.

'You're playing great!' Brown enthused as the team rested. 'I know they've just equalised but that was out of luck more than anything. You've got them on the run. Stick with it and we'll be back ahead in no time.'

With Brown's words ringing in his mind, Greg became like a dynamo from Weston's kick-off. He played smoothly and sharply, as if he was aware of every man's position on the pitch. Soon City's entire game centred on his skills, and he was aware of the step up the match and his talents had taken. It reached the point where he felt he barely had to think about what he was doing, that he was truly at one with the ball and what was required of him. Before long he had scored a second goal, a truly superior shot developed out of a corner kick. He felt on top of the world seeing the ball pound into the net once more. Now that City were back in the lead, he was determined that they would stay there.

Though beginning to tire, both teams put up a frantic fight for the remainder of the match. Darley played excellently. There were many near misses, and against many other teams they would have been the victors. But that Saturday afternoon, Weston City had the mix of technique, team spirit and magic present in all of the finest football, and in the eighty-second minute came the match's defining moment. A run of stunning crosses right from deep within Weston's own half sent the ball across most of the pitch to land at Greg's feet. His heart hammered with excitement as he sprinted into the penalty area then, knowing the time was exactly right, he chipped the ball over a defender and into the goal.

Greg exploded with a yell of rapture as the crowd went wild. He had done it, scored a hat trick in the cup final! He ran towards the opposite end of the stadium, towards the thousands of joyous people who were shouting his name. He had made it, he knew right then as he heard the chants. He had become what he had always wanted to be. He was a footballing hero at last!

The atmosphere was crazy as the final whistle blew. Greg felt dazed as he shook hands with the Darley players, in a state of disbelief at what he and his team-mates had achieved. Greg's elation at having won was at an intensity he had never experienced before and, in the moments afterward, with the stadium in uproar as he held up the shiny silver trophy to display it to the ground, he felt happier than he had ever been. Greg had no doubts that it was the greatest day of his life and the impending meeting could only serve to make it even greater.

The electric air of celebration continued off the pitch. Brown made a beeline for Greg as he arrived back into the changing-rooms, the manager pulling his star striker into a big embrace.

'Well done, my son.' He patted Greg's back with hard slaps. 'I knew you'd pull through for us.'

'Thanks, boss.'

Just as he had done when they had first met, Greg became aware of how attractive a man Brown was. Though his dark hair was greying, his once-trim footballer's body had thickened, and deeper creases had appeared on his handsome face, Brown remained masculine and appealing. Being in his manager's arms like that, his sweaty naked torso against Brown's big sports jacket suddenly seemed very, very thrilling. All too soon Brown pulled away.

'Listen.' He headed off to congratulate the rest of the team. 'I want you to stick around a while after you've changed and we'll have a quiet little get-together. I've got the press to deal with next, but if I'm not around here in the next forty-five minutes, you come and find me.'

Greg assented, wondering what lay in store for him. He undressed quickly. The noise in the changing-rooms was deafening and cheerful, the songs and chants continuing in the showers where he was pulled into hugs, kisses and dancing by his team-mates. He couldn't help but become aroused by it all. Fortunately, with much concentration, he avoided an erection, but his mind began to wander on to thoughts of the League and the events that were certain to follow such an important match. He managed to collar Grenet as he towelled himself dry, attempting to glean some further details from his friend.

'Psst, Grenet,' he whispered. 'What about tonight?'

But Grenet didn't seem prepared to divulge much information. 'Not here, my friend,' he replied, as Charmers, dressed only in his football socks, dragged him away. 'I'll be in touch.'

Greg changed into posh suit he had arrived at the stadium

in, then seated himself on a bench as the happy faces and partially clothed bodies of his team-mates bustled around him. As he waited, drinks were opened and passed around, expressions of admiration and gratitude were exchanged, and invitations to nights out were offered, Greg side-stepping the latter well aware that he would be otherwise occupied. Eventually his friends began moving on. He waited a full twenty minutes after the last of them had left before he decided he should try and find his missing manager himself. Quick checks of the immediate vicinity revealed nothing. The place seemed mysteriously quiet, as if it had been cleared for a purpose, and he discovered no sign of anyone until he returned to the changing-rooms with the idea of contacting Brown later. As he picked up his sports bag he heard a repetitive, rumbling noise coming from beyond the large doors that led to the pitch. Intrigued, he followed the source of the sound. Soon enough the echoes became clearer and he became able to make out distinct voices.

'Will-y!' they chanted in a two-beat time, following his name by three quick claps just as the City fans had done at the end of the match. 'Will-y! Will-y!'

Outside on the pitch he found a group of men on the goal-line shouting towards him. He ran up to meet them, recognising immediately several of his team-mates and a number of that afternoon's opposing side. The Darley players were still in their kit. Greg quickly surmised that he had discovered the whereabouts of his League meeting, but was rather confused to find his manager there alongside the usual members. As Greg reached the crowd they let out a final roar of approval before the Weston boss began to speak.

'Sorry about the secrecy, mate,' he began. 'But we wanted to give the man of the match his proper, respectful entrance ceremony.'

'But what are you doing here?' Greg asked. He had no idea that Brown was involved in the League's activities.

'It's the final, my friend.' Grenet sauntered over and wrapped an arm around Brown's shoulder. 'The big one. The time when the highest-ranking members of our society get their reward too.'

'Or otherwise!' Greg looked around to see who had cracked the joke. It was Ken Holbeck, Darley's manager, who was leaning against a goalpost with his arms folded. Like Brown, Holbeck was an ex-player with similar 'older man' appeal, and Greg was happy to see him in the selection line-up.

'So.' Brown slapped his hands together and rubbed them against each other eagerly. 'Shall we get down to business?'

'*Mais, oui,*' Grenet pushed his boss forward. 'You pick first, being manager. Sorry, Greg, you're second this time, but I swear you won't have to wait long for your turn.'

Greg didn't mind, relishing the chance to watch Brown in action.

Darley's men lined up in the net on the goal-line, side by side, as if they were forming a wall. There were five of them, including Holbeck, and Greg eyed their attractive faces wondering who his boss would pick.

'So, chief.' Grenet leaned on Brown from behind, his head on the older man's shoulders. 'Who is it going to be?'

Brown rubbed his chin a couple of times. 'It's a difficult decision. Were I a younger man I'd take all of you on at once.' The line up sniggered as Brown continued. 'But I'm not so I'll just have to pick the one that can take on all of me at once. O'Dowd, you're a sturdy fella. It's got to be you.'

There was a rumble of approval as Brown approached his choice. O'Dowd, a Darley midfielder, was a huge slab of a man in his early thirties. Around six-foot-five, and broad, he towered over most men and was several inches above Brown. His smile indicated the fact that he relished their imminent union.

'Ah, I forgot.' Grenet began rustling in his pockets. 'Protection and preparation!'

'Don't worry, mate.' Brown delved into the inside of his jacket before taking it off and laying it on the grass. 'I've brought my own!'

He held up some condoms and sachets of lubrication to the amusement of all around and then returned his attentions to his pick.

'If you'd just like to get into position,' he began.

'It'll be my pleasure.' O'Dowd beamed. He knelt down over the goal-line, hands in front of him, his big, fleshy arse sticking out behind.

'Now excuse me, gents,' Brown addressed the gathering in general. 'I've just got something to take care of.'

Greg watched as his boss pulled down O'Dowd's shorts, exposing an arse that was sizeable but taut. Brown opened it, pushing the cheeks away from each other so that the dark furry area surrounding O'Dowd's arsehole was on display to all.

'Not bad, eh, guys?' Brown sank his face deep up O'Dowd's crack so that his chin and part of his nose disappeared within the buttocks. Greg could hear slurping noises as Brown nuzzled around and both men uttered pleasured, furtive sounds at the joining of their bodies. Brown began easing his neck back and forward in controlled but forceful motions: Greg guessed he had inserted his tongue up O'Dowd's chute and was fucking him with it.

Greg felt a nudge at his elbow. It was Charmers, wearing his usual cheeky expression and, seemingly as always at League meetings, giving his crotch a good old tickle.

'I bet you never thought you'd live the day to see that.' He grinned. It was true enough. Greg had never imagined he would see his old football hero with his face up another man's backside but at that moment feeling his horny tremblings within he was very glad he had.

Brown moved to an upright position again and lowered his trousers. As he had been wearing a suit that day, his shirt came a certain way over his arse but at the front his prick stood proud, lifting the material of his clothing and sticking out beyond it. His knob was about six inches long, coffee-coloured, and it had a dark round head. It looked very appetising in Brown's hands as he rolled on his johnny.

'You ready?' he asked O'Dowd as he squelched out some lube over himself.

'You bet,' O'Dowd replied, flinching a little as Brown inserted.

Greg looked on as the first, then the second inch of Brown's thing slid upward into O'Dowd until all of it was fully buried in his willing tunnel.

'I'm in,' Brown revealed and, as he started to pump, his buttocks bounced out from underneath his shirt-tails.

'OK, man of the match.' Grenet gave Greg's bum a quick slap. 'Now you choose.'

Greg was confused. 'Already?' he asked. The other League get-togethers had all begun with the first sex session being watched until it had ended.

'Yes, my friend,' Grenet explained. 'Tonight we all celebrate together. So pick a man. And be quick about it.'

Greg checked over the line-up once more. He knew instantly who his choice would be. 'Newell. I'll take Newell.'

'You have good taste, to my disappointment. I guess I'll just have to take him later,' Grenet ribbed. 'OK, move around, guys. Time to get some more action on the pitch.'

The Darley players did as they were told, Greg's man standing right next to where Brown and O'Dowd were screwing. Newell was a midfielder of average height. He had a good-looking face with pronounced cheekbones. A man of Afro-Caribbean descent, his dark-skinned face revealed a big ivory grin as Greg winked at him.

'Enjoying the show?' Greg asked, looking down at Newell's

shorts. The material at the front of them was not so loose any more, being occupied by a notable curve of hardening cock-flesh.

'I certainly am.' Newell turned around and knelt in the same position that O'Dowd had before him. 'But I think I'm going to enjoy you more.'

Newell's cheeks looked like two half-melons under silk stuck out like that and, kneeling between his pick's shapely, football-sock-covered calves, Greg touched and fondled them before letting them free. He pulled Newell's shorts down to the ground so that the taut glutes were fully exposed and he could see the man's hairless, chocolate-coloured testicles dangling between his thighs. Greg played with, slapped and pinched the buttocks while he watched the two men fuck at the side of him.

'Doing all right for an old guy,' Brown panted, catching Greg's eye. Brown's face had reddened, and his forehead was slightly damp with sweat. Greg liked to see him in such a state of titillation and looking downward liked even better the sight of Brown impaling O'Dowd's bum with his hairy, solid member.

'Get on with it, Williams,' Greg heard Charmers complain. 'Some of us are still waiting, you know.'

Taking the hint, Greg focused on the anus in front of him. He let a spindle of dribble drop from his mouth on to the base of Newell's spine so that it ran directly down the split of the midfielder's arse. He met the saliva at Newell's tender entrance with his fingertips, wiped it around a little and then shoved inward. He found Newell's rectum pleasantly tight, gripping and almost sucking him inward. He shafted in and out a few times with his hand, but before long Newell revealed he was ready for more.

'Please, Greg,' he murmured, pushing backward. 'Less of the fingers and more of you for real.'

Never one to refuse the plea of a sexually desperate man,

Greg withdrew his digits. He undressed completely. Despite his eagerness, and the taunts and encouragements from his team-mates, he knew the sex would be better if he were naked. He liked the idea of exposure in front of the other men and knew the feel of Newell's kit against his skin would be simply exquisite. Most of all, he felt he couldn't miss the chance to be stripped down on the world-famous football pitch where he had played that very afternoon. He imagined the stadium was full and that the audience around him were no longer cheering him on to score a goal but to shaft Newell, all the male fans out there crazy at seeing him, erection in hand, poking up another man's backside. His dick aching with need, Greg rubbered up quickly and began pressing his end at Newell's oscillating hole. The arse-ring stretched eagerly and soon, Greg was deep inside.

'That's right, Willy,' Newell encouraged. 'Just leave it there a second. Oh, it hurts, but it hurts real good.'

From behind him, Greg heard Grenet ask whether he was in or not. After Greg answered in the affirmative, there was some shifting around of the remaining Darley players as Charmers made his selection. Becoming less and less aware of those around him, and more concentrated on his own prick, Greg began to pump. The action took some effort at first. Newell was tight and took a while to relax. But soon the drive inward became easier and Greg was ploughing with speed, the soundtrack of their lovemaking becoming the grunts at every fuck, the soft squelching of hard flesh entering soft, and the regular slap, slap, slap of skin pounding skin. Greg leaned over, taking the man in front of him into his arms. The silky feel of the football shirt against his chest and belly felt fantastic. He nibbled at Newell's neck just above the collar as he fingered the man's pecs and the hard nipples like studs underneath the material. Greg moved his hands downward to the firm muscle that danced between Newell's thighs. It was wet at the end as if covered in shower gel, and Greg wanked it, feeling Newell's compact, meaty balls as he shagged.

'That's it, Greggy-boy!' Greg was brought out of his reverie by a hard, resonating spank across his arse. 'Give him what for.' It was Charmers on the ground beside him, his fingers up the behind of yet another Darley player prostrate on the goal-line. Charmers wiped his short, stumpy dick on the backside in front of him a few times, then quickly put on a condom and entered.

'Ah.' He sounded like a cold man who had just got in a hot bath. 'Beats pussy any day.'

He began to hump, and Greg's eyes fixed on the man's cock disappearing and reappearing up the arse-crack.

'Like what you see? Or just after some tips on how to do it properly?' Charmers joked, obviously relishing being watched like that. He had a rough-looking face and an impudent, lop-sided smile that was always surrounded by a good couple of days' stubble. Greg had always liked the look of his friend. Charmers had a sexy, regular-guy appeal and though the two had never had full-blown sex there had been much flirting between them. Needing another man's mouth on his own Greg lunged for him. Charmers responded ferociously and the two men began eating at each other's face with wild lust.

'Any chance of some of that coming my way?'

Greg was interrupted by a request from his left-hand side. Brown was now banging the bum in front of him with fast and heavy bucks. His face was deep red and sweat stains were showing on the back and armpits of his shirt. Greg could smell his beefy, salty odour and, feeling a wave of attraction for the man, leaned across to do to him what he had just done to Charmers. Brown's face was covered in the kind of stubble that never shaves away properly and it scratched Greg like fine sand-paper as he slipped his boss the tongue. The sensation of snogging an older guy, one whom he had fancied from afar for so many years while he was shagging someone else, brought Greg to another level of sexual pleasure and he felt the building up at the end of his penis. Brown's short uncontrolled breaths puffed out against his face as they kissed. Suddenly the man stopped his pistoning and shook violently, obviously having been brought off. Greg watched as the tremors subsided, Brown giving a few more shafts to finally drain himself, then finally pulling out with a sticky exiting sound.

By this point the goal-line was full, all members of the League having been matched up and at some stage of sex-play. Greg looked down the line at the glimpses of erections, some inserted and fucking, some unbounded and throbbing at the arses, raised and primed between football shorts and shirts. He returned his gaze to Brown's prick. Still hard, the nipple end of its johnny was now heavy with come and it drooped downward from Brown's bell-end. It looked so pleasingly dirty like that. Brown unsheathed himself, and his naked dong shimmered with fluids, some blobs of white remaining spotted over him. Greg reached over to take the thing in his hand. The touch of the slimy, steely pump was just too much for him to take and he too began to shoot, every throb coupled with a shunt up Newell's vice-like tunnel. He found himself crying out with bliss at every release, his body spasming with uncontrolled, repetitive movements that gradually reduced in strength to be replaced by the dreamy burn of afterglow.

Newell turned over after Greg withdrew. The man's body was covered in come and he had a lost expression on his face, obviously completely blissful. Not wanting to disturb the man's peace Greg instead turned his attentions to Brown. They kissed once more, only this time the collision was not so furious. Time and care was taken over it and it felt a shared, warm experience.

'If that's a get-together I can't wait to see what you get up to when you really celebrate.' Greg grinned, referring to Brown's invitation back in the changing-rooms.

'It's not over yet.' Brown nodded towards the queue of footballers that still rammed together at their side. 'I think you should consider this as merely half-time!'

Greg took in the view of thrusting and penetrated bums once more. 'Oh, I was. I wouldn't miss this for the world.' He paused to consider his next move. 'I was just wondering though. Any chance of kick-off being with you?'

'I'll see what I can do.' Brown smiled.

Greg leaned inward and his mouth met his manager's again.

Fourteen

Half an hour later, Greg had recovered from his earlier session and was ready for another. He knew exactly who he wanted to share his time with and he found the man sat in the dug-out at the side of the ground.

Brown was alone and watching the rest of the League's action, just as he had the football match that afternoon.

'Having a rest, boss?' Greg asked as he sat down on the bench next to his manager.

'Yeah. I can't keep up with you young 'uns,' the manager chuckled. He had partially re-dressed during his break and now was wearing a light-blue shirt opened at the front and a pair of black silk boxer shorts.

'Young 'uns!' Greg exclaimed. 'Don't be daft. How old are you now? Forty-two?'

'Forty-three, actually,' Brown corrected.

'That's not old. All those years of exercise when you were a player, you must be twice as fit as most men your age. And you've kept in condition as well.'

Greg had not lied. Despite his busy career as a manager, Brown had kept up a rigorous exercise plan. Greg had often seen him in the club's gym and sometimes he even joined City on their training days. His efforts showed on his body, which had grown larger with age but displayed his active nature. He was not overly muscular, but he was still quite a big man with chunky arms and shoulders and a nicely solid chest that poked outward at the gap at his shirt. Greg could see a sprinkling of curly chest-hairs at the mid-point of his pecs, some dark and some white. Brown's legs were also still worthy of more than a second glance. Stockier than they had been in past years, they retained the extended hour-glass look that resulted from their increased muscle size. Greg remembered that, not so long ago, when watching Brown play, or when he would spend hours daydreaming and looking at a poster of his hero, so much of his focus would be on the man's swarthy striker's pins. That they were so close now thrilled him, and he could barely wait to bring them even closer.

'I'm still twice as old as you are,' Brown continued.

'Do you think that matters?' Greg asked. 'Some men look great as they mature. Age gives them that worldly air as if they know what they're doing with their lives, as if they know how to take charge. And it looks good on you. Really good.'

'I try my best.' Brown had a wide, handsome face that seemed to be growing sexier as the number of wrinkles on his face increased and his hair became greyer. A permanent stubble darkened his cheeks and neck and caused the deep dimple in his chin to look even more pronounced. He tried to explain himself again. 'But I just fancied a bit of a breather, you know. A chance to watch the action as well.'

Greg had also been voyeuristically enjoying the footballers' antics. 'Did you see Charmers shagging Holbeck?' he asked, referring to one of the more notable events of the past thirty minutes of orgiastic sex.

Brown laughed. 'Yeah, he gave him what for, didn't he? He's a dirty fucker that Charmers and no mistake. But I know Holbeck. That's how he likes it!'

Greg could hardly believe that his boss was talking in such a way but at the same time he was enjoying it immensely. He too had re-dressed a little, having borrowed a pair of shorts from one of the Darley players and put them on. He could feel the material becoming rather tight around him as he spoke to Brown and he wondered just how much the man had meant what he had said earlier on.

'It's great being a winner, isn't it?' he said.

'That's us, mate,' Brown said. 'Champions of the fucking

world. You know that's one of the real reasons I came back down here to sit on this bench. Seeing that match today, seeing City playing like they did, and you playing like you did was one of the greatest things that has ever happened to me. And to have a chance to see my boys on this pitch as victors again. I just didn't want to miss it. You've made me a proud man today, Greg. You've made me very proud.'

He slapped a hand down on Greg's knee and gave it a squeeze. To Greg's delight the hand stayed there, and his erection increased in persistency at the touch. He widened the splay of his thighs so that his shorts became tighter against him, all the time looking into Brown's gorgeous eyes.

'So when do you think that you will have finally recovered, boss?' he asked, feeling rather eager.

The hand wandered further up Greg's leg until it was caressing his upper thigh with firm massages.

'Oh, I don't know.' Brown feigned nonchalance as his face neared Greg's. 'How does right now sound?'

The two men kissed ferociously. Greg felt the hand slip up the leg of his shorts and begin to grope around.

'I'm going to make you proud again, mate,' he said as his balls and member were tickled. 'I'll make you the proudest man alive.'

He fiddled with the button of Brown's boxer shorts. His boss had obviously recuperated enough already as his prick was erect and causing his underwear to distort to fit around it. Quickly, Greg opened the fly and the thing popped out, a good growth of pubes poking out of the hole along with it. Again, like on Brown's chest, the hairs were mainly dark but he had some greying and white sprigs showing through and Greg felt extremely titillated at the thought of being with an older man. He took Brown in his hand and slowly rolled down the man's foreskin so that his dark bell-end was exposed.

'You know how to handle a cock as well as you do a football,' Brown murmured.

'You've got a good one,' Greg teased. 'For an older guy.'

Greg pushed his shorts down to mid-thigh so that his dick and balls were freed though he could still enjoy the feel and sight of sports kit on his body. Taking Brown's penis in his left hand he repositioned his boss's clutch upon himself so they could wank each other off simultaneously as they kissed. Brown had a wandering, dancing touch that some-times lightly stroked over Greg's erection, sometimes delved down between his legs and sometimes took full, strong tugs that almost took his breath away.

'Looks like I'm not the only one who knows one end of a dick from the other,' he gasped in between snogs, pleased and amazed at Brown's hand-jobbing technique. 'I think you're going to teach me a trick or two.'

'It all comes with experience,' Brown began. 'When you've been around as long as I have –'

He stopped. Greg had got on his knees in front of him and was heading directly for his dick. He could hear the other men on the pitch making sexual noises behind him.

'But what will the League say?' Greg asked sarcastically, not really caring about the answer.

'I'm the highest rank here.' Brown reassured him. 'I can do just about what I bloody want.'

Greg delved inside the fly of Brown's boxers and brought the man's balls fully out of his clothing.

'You know I was never as forward as you when I was twenty-one,' Brown said, amazed at Greg's sexual confidence.

'I don't feel like waiting around. I've dreamed of this moment for years,' Greg explained. 'Trevor Brown inside me. Who'd have thought it?'

Suddenly Brown's legendary gruff, managerial skills came into action. 'Right then. If that's what you want.'

He sat himself up, as if transforming himself into his usual authoritative self.

'Shut up and suck,' he said. His voice was stern, and demanded respect, just like the time he had scolded Greg for drinking before the final. Greg liked the sense of being dominated and immediately went for the cock, his own piece aching as he did so.

'That's it, kidder, take it in.' Brown's encouragements electrified Greg, sounding like the words of support he would shout from the sidelines during a game. Greg did as he was told, immediately pushing downward on the length until he felt it right at the back of his throat. He sucked hard, then pulled back and off so he could waggle his tongue over the greasy head. He looked up at Brown's desirous face as he did so, realising he was experiencing the double fantasy of giving head to his football hero and of making it with someone so much older than himself.

'And again.' Brown nodded, then exhaled heavily as Greg slid back down once more. This time when he came back up he dribbled at the top of the thing, his saliva streaming down over Brown's blue veins, collecting in pools on his boxer shorts and running into his pubic hair.

'Come on, Trip, like you mean it!' Brown coached, almost aggressively. Fully aroused now, Greg gave the blow-job all he had got, deep throating it, swallowing and gumming it. He would ram himself up and down it as fast as he could for a while then just lightly rub the end with his tongue, knowing how delightful the mixture of sensations would feel. He loved to look up at Brown's half-closed eyes as he wanked the man off into his mouth, tasting the viscous goo that had started to ooze out of him. He found his manager's balls were still scented with sweat from his earlier sex session and he licked and sucked at them, enjoying their saggy skin in his mouth and their pungent smell. He raised up Brown's legs so he could nuzzle the man's bum crack, sniffing away at it and lapping at it until the silk that covered his anus was well and truly damp with spit.

Brown had begun taking deeper and deeper breaths and now he sounded less demanding and more approving.

'Fucking hell, you know how to play, Williams. Best I've known of in a long time.'

'That is something.' Greg lowered the man's legs once more. 'Considering how long you've been around.'

'Hey! Cheeky!' Williams clipped Greg around the head with the back of his hand. 'I thought that's how you liked it.'

He took hold of his cock and whacked it a couple of times against Greg's face.

'Just kidding, boss.' The situation was actually extremely enjoyable to Greg and he was simply attempting to get a rise out of his manager so the man would start admonishing him again.

'I bloody hope so! I didn't get where I am today for nothing you know.' It seemed as if Brown had caught on and was becoming an austere figure once more.

'Really?' Greg sat back, attempted to look self-satisfied. 'How did you manage it then?'

Brown looked shocked. 'Get on this bloody bench and I'll show you what I can do.'

Greg removed his shorts once more and moved towards the bench. Brown stood up and without warning, gave Greg's backside a hard whack with the palm of his hand.

'That's for your disrespect,' he growled.

The slap began stinging immediately, but the slight, warming pain, and Brown's grumpy demeanour felt too good for it to really hurt.

'Get a move on,' Brown said harshly. 'On your back. Legs up. Let's see that arse of yours nice and open.'

Greg did as he was told, taking hold of the back of his legs so his backside spread wide.

'So you've always dreamed of having me inside you then?' Brown remained gruff and Greg answered quickly.

'Yes, boss.' He felt like a scolded dog and all the hornier for it.

'Well, let's see what I can do about that.'

Brown gave Greg's rump another quick spank. 'And that one's for luck,' he said as he crouched down.

Greg's bottom smarted hot and stingy, and the touch of Brown's face upon it felt wonderful. He could feel some tender wet kisses upon his cheeks that contrasted with the prickly pain, before the sensation of a wet tongue on his bottom sent him reeling into ecstasy. Brown was burrowing up his crack, his extended mouth-muscle exploring around with the same proficiency that his hand had examined the inside of Greg's shorts. Greg felt a wetness at his anus, fingers poking and stretching him open. There were more licks and laps and then an insertion, a dampened prodding, wriggling thing inside him that produced some devastating effects upon his rectum. Greg found himself swearing and groaning as Brown ate him out, realising the man's talents weren't just restricted to football and business.

'Not so cocky now, are you, young man?' Brown climbed on top of him and Greg could feel the man's steaming erection pressing against his groin, the bulk of his body weighing down on his legs.

'No, sir.' And then, desperate for his anal joys to continue: 'Come on, boss man. Finish what you started. Show me you've still got it in you.'

'It's other way around, mate.' Brown took a condom from his shirt pocket and Greg saw him fiddling with himself to put it on. 'It's you who are going to get it in you. And you're going to fucking love it as well.'

Brown sat back and looked downward at Greg's arse. He had his hand below waist level, obviously directing his cock, and Greg felt a pushing at his tender entrance. The rod was nicely hot and very hard and it slowly forced him open until it had slipped fully inside. Brown steadied himself by placing his hands on the bench at the side of Greg's back and made his first shaft. Greg still felt tight, but the pain was good, and he made his arse muscles grip the penis harder to gain even greater sensation from it. Brown's initial bucks were tentative, as if he sensed Greg's rectum was not fully relaxed yet, but soon he had picked up speed and Greg could feel his chute opening and closing around the inserted thing. He looked down to see Brown's belly beating against him, the line of greying pubes next to his balls, then began feeling his manager's body. He ran his hands over Brown's pectorals, over his back and thick arms. The skin was a little looser than a younger man's and all the more appealing to Greg for it. He arched his neck forward to kiss Brown once more and their mouths met with savagery, eager for each other's contact.

'How does it feel?' Brown's words were punctuated by his pants of pleasure and exertion. 'Is it how you imagined?'

'It's better.' Greg stared into Brown's reddening, sweaty face. 'It's better than I ever dared hope.'

They kissed again and Brown's humps increased in speed. Greg put his hands behind the man's bum to feel it boring into him. Brown grabbed hold of Greg's cock and began to pull it as he screwed, and before long, the sex had overwhelmed Greg and he began to shoot. As the pumps showered up on to Brown's chest and belly, Greg could feel his rectum squeezing uncontrollably at the dick inside him. He was euphoric as the man on top of him grimaced, stopped his bucks for a second and then began shuddering in his arms. He felt Brown's member flickering inside him as it let its contents fly, the movements adding to the joys of Greg's orgasm as it did so. He was sad to let the thing go from him, but the warm soreness he felt at its exit was buffered by the steadily increasing heat of satisfaction and he began to feel rather wonderful as Brown eased himself off and, exhausted, lay at his side.

The two faced each other, embraced and smooched a little while longer.

'You're a fuck and a half, boss,' Greg said, feeling awed by Brown's abilities.

'Not so bad yourself. For a young 'un,' Brown ribbed.

'You ought to stick around after matches, you know. Give the press a miss for once. Me and Grenet would be very appreciative of the company if you were to show your face in the showers.'

Brown laughed. 'Maybe, mate, one day. I do have some good memories of what it was like when I was professional.'

'Really?' Greg felt excited by the news, wondering just which of his other football idols in the past had the same little secret Brown had. As Brown began to spill the beans, he felt truly glad he had had the chance to play around with the man. It was one of many highlights his membership of the Secret League had brought and as he placed his hand on the man's crotch and gave it a friendly feel, he felt exceptionally lucky that the seasons ahead would no doubt be bringing many, many more.

Fifteen

'Oh, I don't know, Greg.' Becoming more involved in the conversation, Lila picked up the remote and turned the television down. 'I just think it's all getting a little too much.'

Greg sank back into his comfortable chair. 'That's putting it mildly.' He was in his mother's lounge, having returned to the house in preparation for Matt's stag night, only to find that Lila had something serious to discuss.

'They were coming and going till half past two in the morning, dancing on the front garden, knocking on the window, shouting. I would have called the police but, well, it all seemed in such good spirits.'

Lila was revealing what had happened after the final, and how certain fans were a little too forthcoming in sharing their joy with her. Although Greg knew nothing too bad had happened, he was aware of how tired his mother looked in the flickering light of her television set and was worried that the side effects of his success were starting to get to her.

'I'm sure it was. I'm sure you were in no danger,' Greg reassured her.

'Of course I wasn't.' Lila shrugged, as needy to show her independence as ever. 'But at my age I suppose you just start to be fond of your peace and quiet.'

'You just don't need it, Mum. It's your right. Nobody deserves to have their privacy invaded like that no matter who they are.'

'Maybe.' Lila paused thoughtfully. She crossed her legs and began bouncing one of her slippers as she continued. 'And maybe privacy in this house is a thing of the past.'

'What do you mean?'

'It set me thinking, Saturday night. Perhaps I'm trying to

hold on to things long gone, living here. Times have changed lately, one hell of a lot. But I don't seem to have changed with them. I'm just stuck in my old ways, same as I always was. And it's not only starting to feel wrong, it feels stupid, especially considering the opportunities I've got, that you've brought about with your career.'

'Are you saying you want to move?' Greg hoped that at last Lila was ready to make a break from Middleton.

'I'm saying for the first time I'm seriously thinking about it.' Lila raised her eyebrows as if she herself was surprised at what she was saying. And then, something else having caught her attention, she cried, 'Oh look, we're missing it!'

She turned the volume up again. The screen showed a close-up of two faces kissing.

'Sheila, not with him, please. He's a bad 'un!' she pleaded, lost in the story.

Greg watched his mother's preoccupied face, pleased with the turn the conversation had taken. That his mother was considering leaving the old house behind was a giant step forward and all he had to do now was provide the right direction for her journey to take.

An hour later, Greg left his mother with her thoughts. As Matt's best man and organiser of the stag night, it was time he got involved in the evening's fun. The Black Bull was darkened when he arrived. The windows were blocked out and a number of primary-coloured disco lights provided the main illumination. The jukebox was much louder than usual and was playing recent upbeat pop hits. But despite the changes, the pub still retained its provincial feel, and Greg was pleased of the familiarity.

'Over here, mate!' Greg heard Matt call his name over the noise of the jukebox. He looked across the pub to find his friend by the bar. His arm was raised and he was waving so that his thick bicep was accentuated at the end of the sleeve of his short-sleeved shirt. Matt looked good, really good and

Greg made his way over quickly, taking his friend's brawny body into a friendly hug.

'Thanks for sorting all this out.' Matt seemed very happy and slightly drunk. 'It looks like we're in for a good one.'

'Good?' Greg feigned shock. 'We're in for the time of our lives. Couldn't send you off any other way. You're my best mate, after all.'

'And you.' Matt's dark eyes gazed into Greg's for what seemed like eternity and his thick forearm stayed wrapped firmly around Greg's back. 'You're mine. I don't know what I'd do without you.'

'Hey, break up the love affair, boys.' A beefy, deep-voiced man interrupted the pair. 'You're spoken for, don't forget.'

'Sorry, Luke.' Matt released his grip and began making introductions. 'Greg, this is Luke from work. Luke, this is –'

'I know very well who this traitor is.' Luke stuck out a cumbersome hand. He grabbed and shook Greg's own with not a little strength.

'You're a Middleton fan, then?' Greg asked. He felt rather mesmerised by the bulky, handsome labourer. Luke was around six and a half feet tall and appeared to be in his late twenties. Life had blessed him with a naturally large build that had been exaggerated by his work on the building site to the point where his hardy shoulders and arms looked as if they would have trouble squeezing through most doorways.

'Aye. But we'll put that aside for the evening, seeing as we've got other things to bring us together.' Luke's green eyes twinkled, showing his aggression was fake and he was simply teasing. 'Now who wants a drink?'

As a round of whisky shots was ordered, Matt continued to present Greg to the people in the vicinity, many of whom Greg knew, being friends or work-mates of Matt's he had met previously or men he knew himself from their home town. Others he had briefly to make the acquaintance of: despite having sent out the invitations himself not even he knew all the forty or so men there. Greg enjoyed seeing all those male faces together. The group seemed to cover all the bases of masculine appeal. There were the archetypal hunks of guys like Luke, the more pretty, slight and well-groomed types like the group that sat boisterously swigging at one table, and rough, quiet, almost threatening men that eyed Greg with a look that was impossible to discern as caused by attraction or aggression, but that was enticing all the same. All in all, he thought to himself, as he received his first drink, the men were a very attractive bunch and a perfect selection for what he had planned for the evening.

A couple of hours later everyone was in good spirits. The drink was flowing, the music was good and a hearty laugh never seemed to be too far from anyone's throat. Greg took some ridicule about being a footballer, mostly from the Middleton fans and from Luke in particular, but it was all good-natured. He enjoyed the bonding process, the jokes and mickey-taking that covered up the man's embarrassment as he and Greg got to know and like each other. He was glad of the happy atmosphere, knowing that it would provide a better setting for what was about to happen next.

At half-past ten, as scheduled, his plan began clicking into action.

'Hey, Willy!' The barman poked at Greg's shoulder in an attempt to pull his attentions away from the group of men around him. 'This fella's wanting to know where he can get changed. Anything to do with you?'

Standing at the ordering side of the bar was a man with a face Greg was very familiar with. It was a good-looking face, with Mediterranean features, olive skin, and dark hair and eyes. Greg had not seen his friend enter the pub and he gave him a quick acknowledging nod before he began to feed the barman a little white lie. The new arrival was everything to do with him despite his denial of responsibility to the pub's owner. The man was the stag-night stripper.

'Get changed?' Luke, having obviously overheard part of the conversation, butted in with his booming voice. 'Don't tell me you're the entertainment, pretty boy!' Luke took a pinch of the stripper's face and tugged at it.

'Actually, I am,' the stripper replied, pulling away.

'What the hell?' Luke began.

'I think there's been some kind of mistake,' Greg lied. 'I saw an advert in the paper. When I read the name Jules I just presumed it was a girl. It was a bloke who answered the phone call but I just thought he was her manager.'

In truth, Greg knew exactly what was going on. He had known Jules a good couple of years and had asked him to the party to throw a rather large spanner into Matt's works.

Luke let out a loud, reverberating burst of belly laughter. 'Greg, you daft sod! Your brains are in your feet, eh?' He clipped Greg over the head with one of his huge paws. 'We've all chipped in for a bit of skin and this fella's what you get us? Classic!' He turned to the crowd around them. 'Hey boys!' he yelled. 'Get a load of this!'

Shouting over the noise of the music, he informed the rest of the men of the little mishap. It was the moment of truth for Greg. Luckily the news was taken with amusement rather than disappointment and the pub exploded in raucous good humour. Insults and beer mats began to fly Greg's way.

'Hey, hey, lads, quieten down a minute.' Luke tried to calm the guests and when their noise had levelled to a mere rumble, he put a hefty arm around Jules' shoulder.

'Right then, bud. Whereabouts have you come from to be here with us tonight?'

Jules gave the name of a town a good forty minutes' drive away.

'Blimey, fella! You've come all that way just for us! I don't blame you actually. I've been there and it's a shitehole!'

The men roared once more as Luke continued. 'And I suppose we've paid for you up front already.'

Jules looked sheepishly at Greg, then nodded.

'Well, we can't send you away without you showing us what you can do, can we? And our hubby-to-be deserves a decent show of flesh while he's still allowed, doesn't he, lads?'

The crowd cheered drunkenly, whether out of the desire to humiliate Matt or whether they were eager to see Jules naked Greg couldn't tell.

'Go on then, mate. You can get changed. Toilets are through there.' Luke pointed over at a side door. 'Got any music?'

'Put this on when I say.' Jules took a tape out of his jacket pocket and handed it to the barman before leaving.

'Right then, Matt.' Luke picked up a chair and placed it centrally in the room. 'Pride of place. Come on everybody. Clear a space for the bridegroom.'

'I'll get you for this!' Matt half-smiled, half-snarled at Greg as he planted himself down in his seat. Tables and people were quickly moved out of the way and before long, Jules made his reappearance, receiving a mighty roar of approval as he did so. He was dressed in Middleton kit: red shirt, white shorts and socks and shiny black football boots. He carried a ball, giving it a couple of spun throws in the air as he walked into his position directly in front of Matt. His audience clapping, cheering and egging him on, Jules tapped the ball around his body a few times, from knee to foot, to the back of his neck and then down again.

'Good control!' Luke shouted across, obviously enjoying the act. He turned to Greg who was standing beside him. 'Very appropriate choice, a footballer. He's a Middleton fan as well, I see.'

Greg watched as Jules deftly kicked up the ball into his hands then lobbed it at Matt's chest with a short, fast throw. Matt caught it, then lowered it to his lap, spinning it around with his fingers as if he didn't quite know what to do with his hands.

'Get on with it, then!' Luke growled. 'We've paid good money for this!'

Jules signalled the barman and his music started. It was a familiar, brassy, blues number and Jules began moving to it as the first notes sounded. Greg had seen the stripper dance before, and knew he was good, but still somehow was unprepared for the erotic show he saw in front of him. Jules had a fantastic lithe and muscular body, and it looked great in his costume. He knew how to move too, and was rolling his hips around and around, fucking the air with his crotch inches away from Matt's face. He turned around so that Matt's head was level with his arse. The waggling behind was as perfect as Greg remembered it, the two half-spheres of man-flesh side by side jiggled and ground enticingly, and then as Jules bent over to show them off fully, the split was traced beautifully by the indentation in his shorts.

By this point, Matt was looking a little embarrassed. The whistles and jeers of his friends sounded all around and he shuffled uncomfortably in his seat, glancing about for support as Jules' cleaved backside wriggled in front of his face. But Greg could see something else in Matt's expression, something he had seen before during the times they had spent alone recently. It was a look of desire. Matt couldn't take his eyes off his stag-night present no matter how much he pretended otherwise.

As Jules stood up and turned around once more, the changes in his body became immediately obvious to all those watching, and the laughs and cheers signalled their appreciation and amusement. His shorts, although previously occupied by quite a bulge, were now much more packed and a semi-hard, monster-sized manhood dangled at his crotch as he danced. It looked like a living, independent thing, writhing around to Jules' gyrations, and Greg could hardly wait to see it exposed. Aroused, he too felt a rising just below waist level and he just hoped it was happening to him in the right surroundings.

At his side, Luke put a circle of fingers in his mouth and blew an ear-splitting whistle. 'Come on, mate. Let's see the rest of you,' he encouraged.

Swaying to popular opinion, Jules started taking off his shirt. He did it slowly, first displaying only his upturned-eggbox-shaped abs, then his chest, then peeling off completely to show off just how good his upper body looked. He began rubbing his hands over himself suggestively. His skin was shiny and Greg surmised the man had oiled himself up before coming out on the floor. He continued to look on as Jules explored himself lower and lower down until he was grabbing at the ample bundle between his legs. The package was too much for one handful and the fully erect prick pointed diagonally out from his grip restrained by the material of his shorts.

'Go on, Matt!' Luke was apparently as desperate to see the cock uncovered as Greg was. 'Give the boy a break. Get it out!'

Matt once more appeared embarrassed, but a quick flick of his tongue to his upper lip revealed to Greg that other things were also on his mind. Encouraged by Luke, the partygoers began chanting and hand-clapping and unable to ignore such encouragement, Matt took hold of the man in front of him. At first he just held Jules' swaying hips, then gingerly he eased his fingers to the elasticated waistline of the shorts and began slipping them downward. Centimetre by centimetre, Jules was exposed. A curly black patch of hair burst into view and was immediately followed by more and more of the man's mammoth erection, light brown in colour and covered in criss-crossing veins. Matt had to pull the shorts far outward to get them over the sizeable length and when he finally managed the task it sprang up and outward, banging into his chin as it flew free. And then, there it was: nearly a foot's length of phallus throbbing above two huge low-hanging bollocks. It was proud and rude-looking, its wrinkled foreskin having rolled back partially to reveal a bulbous pink head shimmering with pre-come.

The music had stopped and, perhaps in awe, everyone in the room was silent waiting to see what would happen next. Greg's heart beat faster as he watched the two men in the centre of the room. Both were dark and handsome. Jules' naked athletic body looked fantastic at the side of Matt's chunky, clothed build. Matt's hands were shaky now. He let the ball on his lap roll down his thighs to the floor so that the mighty bulge in his jeans could be seen by all. He was now no longer looking to his friends for aid. Instead, his gaze was mesmerised by the great rod that flicked up and down in front of him. He appeared to be in a daze. He inched his head further and further forwards until his lips brushed against the tip, the contact bringing hushed sighs and murmurs of surprise from the onlookers. A cautious tongue slowly poked out of his mouth and took the first apprehensive lick, sliding over the bulb from underneath, over the piss-slit and then back again. Becoming less reserved, Matt tasted the member once more. He rolled his tongue around and around it and Greg could see strings of saliva and clear juices dangling in the air every time he pulled away. Matt reached up and gripped it at the base and then, closing his eyes, opened his mouth wide and took it in. His cheeks hollowed as he began to suck, his head sliding back and forth either no longer aware or no longer caring who surrounded him.

'You get what you pay for with this fella, don't you?' Luke whispered in astonished tones, breaking Greg's concentration. Greg looked at the man at the side of him. Luke's eyes were as wide open as his mouth and his gaze was glued to the impromptu sex-show.

'You like it, then?' Greg asked.

'Like it?' Luke at last managed to turn away. 'Look at what it's done to me!'

He took a handful of his crotch. Though obscured by the material of his jeans, a large, hardened prick was outlined and two big nads overflowed out at the sides of his grip. Somewhat surprisingly to Greg, the man kept his thick fingers there and he started to play with himself, the calluses on his wide, manual-labourer's hand looking great stroking over his denim-covered package.

Greg moved closer. Tentatively, he ran his own hand over Luke's giant, sculpted thigh and then upward, replacing Luke's tender, tickling touches with his own.

'I was hoping you'd do that,' Luke growled before placing a forceful clutch between Greg's legs. 'Mmm, that's nice, footy boy. That's really fucking nice.'

Greg looked around the room. Just like he and Luke, the other men had become aroused and involved in sex-play, some kissing in pairs, with their hands at each other's crotches, some simply continuing to watch the show rubbing their own genitals as they stared transfixed.

Jules was now helping Matt undress himself. He removed the man's shirt then ran his cock over Matt's bare skin, over the bulky builder's shoulders then down across the pair of moulded man-tits. He paid particular attention to the nipples, wiping his dick-end upon the sturdy points, so that they stood out like bolts on a girder. Feeling horny at the sight, Greg re-focused his attention on Luke.

'Let's see what else I can do for this thing of yours,' he said, unzipping the man's fly. The bulge in Luke's boxer shorts poked through the opening, a section of skin and hair peeping through the hole in the front. Greg undid the jeans fully, then pulled them down with the man's underwear in one go. Luke appeared nervous and quickly checked around as if to see if anyone else had noticed what they were up to.

That the other men were in similar states of undress seemed to calm him and he let Greg continue unheeded.

'That's a beautiful piece you've got there.' Greg manhandled the hot joy-stick causing a wincing expression of pleasure to appear on Luke's face. The cock was a fat one and it poked out under the hemline of Luke's shirt as Greg slid the skin back and forth over the head. Luke's hairy balls were sweaty and Greg fondled them, enjoying the dampness upon his fingertips.

'I bet you like it when the girls do this to you, don't you?' Greg asked, increasing the tightness of his grip.

'I like it even better when they suck me off,' Luke replied, his thing jumping in Greg's grip as he spoke.

Greg fell to his knees, immediately shoving his chin deep between Luke's brawny thighs so the man's testicles rested on his nose and mouth. He began munching, his tongue rasping over the curly hairs, up the crease at the top of Luke's legs, sucking one ball into his mouth as if to swallow it. The smell and the taste were incredible: a salty, meaty musk on his taste buds and up his nostrils that made his mouth water with the sheer testosterone-filled rush of it. He began lapping at the shaft itself, right from base to tip, Luke shuddering as he reached the end. He put it in his mouth properly then grabbed at Luke's massive buttocks, drawing him inward then pulling him back. Getting the message, Luke began moving of his own accord, fucking Greg in the mouth with slow easy shags then hard, fast ones, his balls slapping against Greg's chin with every pump inward. Luke started to make little animal-like noises of approval that mingled with the moans and groans of the many men in the pub. Greg felt the cock in his mouth thicken and stir. He was glad when Luke withdrew, as he didn't want his new friend to come so soon.

'Nearly there,' Luke panted, rubbing himself over Greg's pouted lips. 'But I want to hold on for more if I can.'

He took hold of Greg's arm and lifted him up to a standing position once more.

'Why don't we have a look and see what you've got to offer?' he said, fiddling at Greg's groin with heavy-handed touches. Luke pulled down Greg's clothing quickly. The builder didn't have much grace in his lovemaking but Greg liked his brutish, clumsy movements. They seemed to emphasise the strapping nature of the man and make their time together all the more erotic.

'Fuck me!' Luke gasped as he took Greg's erection into his palm. 'If you'd have told me yesterday that I'd be up to this sort of stuff today, I'd have never believed you, never in a million years. But I'll tell you what. I'm bloody glad I'm here. Because I've never seen anything as gorgeous as your prick looks now.'

Greg felt himself pulsate as Luke's heavy fingers ran coarsely over his genitals, then began wanking more readily. He saw Luke's expression turn bashful as if he was working up the effort to ask something.

'Can I kiss it?' he finally questioned.

'It'll be my pleasure,' Greg smiled.

Luke squatted, pushing his trousers and pants down around his ankles. His huge thighs splayed and his dick pressed upward against his belly, a little dribble oozing out on to his shirt. He took Greg's prick into his mouth immediately. Unpractised, he slid down it too fast and he made a little choking sound, having taken in too much. Greg took the man's head in his hands and began guiding him up and down his length, teaching him how to blow with care and precision. Luke's reddening face, his local-lad, handsome looks, looked great impaled on a hard cock like that, his cheeks being regularly pushed outward by Greg's horn. Soon Luke was sucking like an expert, and the hungry sound he was making showed he was enjoying giving almost as much as Greg was receiving.

'You're a fast learner,' Greg panted, near-exhausted. Suddenly Luke grabbed hold of him, took him into a rough bear hug. They kissed with abandon, Luke's tongue attacking Greg's own in a boisterous frenzy.

'You're a fucking animal!' Greg exclaimed as they parted. He felt in a dream state encountering such a wild, masculine beast, and his legs were weak with want. Luke simply smiled benignly at Greg's comment, as if totally unaware of his beauty or his abilities as a lover.

'Come on.' Luke took off his shirt revealing a perfect torso and a large Middleton United tattoo on one arm. 'Let's join the guest of honour.'

Greg undressed himself totally, then hand in hand with Luke went over to where Matt and Jules had put on their display.

All around the pub the guests were in differing states of nudity and were involved in intercourse. Matt had removed all his clothes and was lying on his back on a circular table. He had his hairy legs folded on top of him and Jules was bent over with his mouth up the crack, greedily devouring the shitter with loud wet slurps.

'Still gonna get me for this?' Greg asked his friend, before giving him a firm loving kiss.

Matt closed his eyes and moaned, obviously too far lost in the joys of being eaten out to answer. Luke and Greg moved round to Matt's arse to watch Jules' rimming from a better angle.

'What do you think then, mate?' Greg asked, seeing Luke's awe-struck gaze.

'I tell you what I think.' Luke began masturbating again, then reached over to Matt's prick to feel that at the same time. 'I think I could get used to this.'

'He's ready.' Jules stood up. The anus he left was red and widened from having a tongue and fingers penetrate it. It shone with saliva and some of the hairs that circled the hole were sticking directly to the skin with wetness.

'You're too big,' Matt mumbled in an ultra-pleasured,

hazy, only half-complaining state. 'I'm not sure if I can take it.'

'Relax,' reassured Greg, tickling Matt's balls as Luke wanked him. 'You'll love it once it's inside.'

Jules rubbered up, his gigantic cock looking almost artificial in the condom. Greg knelt on his haunches so that he could see right up the opened buttocks. He took hold of the approaching penis and guided it to the raw hole. He could hear Matt groan at the first penetration, his ring stretching to fit the thing's impressive width, then watched as Jules pushed in further so that more and more of the meat slid up and inward. Matt was moaning at every extra inch inside. Greg did begin to wonder whether his friend could take it after all. But eventually Jules' sword was fully enveloped and Matt's pained utterances ended in a sigh of grateful relief.

Greg stayed at that level for a while, masturbating while watching his lover's hirsute pucker get pummelled by the mighty tool, Jules' shaved balls banging again and again against Matt's cheeks. Sometimes he would reach up to feel the hard rod ploughing inside or, if Jules pulled too far back and slipped out, he would help the two men by directing him into place once more. He liked watching Jules' jiggling arse pumping away like that, the buns squeezing together and dimpling at the sides with every rut. But eventually the time came when his voyeurism alone wasn't enough and he too needed a piece of the action.

Luke was snogging Matt enthusiastically as Greg stood up again, jerking himself off with fast, desperate shakes at the same time. They broke apart on noticing Greg's return. Matt looked absent with physical joy and his body was rocking heavily with every fuck he received.

'Yeah, I'm still going to get you for this, Greg,' he purred, licking his lips. 'I'm going to get the both of you. Right in the back of my throat.'

Matt opened up his mouth big and wide, sticking out his

large wet tongue so that it curled downward over his chin. Greg and Luke placed their pounding things upon it, sliding them around and over Matt's face, slipping into his mouth fully and giving his gullet a fuck or two. Matt grabbed hold of both cocks simultaneously and, keeping them in position, pressed the ends into his mouth, gobbling away at them and obviously loving having three cocks inside him all at once. Greg thrilled at being inside Matt once again, and the fact that he was rubbing his prick against another man's at the same time made the experience all the more enjoyable. Before long Greg noticed that Luke was entering the same state of arousal he had been in earlier, becoming all short, panted grunts and snuffles, and his eyes from time to time falling shut. He realised that Luke was ready to blow. Taking Matt's jawline in his hand, he positioned it to one side so that his lover's mouth took in only Luke's meat. Luke screwed in and out for a while but he didn't last long. He yelled with release, his cock shaking violently, constricted by Matt's lips as he came. Greg watched Matt's protruding Adam's apple rise and fall repeatedly as the man swallowed the contents of pump after pump, until Luke was spent and he withdrew. A sizeable blob of goo oozed out of the builder's knob hole as he pulled out and Greg watched as a darting tongue reached out to clean it up.

'Not wasting a drop,' Matt husked, turning once more to Greg. 'Now you.'

Greg did as he was told, putting his hard-on back inside Matt's pursed lips. The opening was sticky with come and the sensation brought Greg to higher levels of pleasure. Matt was looking directly at him as he began to shag and their gaze deepened and seemed to take on significant meaning as his cock slid in and out. Matt was so sexy, so good-looking, so manly and Greg knew, as his dick battered into those stubbled cheeks, that their love was true and would last forever.

Matt was tugging at himself now and it was the sight of

his hand upon his prick while Jules' stomach pounded against his balls and thighs that finally brought Greg off. The orgasm was earth-shattering, starting right at his balls and then pulsating through the entirety of his body as his cock jumped frantically inside Matt's hungry mush. He quaked uncontrollably with sheer happiness. Pleasure and emotion became all, each throb blanking out more and more of his surroundings. He was unable to take his eyes off Matt or think of anything but his affection for him, until the ejaculations began to decrease their intensity. Eventually he became able to withdraw, rubbing himself over Matt's extended tongue, several creamy dribbles creeping out as the climax ended.

Greg felt like a sledgehammer had hit him. He bent over to kiss his lover, tasting the mess of his own fluids as the smooching began.

At the first contact of their mouths, Matt started to convulse. His time had arrived too and Greg felt a hot wet stream fire over his back and shoulders as Matt's dick shot off a long-reaching round of come on to his body. It felt great to be showered like that: the streaming sticky drips that coated his skin felt like bursts of pure masculine emotion. Eventually Matt stopped shaking and after several deep kisses, the two men pulled apart to look into each other's eyes.

'I love cock,' Matt said, his body still bumping with Jules' every shag. 'And I love you, too.'

An almost agonised sound from the other end of Matt signalled that Jules had made it at last. Greg watched as Jules' face contorted with delight, the stripper giving a few more deep, hard rams and then slowing down, his sweating body relaxing and a relieved, satiated smile spreading across his face.

'Now this is what I call a stag night.' Luke, still standing at the side, had obviously enjoyed what he had seen immensely. He grabbed hold of Jules' enormous prick. It was becoming flaccid but it was still an astounding-looking organ.

'How long till this thing's ready again?' he asked.

Jules looked tired, but after giving the gorgeous man a full look up and down, he shrugged. 'Not long at all. For you.'

'Good stuff. I want to see if I can handle it as well as he could.'

On registering Matt and Greg's intimacy, he took hold of Jules' hand and began leading him away. 'I think we better leave these two to it for a while. Thanks for everything, lads. Don't leave too soon. There's time for a rematch before last orders.'

Greg nodded a goodbye, then took a quick scan of his surroundings. All around him men were still getting it on, buggering, sucking, fingering in a full-on orgy. Horny smells and sounds filled the air. It seemed like the party would be continuing quite some time, but knowing Matt and how strange he could act after the two of them had sex, he had no idea how long they would be staying.

Matt removed himself from Greg's arms, sat up and wiped some of the come from his hairy belly. He appeared distant and forlorn and Greg took it as a bad sign.

'I get it,' he said. 'You want to make a move. It's all right. You can leave whenever you want to.'

Leave and go back to the wrong decision, Greg thought. He felt suddenly despondent. His plan had obviously not turned out as he had wanted.

'Leave?' Matt seemed surprised. 'But I was enjoying myself. I thought we'd stick around for a good while yet.'

Greg grabbed hold of his lover once more. A tear came to his eye. He was as happy as when he had held up the cup at the final. He had been wrong. Matt had come to his senses after all.

'Oh darling, we'll stick around all right.' He cried and laughed at the same time. 'We can stick around here just as long as you'd like!'

Sixteen

The sun was beaming down on the beach with a baking, luxurious heat. The surroundings were beautiful: miles of white sand, a calm sea of almost neon blue and an impressive set of cliffs that were spotted with greenery. The place was like heaven, and Greg couldn't imagine anywhere better to be spending a holiday with his new boyfriend. The rest of the world seemed so far away, and he was relaxed to a degree that, as a result of the recent cup win, he had not really experienced for several months. He felt as if he could just lie on his sun-lounger like that forever, the weather and location were so wonderful. And as for the company – he picked up a bottle of suntan lotion and squeezed some into his palm.

'Want a bit?' he asked his drowsy lover, who lay face-down with his head upon his crossed arms.

Receiving a nod and a sleepy 'Mmm', Greg began massaging the strong, muscled and recently tanned back, his slippery, creamy fingers tickling the hairy armpits and sliding underneath the waistband of the tight black swimming-trunks to cop a quick feel of the well-toned buttocks, half as a joke and half because he just couldn't resist. His frolicking didn't go unappreciated. It elicited laughter and responsive, undulating movements from his dark-haired friend. But before the two men could go too far in their playfulness they were interrupted by a voice heading towards them.

'Coo-ee!' It was Greg's mother's arriving with a tray in her hand. 'I thought I'd bring some drinks back down with me.'

'Thanks, Lila.' Greg took a couple of glasses and passed one over to the man at his side. 'I was getting a little thirsty.'

Lila sat down, her light summer dress billowing in the slight, warm breeze.

'It's a bit of a change from Middleton,' she said taking a quick sip, then looking out to sea.

'You can say that again!' Greg chuckled. Sensing a pensiveness in his mother he added, 'Not having second thoughts, are you?'

'You've got to be kidding. 133 Goldstone Avenue instead of that.' She pointed back to a white, villa-style house that overlooked the beach. 'I only wish I'd taken you up on the offer sooner. I've got my peace and quiet now. And more than I'd ever dreamed of.'

'Happy, then?'

'Happy, duck?' Lila lay back, closing her eyes to block out the sun. 'I'm not just happy. I feel blessed.' She paused before continuing. 'And how about you? How's things in the land of my favourite striker?'

Greg took hold of Matt's hand. As always when he shared the smallest of intimate touches with his boyfriend he became overwhelmed with joy, and he found himself instantly smiling.

'Oh, they're merely fantastic, Mum. Merely fantastic.' He too looked out to the waves, then lay back in the warmth. He felt luckier than he had ever felt before. 'In fact you could say I'm the happiest favourite striker in the entire world!' he laughed.

Coming Up from Idol

SUREFORCE ☐
Phil Votel
ISBN 0 352 33736 2
10 October 2002
£6.99

Working-class Manchester. A seedy underworld populated by rough, butch security guards and club owners. Amongst its denizens is Matt, recently discharged from Her Majesty's armed forces and now employed by the security firm Sureforce – a company ruled by an iron-fisted, well-muscled boss. It's good money and there are plenty of perks – including hanging with the beefiest, meanest, hardest lads in town.

STREET LIFE ☐
Rupert Thomas
ISBN 0 352 33741 9
7 November 2002
£6.99

Ben is eighteen and tired of living in the suburbs. As there's little sexual adventure to be found there, he runs away from both his A-levels and his comfortable home to a new life in London. When the friend he'd hoped to stay with is away, Ben is forced to spend the night on the street, cold and afraid. He's befriended by Lee, a homeless Scottish lad who offers him the comfort of his sleeping bag. Both become involved in a web of prostitution and sexual conspiracies, but when Ben is taken hostage by a mysterious client, Lee takes it upon himself to help Ben escape.

BOOTY BOYS

Jay Russell

ISBN 0 352 33747 8

5 December 2002

£6.99

Hard-boiled, hard-bodied black British private eye Alton Davies can't believe his eyes or his luck when he finds muscular African-American rapper Banji-B lounging in his office early one morning. Alton's disbelief – and his excitement – mount as Baji-B asks him to track down a stolen videotape of a post-gig orgy in which his homeboy, the notorious ladeez man Karamel, plays a revealingly man-pleasing role. Alton has just twelve hours to catch up with the thief, exotic dancer Champain Blue. And while the rappers cruise the London streets in their twenty-foot Caddy, hungry for sex and distraction, Champain keeps one well-lubed move ahead of the increasingly stretched Alton. The tension mounts as time, and Karamel's reputation, ticks away.

------- ✂ ----------------------------

Please send me the books I have ticked above.

Name   ....

Address   ....

....

....

....

.... Post code ....

Send to: **Cash Sales, Idol Books, Thames Wharf Studios, Rainville Road, London W6 9HA**

US customers: for prices and details of how to order books for delivery by mail, call 1-800-343-4499.

Please enclose a cheque or postal order, made payable to **Virgin Books Ltd**, to the value of the books you have ordered plus postage and packing costs as follows:

UK and BFPO – £1.00 for the first book, 50p for each subsequent book.

Overseas (including Republic of Ireland) – £2.00 for the first book, £1.00 for each subsequent book.

If you would prefer to pay by VISA, ACCESS/MASTERCARD, AMEX, DINERS CLUB or SWITCH, please write your card number and expiry date here:

....

Please allow up to 28 days for delivery.

Signature ....

Our privacy policy

We will not disclose information you supply us to any other parties. We will not disclose any information which identifies you personally to any person without your express consent.

From time to time we may send out information about Idol books and special offers. Please tick here if you do *not* wish to receive Idol information.   ☐

------- ✂ ----------------------------